# ABOUT THE AUTHOR

Janelle McCurdy is an author and fully fledged gamer. After graduating from Royal Holloway University with a Criminology and Sociology degree, Janelle moved back home to London, and began writing middle grade fantasy. In her free time, you can find her holed up in her room, gaming and watching anime, or attending numerous comic cons and gaming events. Her FAB Prize winning story, *Mia and the Lightcasters*, was acquired by Faber in a major auction.

# ABOUT THE ILLUSTRATOR

Ana Latese is an illustrator based in North Carolina. She has illustrated *Boys Don't Cry* by Malorie Blackman, as well as working with editorial clients including *The Washington Post*. When she's not illustrating, she enjoys playing video games, bundling up with her dogs and watching *Criminal Minds* 24/7.

*To my Nan, my beautiful star in the sky.*

First published in 2023
by Faber & Faber Limited
The Bindery, 51 Hatton Garden
London, EC1N 8HN
faber.co.uk

Typeset by MRules
Printed by CPI Group (UK) Ltd, Croydon CR0 4YY

Text © Janelle McCurdy, 2023
Illustrations © Ana Latese, 2023

The right of Janelle McCurdy and Ana Latese to be identified as author and illustrator of this work respectively has been asserted in accordance with Section 77 of the Copyright, Designs and Patents Act 1988

A CIP record for this book is
available from the British Library

ISBN 978–0–571–36845–7

MIX
Paper | Supporting
responsible forestry
FSC® C171272

Printed and bound in the UK on FSC® certified paper in line with our continuing commitment to ethical business practices, sustainability and the environment.
**For further information see faber.co.uk/environmental-policy**

2 4 6 8 10 9 7 5 3 1

**FABER** has published children's books since 1929. T. S. Eliot's *Old Possum's Book of Practical Cats* and Ted Hughes' *The Iron Man* were amongst the first. Our catalogue at the time said that 'it is by reading such books that children learn the difference between the shoddy and the genuine'. We still believe in the power of reading to transform children's lives. All our books are chosen with the express intention of growing a love of reading, a thirst for knowledge and to cultivate empathy. We pride ourselves on responsible editing. Last but not least, we believe in kind and inclusive books in which all children feel represented and important.

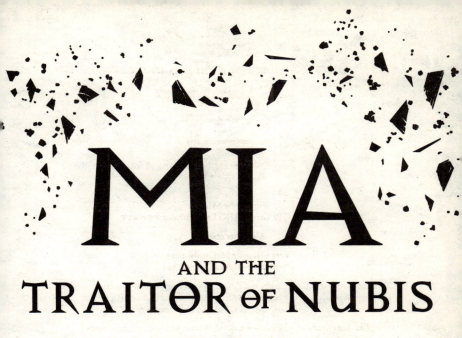

# MIA
### AND THE
## TRAITOR OF NUBIS

## JANELLE MCCURDY

### ILLUSTRATED BY ANA LATESE

## faber

# CHAPTER ONE

Screams pierce the air and flames crackle around me. In the alleyway, I crouch behind some bins with my little brother Lucas close by my side. His tiny hand clutches mine and I squeeze it back. *I won't let anything happen to you. I promise.*

The hot stench of garbage invades my nose and thick black smoke burns the back of my throat, making it hard to breathe. Behind us, at the other end of the dark alleyway, children scream and cry for help as they're snatched away by men and women dressed in huge red cloaks that flap in the wind. With sinister grins, the adults thrust shadowy smoke from their hands in front of the children's faces, like monstrous beings that only belong in the Spirit Plain. Reapers.

My grip on Lucas's hand tightens. *We've gotta get out of here!* I go to run but stop myself and clap a hand over Lucas's mouth as a gutterslug red-cloak steps in our path in front of the alleyway, his back to us. In the distance something clangs loudly, coming closer and closer, like metal chains or iron bars banging against each other.

'Stay close,' I whisper to Lucas. He nods and I slowly remove my hand from his mouth. Black, shadowy snakelike creatures skitter past on giant spider legs. Beasts made of shadow and stars: umbra. They search the area with their blood-red eyes and I pull Lucas down. His tiny hand shakes in my grasp, and I gently kiss his head. *I'm gonna protect you no matter what.*

A huge cage slams against the concrete in front of us, and we jump. My breath hitches in my throat and my hands feel clammy. I look ahead and freeze. Trapped within the metal cage like animals are the protectors of our city. The tamers. The very people who fight against the Darkness of the Reaper King, and all the other dangers out in the Nightmare Plains. Their shadowy umbra, with sparkly golden eyes, are pinned to the ground by strange blue spiked collars chained around their necks. *What the flip is happening?*

Within the cage, oh-too familiar hazel eyes connect with mine, and my gut twists into a knot. *Mum.*

She grasps at the metal bars and quickly turns to whisper something to Dad. He nods and slinks away into the crowd of prisoners. Loud bangs sound from the other side of the cage and the red-cloaked guard cusses under his breath and moves to investigate. *Now!*

I tug Lucas's hand and we quickly, carefully, make our way over to Mum. Her hands shoot through the bars to caress our faces.

'My babies.' Her eyes fill with pain and mine sting with tears. Her palm is cold against my burning hot cheek, and I rack my brain trying to think of a way to get her and everyone out. Lucas sniffles and rubs his cheek against her other hand.

'Listen to me,' Mum whispers. 'You need to go. He's coming for you.'

*What?* I shake my head. *What's she talking about?* The way she holds us feels so familiar, yet something feels wrong. So wrong.

'You're a lightcaster, Mia, and you need to master your powers! You'll never be safe until you do. Take Lucas and go! Now!' Mum yells, but it doesn't sound like her voice. What's going on? She pushes us away and I let go of Lucas's hand.

'Mum, what are you talking about?' I grab the

bars but I'm yanked back, snatched from her. I look down and scream at the skeleton fingers latched on to my arms.

'Mum! Help!'

A sinister chuckle and a venomous voice seeps into my mind.

*'I'm coming to find you.'*

*Don't turn around. Don't turn around.*

*'You can't hide.'*

'Mimi . . .' I hear a small voice call out from behind me. 'Mimi . . . Help.'

I look over my shoulder and the bony hands that grip me crumble to dust.

A few feet away, Lucas stands with his little fists pressed against his eyes.

'Lu-Lu?' I walk over to him cautiously. The flames around us flare higher with every step I take. I crouch down and place my hand softly on his head. 'Lu-Lu, we have to—'

His face changes, halting my words. Blackened eyes stare back at me and ink-stained tears streak his cheeks. A bright shark-tooth smile spreads across his lips. 'Mimi . . .'

I stumble back, crashing against the floor. 'No!'

'MIMI!' He sprints towards me, grinning like a monster and I scream.

'NO!'

*'Mouse!'*

I jerk awake and gasp. The flames and Lucas's distorted face vanish into thin air as soft moonlight shines through the curtains. I heave, trying to catch my breath. My clothes stick to my sweaty back and I shiver.

*'Another nightmare?'* Nox asks from the floor.

My eyes snap to the shadowy creatures that shimmer like stars in the forever night. One black and one white. My umbra, Nox and Lux. Their worried golden eyes stare from foxlike faces. I nod and bury my face into my knees.

*'You may think it is nothing, young one, but perhaps you should speak with your parents. These nightmares have been non-stop since the attack.'*

Yeah, non-stop for three months and fourteen sky connects. That's how long it's been since my whole life changed, and definitely not for the better. Three months and fourteen sky connects ago me, Lucas, TJ, and Jada escaped Nubis and arrived at the City of Light with the weight of Mum, Dad, and hundreds of other people's lives on our shoulders. I still remember the warmth of the sun on my skin for the first time ever. And even though there's been no sign of the Reaper King since, I can't stop counting the days and wondering if that victory is just temporary. Despite making that gutterslug king eat dirt, and knowing his Elite minions are locked up, bad memories still haunt my dreams and they're getting worse.

*'So, what happened this time?'* Lux asks. *'Or am I going to have to dig in your mind and find out.'*

I scrunch my nose in protest. Since Lux and Nox came home with me, we made a promise not to access each other's minds without permission unless we think the other is in danger. They slip up sometimes, but for the most part it's been OK, and it's nice having my mind to myself again.

'It was pretty intense,' I say, rubbing my clammy cheeks. 'It was about the day the Elite first attacked and caged all the tamers. But it was different too. Mum was saying things she didn't say, and it didn't even sound like her voice at one point.'

*Nightmares are often warped versions of old memories from traumatic events. Best to keep an eye on them though, given what you are,'* Nox says.

Yeah … A lightcaster. I sigh and lean against the wall. A child born with the powers of the moon and the sun, with a light like no other. Yet so far it feels like only negative things have come from it. Powers that have chained and shackled me and Lucas to a fate we didn't ask for. A fate that potentially endangers us for the rest of our lives if the Reaper King isn't really gone.

I grit my teeth at the thought. Even without the Reaper King, there's no way me and Lucas can control these powers if we don't know what we're capable of. Especially with the way everyone's been acting since the news came out in the city. We've been standing out like an extra moon in the sky.

The only clue we have is that these powers began, or at least are connected to, the founders of our kingdom and two special crystals. That's what Mum said from what little she and Dad translated from the *Legends of the Lightcasters* book they have.

'All I've flippin' done is monitor these nightmares. I wish they would bog off already,' I say with another sigh.

'*Still, you should probably stop being stubborn and tell your parents about them,*' Lux says.

I roll my eyes. 'And have them even more worried

than they already are? Forget it. They're just nightmares,' I say.

Right now, Mum and Dad need to stay focused on what they're going to do with all the Elite that are currently locked up in the hold. Not to mention, I've got bigger problems. I flex my hand open and closed. *Like figuring out how to stop these stinkin' powers of mine from flaring up at the wrong moment, making me look like even more of a freak.*

*Then there's Miles ...*

I grip my bed covers harder. He's still out there somewhere, my old best friend who disappeared almost as quickly as he came back into my life.

*'You're still thinking about that Elite brat, aren't you?'* Lux asks. I sigh and nod.

*'Where do you think he went?'* Nox asks.

I shrug. 'Who knows. Maybe he needed space to clear his head in the Nightmare Plains, or maybe he went home to Astaroth.' *I just wish he'd come back already.*

I throw myself into the comfort of my pillows and pull the covers over my head. My bed shifts and I peek out to see Nox settling down by my feet, wrapping his long busy tail around himself. Even in his baby form, he takes up almost half the bed with his black deer-like body. I smile and stroke his head.

*'Goodnight, young one.'*

*'Try not to make us jump with your nightmares,'* Lux huffs from his spot on the floor. His white shadowy fur glows like a little lamp in the room and a chuckle almost bubbles up, but I swallow it.

'Sorry. I'll try my best,' I say.

Lux harrumphs, but I catch him checking on me one last time before laying his head down.

Next time I wake I catch the last of the silver line that joins the stars for sky connect. The start of a new day. Nox shakes his shadowy body and jumps to the floor.

*'No nightmares?'* he asks.

'None,' I confirm. *Thank Lunis.*

*'Good. Then it's time to get ready for class, young one.'*

I grimace. 'Don't remind me.'

But I force myself up and roll my shoulders back. I throw off my hair bonnet and walk to the bathroom to splash my face with cold water. *Today'll be a good day. You got this, girl.* I stare at my reflection and nod.

I get changed into a white blouse with black shorts and leggings. Nox brings me my butterfly hairband.

I take it from his mouth and tie my dark curly hair back into a low ponytail with bangs. I wrap my purple hoodie around my waist and head towards the door.

I stop with my hand on the door handle, spotting something on my desk, and I can't help smiling when I realise what it is. I run over, scoop up the small butterfly-shaped note and read it:

Have a good day, Baby-girl. You'll smash your classes as always. You're a star,
    Love Dad x

I look back at Lux and Nox. 'I bet you guys saw him leave this one, huh?'

*'Yes, it was just after you fell asleep,'* Lux muses.

Ever since the battle against the Elite and the Reaper King, Dad's been leaving these cute little notes for me to find in the morning. I'm glad he didn't come in when I was having that nightmare.

'All right, let's head to breakfast. I bet Lucas is already waiting for us,' I say.

We step into the hall and immediately Lucas's door clicks open. He stands in the doorway in his blue PJs, yawning. 'Morning, Mimi. Morning, Luxy, Morning, Noxy.'

*'Morning, tiny human,'* Lux greets. Even in his baby form, Lux still towers over my little brother. Nox walks over to Lucas and licks his cheek. He smiles and strokes Nox's head.

'Morning Lu-Lu. You ready for breakfast?' I ask.

'Yeah.' He rubs his eyes and walks with me downstairs.

Every sky connect, Lucas has been getting up the exact same time as me. Apparently it's his attempt at being a 'big boy'. Not sure I understand why it's so important to him, since he's only four, but I don't question him about it either. *Whatever floats his boat.*

We walk into the kitchen, passing Mum's lab coat hanging by the front door, and the smell of chocolate cinnamon buns hits my nose. A bright smile spreads across my face and through the kitchen window I see Spike and Bolt chilling in the garden, enjoying the moonlight. Lux and Nox go out to join them, and a warmth swirls around my heart. They've been getting along so well with Mum and Dad's umbra. I'm glad everything seems to be fitting together, at least at home.

I go to help Lucas on the chair, but he does it himself

and Mum watches him a little longer than normal. She doesn't say what she's thinking, but her eyes do. She's worried about how he's been since the battle. Honestly, sometimes I worry too. He hasn't talked about what happened, but he always wants to do everything by himself now, and sorta feels more distant.

'Where's Dad?' I ask, biting into a toasted cinnamon bun.

'At the hold. He's questioning the Elite again. Particularly the ones who left during the Blood Moon,' Mum says, placing a tray of chopped fruit on the table. 'We need to know whether they left the city willingly or by force, and if by force, then how.'

'Daddy is saving us from the bad guys ...' Lucas murmurs, biting into his bun.

'The bad guys are locked up so we don't need saving any more, honey. Daddy's just making sure nothing else bad happens,' Mum says. She shares a glance with me and sits down at the table with us. Lucas frowns and doesn't look at her. I slide the fruit tray to him. He pushes it away. I lightly flick his cheek.

'Stop, Mimi!' he complains, swatting my hand.

'Stop being grouchy. Big boys eat fruit too, ya know,' I tell him. He scrunches up his face.

'You eat it then.'

I pull a face. 'I'm good, thanks.'

I could've sworn I saw a flicker of a smile, but it's gone the second it appears.

After breakfast I call Lux and Nox back inside. 'We're gonna head out to class now,' I say to Mum and Lucas, grabbing my bo staff by the back door. A gift from the queen to help fight the Reaper King. It shines at my touch and I give it a twirl, then attach it to my thigh strap. I wonder if she's gonna want it back? Too bad, I guess.

Mum smiles and clears the table. 'All right, sweetheart. Have a good day.'

I ruffle Lucas's hair on the way out of the kitchen. My stomach lurches as I stare at the front door.

'You guys ready?'

'*Of course,*' Lux and Nox say together. There's a bright flash as they transform into their adult forms. I take a deep breath, preparing myself. *I got this. I GOT THIS!* I exhale and push the door open, walking out into my sparkling forever-night city.

The moment I step outside, the feeling of a thousand eyes on me hits me like a gut punch. Adults whisper to each other as they walk past. Some make an effort to smile at me, while others stare like I'm a freaky science experiment. One woman hurries her kid away. I grit my teeth and step out on to the road – only to be yanked back by Nox as a travel pod shoots past, beeping. The shock sends a giant beam of light blasting from my palms, knocking back a lamp post and barely missing a second travel pod. My heart pounds against my rib cage.

*'Young one, you need to be careful,'* Nox says, letting go.

The head of the lamp post squeaks back and forth, barely clinging on by a single wire. I stare at the damage, and gaze down at my hands, lip trembling. A woman I hadn't noticed before gasps and clutches at her chest. The fear in her eyes is as clear as the stars in the sky. Shame washes over me, knowing exactly what she thinks. I'm a monster. And she's not wrong.

*'We should go,'* Lux says, growling at a man who shoots me a dirty look.

'Yeah . . .' I mutter.

We start moving again, dodging between strangers. In the space of a few months, our cosy little city has turned into a big, bustling one, apparently like it was before I was born, before the Darkness took over. Before *he* attacked us.

I rub the back of my neck and realise my hand is shaking. Lux taps my head with his horn. *Just concentrate, and stick to the pavements.'*

I shoot him a look, rubbing the spot he hit, but do as he says with a sigh. Nubis has changed. A lot. And so have I.

Colourful fairy lights and glow bugs light the streets like normal, but new lunar road lamps shine for the self-driving travel pods that hover along the road. I keep forgetting about the travel pods. People skate in their own lane on weird shoe skates to reach their destinations, too. All of it technology from Stella, the City of Light, and the capital city of our kingdom, Lunis, where Queen Katiya lives.

Since the attack, many people from Stella have moved here to Nubis. They were curious about the umbra and how we co-exist with them while living in the forever dark. It's all pretty rich if you ask me. They were giving Lux, Nox and Ruby, Jada's umbra, dirty looks when we were in their city. I could understand the fear, but not the disgust. Guess I shouldn't be a hypocrite though. It took me long enough to warm to my umbra at first too.

I cross the road with Lux and Nox, making a point

to look both ways twice. As we reach the other side, a lady purposely crosses the road away from me. I sigh and force my hands in my hoodie pockets.

'Let's get going,' I say, marching past the new hovering city-news board.

Mum, Dad and the other tamers agreed to exchange their tips and techniques for surviving the Darkness for information on Stella's technology. Hence all the self-driving travel pods and skates. Stella's technology and science was always years ahead of ours, but they never wanted to share it before. They and the stinkin' queen were selfish and still are in my opinion. But at least she gave me her staff.

Mum and the other scientists in Nubis didn't just want the blueprints to their technology though, they want to master it and share it with the only other lit city, Nexus, and hopefully bring back the other cities that have fallen to the Darkness at the hands of the Reaper King.

I run and playfully do an aerial cartwheel in front of the huge city entrance gate to help shake off the weirdness of the morning. The walls sparkle with the extra moon crystals reinforcing the concrete to protect the city, an extra safety precaution that hopefully won't be necessary, but better to be safe than sorry.

As always, I examine the ancient engravings on the walls, the images telling the story of old Queen Lucina fighting the Reaper King before originally sealing him away are still clear as the stars in the sky.

Nox nudges me with his nose. I smile and stroke his head. Him and Lux were the only good thing to come out of this mess . . . And seeing Miles again. That meant the world.

I walk past Mum's lab and my heart tugs. They're trying to find out what happened to Nan and Grandad, who still haven't woken up. They were attacked in the Nightmare Plains on the way to Nubis. Mum had them transferred to the newly built medi-centre in Nubis. I just wish there was something I could do to help.

I clench and flex my fingers, and little sparks of energy zap up my arm. I shake them away and carry on walking. Somehow these lightcaster powers and the umbra are all linked in a giant story far beyond anyone's knowledge, connected to the founders of Lunis. It doesn't help me wake up Nan and Grandad though.

Beside me, Lux nips at Nox and the black shadowy umbra growls back. I laugh. It's a good distraction from the stares. I chew the inside of my lip as we get closer to my class. Right now I just need to focus on getting through this lesson.

It's gonna be a long day, that's for sure.

# CHAPTER TWO

The closer I get to my class, the tighter my heart squeezes. We cut through the training field where a crowd of kids practise their kicks and punches while they wait for their different teachers. For umbra-tamer lessons, my old class of five with Jada has now turned into a class of fifteen, but that doesn't include me any more. I miss having class with my friends, but at least we still have martial arts together every day.

Once a week I join Mikasa, Thomas and Lincoln in a special academic class Jada does just for the four of us. I love it, but sometimes the gap where TJ would stand feels so big. I miss that goofball so much – not that I'd ever tell him. Don't want him getting a big head or anything. No doubt, he's training extra hard in Stella to be a Queen's Guard.

*'Ready?'* Nox asks.

I shake my head. 'I'm never ready to deal with *them*.'

Today's class is held in the city's west gymnasium. A huge building with different rooms filled with exercise equipment, obstacle courses and empty training areas. There are only six of us, but most days I'd much rather handle all the other kids from Stella than these grouchy teens.

I open the door to the gymnasium and most of them are already here. Four tall sixteen- and seventeen-year-olds, all training to become official tamers. I've known them for a few months now, but it's still not gotten any easier being here. From the doorway I see that Aaron Wells and Clara Rodriguez sit on the faintly bouncy floor, leaning against the wall. Aaron runs a hand through his curly brown hair as he talks to Clara, whose extra bright green eyes always creep me out. Their umbra sit silently next to them, like statues, in their baby form. Clara's peacock-like umbra has spikes all over his body. Aaron's umbra is like a giant cat with bat wings and horns on her head.

Then there's Elijah Kingsley. He's doing press-ups in the middle of the room. As the top-ranking achiever in our class, and second youngest to tame an umbra – me, obviously, being the youngest – he constantly shows us why he's the best.

Sweat drips off his forehead and I side eye the puddle of sweat gathering beneath him. *He better wipe that mess up . . . Nasty.* I shift my attention to his umbra, Wesley. His razor-sharp fangs and curly horns are nightmarish, along with his boar-like body structure and panda face. But none of these umbra even touch how cool Lux and Nox are.

'*That's right . . .*' Lux says, and I hold back a smile.

*Get outta my head, you joker.*

I walk into the big airy room, and Clara and Aaron stop talking. They stare at me and their dislike of me almost burns. I frown at them. *I'm here, so deal with it, clowns.*

Everyone here has gone through the same thing I did to get their umbra: the spirit calling. But they're mad I got to 'skip' the training beforehand and think I get some sort of special treatment since my dad is head of the tamers.

*They* didn't have to defeat a nightmare king, though, and would probably all be dead if it weren't for Lucas, Jada, TJ, Miles and our umbra. If any of them say anything, I'm ready to fight them. No problem. Even without these silly powers. I won't ever allow myself to feel that fear again, and if that means being alone in this stinkin' class, then so be it. I know who my real friends are anyway.

'Hey, Mia!' someone calls, and my eyes light up as I spot Margaux Tanner alongside her tiger-like umbra, who has shadowy dragon wings and a long spiked tail. I smile and wave back. She's been the only one who's been nice to me since I started in this class. Her long brown hair with stunning blue highlights is tied up high in a straight ponytail with a glowing red bow. She clasps her hands together and bows to me. I bow back and walk across the springy floor to join her. I make a point to step around sweaty Elijah in the middle.

'How's everything going?' she asks as we fist bump.

'Yeah, we're good. I still want that sparring match one day though!' I say, punching the air. I heard from Jada that Margaux's one of the best in martial arts, so she may actually give me a run for my money.

Margaux sniggers and gives me a thumbs-up. 'Of course, but I'm not gonna go easy on you just because you're short. Let's do it after the tamer trials.'

'Deal.' We high-five each other.

'How are you finding the classes? I know it's not been

easy for you, but the others will come around,' she says, looking about the room. 'They just haven't got to know you yet.'

I shrug and follow her eyes. 'It's all good. They don't need to get to know me.'

Margaux gives a soft smile. 'We're supposed to be a team. Once we've finished our classes we're going to be tamers together. We have to get along and trust each other. You never know when you'll need help one day.'

I don't know about that. I've got Mikasa and the others.

I notice a tall brown freckled girl arrive and I kiss my teeth. With a cocky smirk and prissy white trainer boots, Abigail Cartwright flounces across the room with her small raccoon-face umbra on her shoulder. Tiny horns poke out of his head and a long shadowy scorpion tail swishes side to side behind Abigail's back. *Creepy little guy.*

I look away, but in the corner of my eye I catch her quicken her pace towards me. Lux and Nox move protectively closer to me and I cross my arms. *Here we go.*

'Still not quit yet, star brat?' Abigail sneers, and I'm forced to meet her gaze. *Stay calm . . .*

'Oi, knock it off, Abi,' Margaux says, but I've had enough and my body moves before my mind can stop it. I march over to her with gritted teeth and a clenched fist.

'Say that again,' I dare. Every single day it's always something new. Bullying me non-stop. I raise a hand to stop Lux and Nox from following. *I got this, guys.*

The gutterslug's sneer grows bigger and she places her hands on her hips.

'You heard me. You're only here because of your so-called powers. The rest of us actually had to work hard. That's a fact.'

I stare at her, dead in the eyes. Tiny electric sparks tickle my fingers and my fists shake at my side. The faint growls of Lux and Nox rumble in my mind. *Stay . . . calm . . .* I close my eyes and take a deep breath. *Don't lose control.*

'Plus, you're obviously only here on special treatment because of your parents,' Abigail sniffs.

I glare at her. 'I'm a martial artist before anything else, you glutterslug muppet, and I'll kick your butt if you don't back off. SO, TRY ME!'

Red hot anger flashes in my eyes and I feel my powers surge like an erupting volcano. My nails dig into the skin of my palm, but the energy inside me spreads like wild fire.

I'm like a bubbling pot ready to boil over. Burning sparks of light sputter from my palms, refusing to be controlled.

*'Calm down, young one. Your eyes,'* Nox's voice warns in my head, but he sounds so far away and I'm burning hot. And angry. SO ANGRY!

In the corner of my vision I see Margaux's concerned face, and the others have got to their feet, watching us. Like a feral beast, I snarl at Abigail. Why can't she just leave me alone? Every class she pokes, and pokes, and pokes!

*'Mia!'* Lux and Nox yell. My body is ready to burst, but I force myself to spin around and march off.

My feet weigh heavy like bricks, and everything in me cries out to turn back and fight, to teach her a lesson. The further I walk, though, the calmer my body becomes and the light inside me dims. I inhale and exhale strong slow breaths just like Mum taught me, and I feel the sparks in my hands vanish.

'Just because you have two umbra and some powers, doesn't make you better than us! Got it?' Abigail's voice yells after me.

*'Do not let anger consume you. You're better than that,'* Nox says.

*'But say the word and I'll take her out – and her umbra rat,'* Lux quips, and he's only half joking.

*'Remember what your father said. The second your powers flare in class you're out. Everyone will think you're a danger to your classmates,'* Nox warns.

He's right. I wouldn't even be able to do martial arts any more. My fists stay tight by my side, but I don't move. I slowly turn around and look at her dead on, leaving her with four words. 'Didn't say it did.' *Jerk face.* Make that six words.

'Good,' she says with that disgusting cocky smirk again, but I see it. I see the look on all their faces . . . It's as clear as stars. They're scared, and that's the last thing I want. I don't want to be a monster.

The door opens and our teacher Riley walks in with Myla, a fluffy umbra with four legs and giant mouse-like ears. Riley rolls his neck and fixes the sleeves of his dark blue tamer jacket. He's a few years older than Jada, and has been a tamer for a little longer than her too. There's not so much as a smile on his face as he looks at us, but overall, he's an OK guy, I guess. I still wish Jada was my teacher full time though.

Margaux smiles and gives me a small thumbs-up, and I thank Lunis I managed to keep my powers under control. We all stand together and Abigail elbows me purposely when she walks past. I barge her back and Riley clears his throat. He gives us both a look, but I shoot him a dirty one right back.

'Welcome, rookies. As you know the tamer trials are coming up in a couple of days. The exam will test the bond and teamwork between you and your umbra, ensuring that you're both in sync with one another. So, today, we'll be doing something that's kinda like a practice run with a twist.'

I straighten my posture. The tamer trials. A test where a group of trainees are sent out into the Nightmare Plains with their umbra and hunted down by almost every tamer in the city. Lose and you have to redo a year of training. Win and you advance to the next level of classes. Only two people have ever failed the test more than once. Riley himself, and Bently, another tamer. Yet, they didn't give up and still became tamers. Gotta give them credit for that.

'What will we be doing, Riley?' Elijah asks.

A mischievous grin spreads across Riley's face and my eyes narrow. I've seen that look in Jada's eye too, and it's never a good sign. 'Today we'll be playing a simple game of team tag.'

Confusion is written all over our faces at his announcement, but Riley's expression gives nothing away. Whatever it is, I'm still wiping that smirk from Abigail's face. My eyes connect with hers. *You're going down, mate.*

'Come this way.' Riley waves for us to follow him across the room.

I clock Myla bringing something to Riley and squint my eyes for a better look. *A small remote?* He clicks a button and the ground beneath my feet rumbles. Glass walls shoot up from the floor, enclosing us all in a giant glass box while the whole room around us morphs into something new. Short wooden walls burst from the ground, all different shapes and sizes. Trees and bushes emerge from the floor.

'Look!' Clara yells, pointing. A tall structure stretches up with a bird's eye view of everything below. It resembles a watchtower with a balcony and is topped by a huge ticking clock. Tall silver synthetic trees pop out of the ground last, and the glass cage around us drops and seals away again into the ground.

'I figured this would be great preparation for being

hunted in the Nightmare Plains. You never know when you may have to turn the tables on your pursuer,' Riley says. 'Plus, it'll also improve your instincts and reflex skills as a unit.'

'This is actually pretty cool. The best gymnasium I've ever seen,' Elijah says.

'It's not just a gymnasium,' I murmur, pressing my hand gently against one of the fake trees. 'It's an environmental dome.'

It took a little while for me to realise it. I've never seen one so big. Mum showed me one in the early days when she was creating it with the other scientists. I earn a wink of approval from Riley and a smile.

'Good job, Mia. You're right. It's normally reserved for fully trained tamers and is mainly used for the physical aspect of training,' he explains, waving a small remote in his hands. 'With this, I control everything in the room – hot, cold, day, night, you name it. Now, listen up. I'm putting you guys in teams. Elijah, Mia, Margaux, you're team Alpha, along with your umbra. Clara, Abigail, Aaron, you and your umbra are team Beta.'

I love being in the alpha team! Plus having that mudsniffer Abigail on the other team is real motivation.

I'll carry my team to victory and she's gonna be the first to go down.

Riley hands each member of team Alpha a blue glove, while the others get red ones. I slip mine on to my right hand and the little beads inside the glove ooze blue ink when I squeeze my hand into a fist.

'These are your tagging gloves,' Riley explains. 'The objective is simple. Tag members of the opposing team. If you're tagged you're out and you join me in the watchtower. No weapons allowed. Easy, right?' He jerks his thumb at Myla. 'You and your umbra are one unit. If your umbra is tagged, then that means you're tagged, and vice versa. The game is over when a whole team is tagged. Start on my whistle.'

He makes his way to the tower in the centre of the room.

*'Maybe we should make a point . . .'* Nox says and I raise an eyebrow at him. *'If your classmates believe you have an advantage because you have two umbra, then make sure you win with one. I will sit out.'*

*'We'll show them how it's done,'* Lux says. The confidence in his voice pumps me up and I grin.

Nox follows Riley and Myla to the watchtower. Margaux smiles at me and nods at our decision. Across from us, Abigail and the other team shoot daggers at us, and it's my turn to smirk.

A minute or so later, Riley pops up in the watchtower from the stairs inside with Myla and Nox close behind. Feet apart, I brace myself and stare straight ahead at Abigail. The whole room is silent in anticipation of the whistle. I inhale a deep breath.

The whistle presses against Riley's lips. I breathe out and he blows it. Match start!

As the others hurtle towards each other, I spin on my heel with Lux and sprint in the opposite direction. Bodies collide behind me, and members from both teams yell in a mix of frustration and success. From the sound of it, one of my teammates is out already and I turn to see Elijah with a bright red handprint on his arm. He walks towards the tower and punches one of the barriers. I hear Clara loudly cussing at him with a bright blue handprint on her shoulder. *Good job, Elijah. At least you took her out with you.* Abigail's still in. When I'm far enough away to get a better look at the field I turn and see Abigail staring at me with that same annoying look. I ready myself, stretching my gloved fingers.

'Lux, you good?' I ask.

'Yes!'

I see Aaron chasing after Margaux, who front flips over one of the barrier walls, and when my focus switches back to Abigail, I gasp. Her hands are bare.

*Where's her glove?* The bushes rustle to my right and I dive out of the way, barely managing to dodge her umbra. His red-gloved paw skims past me as I roll to safety. *Smart play, you little creep.*

'*But not smart enough*,' Lux finishes. I vault up on to his back and make a beeline for Abigail. Her hazel eyes widen as we charge towards her. I don't want her umbra, I want *her*. She spins on her heel, trying to dip.

We dodge Aaron from the left and Margaux intercepts, slapping him bang in the middle of his back.

'Get her, Mia!' she yells at the top of her lungs, and I grin.

The gap between me and that gutterslug shrinks. I jump off Lux and dash on foot. She sprints for her life, but I'm faster. Way faster. I snap my hand forward to smack her square on the back.

She pivots and leaps back just inches out of reach and her body crashes to the floor. My feet dig into the ground, not letting a second slip, and I charge at her again.

She rolls to safety and I smack the air instead, but jump back, gasping as her sneaky umbra goes to tag me from the right. Lux bashes him away with his horn, growling. *Good job!*

Abigail's attention shifts to her umbra. Now's my chance! I race over and smack my hand hard against her forehead. *Gotcha!*

Riley blows his whistle and I turn around to see Margaux punching her fists in the air, cheering. 'Well done, Alpha team,' he calls down to us. 'Next we'll be focusing on strengthening the bond between you and your umbra through a few other exercises.'

I give Abigail the same smirk she gave me earlier and stunt on her with a little victory dance. 'Better luck next time!'

Nox leaps down from the watchtower to join us. He lands perfectly at the bottom and gallops over to me.

*'Well done, young one. I knew you could do it!'* He nuzzles my cheek and I chuckle at the tickly feeling of his shadows.

I give him the cheesiest grin and line up with everyone again. Abigail's glares burn the side of my head but I can't stop smiling. *We showed her.*

*'Indeed we did,'* Lux says.

My eyes meet Elijah and Margaux's.

'Good job,' Margaux mouths, and a strange warmth fills my chest.

'You know, you're pretty decent for a little kid,' Elijah says, playfully nudging me, and my lips part in shock.

'Er, thanks,' I say. He actually said something nice. *Well, that felt weird in a good way.*

*'Margaux was right. You have to earn the respect of your classmates – they underestimate you because of your age,'* Nox says.

*'Yeah, although, you did save their lives, so you'd think they'd be more grateful,'* Lux huffs.

Honestly, it does feel nice to be included in a team with them. Maybe there's hope yet that I won't be such an outsider in this class.

# CHAPTER THREE

A few hours later, after class, Lux and Nox decide to walk around the city while I avoid Dad's lightcaster training at home. I'm tired of trying to force my powers to come out, and half the time the training doesn't work and my powers end up going wild and hurting someone. Mostly me or Dad. So instead, I head off to meet up with Mikasa, Thomas and Lincoln at the Missing Tree. The silver and blue crystal leaves engraved with the names of those who disappeared during the Blood Moon now hang as memories instead of missing notices.

I think we're all still haunted by the fact that most of the missing people from the Blood Moon were on the side of the Elite and the Reaper King. Especially when the rest were most likely devoured by said gutterslug king. It makes my stomach churn.

'Mia!' Mikasa calls out. She waves and I jog over to her and the others. Lincoln and Thomas stop wrestling each other and we all bump fists.

'Where should we hang today?' Lincoln asks, breathless. He clicks his back like an old man and Mikasa struggles to hold in a laugh.

'How about the park?' I suggest, swallowing down my own chuckle.

'Sounds good to me,' Thomas says.

'How was Jada today?' I ask.

Mikasa sighs. 'Still not that great. When class ends, she runs off to do tamer missions around the city.'

'She's, like, dead-set on trying to find out everything the Elite know after everything that happened with her mum,' Thomas adds. 'I overheard her on the holophone today.'

*I see . . .* She's probably been visiting her mum in the hold a lot too. Ever since she found out that her mum, and so many others who disappeared during the Blood Moon, actually became a member of the Elite, she's not been the same.

We reach the park and take our usual spot on the climbing frame. The place is packed and filled with the happy screams of other kids. A nice distraction from thinking about my nightmares and Abigail's words. *The last thing I'd call myself is lucky...*

My legs dangle from the top beside Mikasa. Thomas and Lincoln take the lower bars and yawn. The ground beneath us, where some kids are jumping and laughing, is made up of blue bounce turf and lilac grass. Others are playing on the huge swing sets and some hover skate around the mini race circuit. The air is electric with screams of joy, yet I can't help the sinking feeling in the pit of my stomach and my smile falters.

I miss having class with Mikasa, Thomas and Lincoln. We're a team. On top of that TJ isn't here any more and it sucks. Like, really sucks. I miss the way he would make jokes about everything. Always making me laugh, no matter the situation. I even miss the way he was always late.

I look up at the stars and sigh. And Miles is a whole 'nother story. *I hope he's OK. He said he needed a break from everything, but he's been gone so long now.* I don't even know where he is. He left almost straight after we stopped that gutterslug king.

'You know, I still can't believe Miles came back to help us. I think about it all the time. He actually helped save us,' Mikasa says, and it throws me off hearing her speak about him suddenly. She's the only other person in our group who knew Miles before he and his parents were kicked out of Nubis.

The twins are from Nexus, which is still lit. Apparently, their parents were intrigued by Nubis after hearing about the tamers. They decided to move here to learn how to live in the forever night in case Nexus was the next target.

If I'm honest, I'm not sure I would have done the same. If the Darkness and the Reapers came again, I would try and fight for my home with everyone else. Or I'd like to think I would. A lot's changed since then.

'Do you think he's coming back?' Lincoln asks.

'Yeah. I'm sure of it,' I say confidently. Miles never breaks his promises. Good or not, he promised he'd be back. So he will.

'We'd probably all be dead if it wasn't for you,' Thomas murmurs. He clutches the frame tighter and stares hard at the ground. 'It was so scary. The shadows in our faces . . .'

'Yeah, that shadow stuff was the worst. It felt like my soul was being invaded and sucked out of my body at the same time,' Mikasa shivers.

'At least it's over now,' Lincoln says, scratching the back of his head.

'Is it though?' Mikasa asks, swinging her legs back and forth. 'How do we know the Reaper King won't just find another way to come back? What do you think, Mia?'

I see Thomas and Lincoln staring up at me too. I throw my head up to gaze at the stars again. That's the big question, isn't it?

'Honestly, I'm not sure, but we'd be clowns if we ruled it out,' I say finally. *Especially if my nightmares are anything to go by . . .*

But I don't mention that.

'Well, hopefully that sucker stays gone,' Lincoln huffs.

The stars begin to shift so we call it a day. I wave goodbye to the others and head for home down the busy street. Like bolter flies to a lamp, people's eyes are drawn to me and the feeling of being stared at hits me again instantly. I catch a group of adults stare and nod in my direction. Someone barges me and I open my mouth to yell but stop myself. *Don't lose control.*

I bury my hands in my sleeves and narrow my eyes to the ground. I head over the bridge and glance briefly at Miles's old house. He should've come back by now.

I cut through the buzzing marketplace. Beads, necklaces, bracelets and earrings hang from shop stalls, old and new. Bright fairy lights decorate them all and big flashy signs hang above them. A lot of strange new stuff came from the people from Stella. Different types of clothes with weird sparkly gems and patterns. Many with extra-long sleeves, which actually look pretty cool. The trinkets are all different too, and one resembling a mini-tornado in a bottle catches my eye. *I wonder what that's for.*

I carry on walking and marvel at what looks like a collection of tiny floating planets contained in a long glass box. I stop in front of the stall and spot a small sphere sitting on a tiny pillow in a dark blue box. Inside the sphere, clouds slowly move.

'It's a weather ball, little lightcaster.'

I jump and look up at the tall man behind the stall. He grins through his long curly moustache and beard.

'Mia,' I correct him. 'So, what does it do? Tell you the weather?'

He wipes his hands on his shirt and I step back a bit as he reaches over and picks up the ball with a bit too much enthusiasm. 'Precisely. This shows it's expected to be cloudy tomorrow.'

He shoves it in my face and I jerk my head back with a frown.

'Here, little lightcaster, you can have it, if you'd like.'

*If this guy calls me lightcaster one more time . . .*

'My name is Mia, and no thanks, sir, I'm good,' I say, eyeing him up.

'Are you sure?' he asks, waving the ball in front of me as if that would make a difference. I stare at him blankly, keeping my arms firmly at my sides.

'Yep, I'm good. I gotta get going. Have a nice night, sir!' I spin on my heel and speed-walk the flip outta there.

I pass Ms Mabel's stand and smile as I spot the pretty elderly lady tie her braids back into a ponytail. There's a long line of customers waiting for some of her sweets and snacks. I don't blame them. If I had more time and tokens, I would queue up too. They're the best and sweetest in the kingdom.

Spotting me, Ms Mabel waves me over. I walk along the line, avoiding the stares. She gives me a big smile when I enter the back of her stall.

I clasp my fingers together and bow. 'Hi, Ms Mabel.'

'Hi, dear. I hear you've been doing well in your new classes. I bet you smashed today's lesson, so here, have these.' She slips a few packets in my hand with a wink. She clasps her hands and bows back to me, then turns to serve the other customers, like nothing happened. I look down to see two bags of precious choco-mallows. Small oval-shaped chocolate filled with gooey marshmallow goodness. The biggest smile spreads across my face and my mouth waters.

'Thank you, Ms Mabel,' I whisper, popping one in my mouth. She gives me a wink as I slip out from behind her stall and run home with my sweets safely in my grasp.

When I get home, Dad's in his study with Lucas sitting on the carpet, flicking through his digital book tablet. I knock on the door and slowly push it open wider. Lucas's head whips up with a big smile. At least he seems to be in a better mood.

'What have you got, Mimi? Can I see?' He tries to eye what's in my hands and I turn my body to keep it out of sight. His big brown eyes stare at me, pleadingly. 'Pleeeease, Mimi?'

*This pipsqueak . . .* I sigh and show him. He gasps.

'You got TWO bags of choco-mallow drops?'

'Yeah, Ms Mabel gave them to me because I've been doing well in my classes,' I tell him.

Confusion spreads across Lucas's face. 'But I did good in my classes too, and I've been doing good in my lightcas-er training. I heard Mummy and Daddy say it,' he says, and my eyebrow twitches.

'Good for you,' I murmur, with a twinge of annoyance. *Little cheeseball.*

'You're both doing well with your lightcaster training,' Dad says, but I press my lips together. *Yeah, right . . .*

Lucas continues to stare at the bags of sweets and I look at them, then back to him. Dad's eyes burn the side of my face. Silently waiting to see what I'm gonna do next, but with a quiet warning not to be mean to my little brother.

'Fine. You can have some,' I say, holding in the urge to kiss my teeth. There's no way Lucas is getting a whole bag though. Dad gives me the nod of approval and smiles.

'What do you say?' Dad prompts Lucas.

'Yay! Thank you, Mimi!' He hugs my legs, and I crouch down and hug him back. I roll my eyes with a smile and open one of the packets for him.

He shoves his hand in and I gasp as he takes out a huge handful.

'Hey!'

'I touched them now,' he giggles, and I shake my head. *Sneaky.* Dad chuckles, but quickly stops when my eyes switch to him. He wouldn't be laughing if it was his honey coffee.

'Is Mum still at the lab?' I ask, glancing up at the holoclock.

'Yes, she's going to be a bit late today. She thinks she might be on the verge of a breakthrough adjusting a piece of technology from Stella to run on moonlight,' Dad says. He takes a loud sip of his coffee and, after a moment, clears his throat. My shoulders tense, knowing exactly what's coming next.

'So, what happened to lightcaster training today?' he asks.

He watches me carefully, waiting for me to fess up. I rub the back of my head sheepishly. What am I supposed to say? That I don't want to train because I hate these powers? That it feels like they're getting even more out of control every single time I try to practise?

I settle for just one word. 'Sorry.'

He nods, but the frown on his face says more. 'You need to take your training more seriously.'

'I know.' *It just sucks.*

My attention shifts to the giant map on the wall. It shows the entire kingdom with pins dotted all over. The cities with a big X through them are the ones taken by the Darkness.

I point to the map. 'What's with the pins?'

'Oh, you mean the pins on the map that you saw when you snuck into my private office that was supposed to be locked months ago?'

I pause, and Lucas stops wolfing down his sweets.

Seeing the look on my face, Dad grins.

'I'm just teasing you, Baby-girl. They're bandit huts,' he says.

'We stayed in a bandit hut when we ran away from the city, but it was completely abandoned,' I tell him.

'They're all abandoned,' Dad says.

'How come?' I ask.

'The truth is, we don't know. We assumed maybe it was the Reaper King, or the umbra, or even wild animals that scared them off,' says Dad, 'but the fact that not a single person lives out in the plains any more is strange. A lot of things have been happening right under our noses, and I don't like it. The only thing we know now is that Astaroth is where the Elite were based. They took some of the tamers there and ...' Dad trails off, but without saying it I know the end to that sentence. Their souls were most likely fed to the Reaper King. I never asked how many people we lost that day. A part of me never wants to know, but since Astaroth was the first city taken by the Reaper King, it's no surprise the Elite lived there.

'Jada's mum, and the others that were taken during the Blood Moon, also confirmed they lived in Astaroth. It's the only thing we've gotten out of them,' Dad adds.

His eyes flick to the map and his lips press into a tight line. 'I still can't believe the Elite fooled us. Ignis was taken over way before our knowledge. It must have been at least a few weeks before they sent the fake distress call.'

'But how did they know?' I ask, following his gaze to Ignis on the map.

'Know what, Baby-girl?'

'How did they know that there was a lightcaster in Nubis? They didn't know it was me until that gutterslug Elite guy stuck his smoke in my face, but they knew to invade here,' I say.

46

Dad rubs his chin. 'It could have simply been a process of elimination and Nubis was next on the list. Or perhaps yours or Lucas's powers sparked at some point. Too subtle for you to notice, but enough to trigger the attention of the Reaper King. Either way, they used Ignis to trick the tamers to leave the city unguarded.'

'How could the queen not know though?' I wonder. 'She's supposed to constantly be checking in with every city.'

'That's the million-token question, Baby-girl.'

Unless she did know . . . and still did nothing to help. The queen said it herself: she doesn't have the power of the lightcasters.

Dad shuts down his holocomputer and gets up while Lucas goes back to scoffing his sweets like a four-eared squirrel.

'Don't finish all of them – we're going to have dinner soon,' Dad tells him.

'I'm gonna change my clothes and check on Lux and Nox,' I say, hearing them upstairs.

When Mum comes home, we eat dinner then listen to music in the living room. We talk about our day and what the plan is for tomorrow in the lead-up to the tamer trials. Most of the evening is pretty chill, but that changes when it's time for bed.

I say goodnight to everyone, but my anxiety spikes the moment I get changed and pull the covers over me. I watch the multicoloured stars dance on the ceiling from my constellation projector, my eyes refusing to shut. Lux and Nox are on the floor by my bed. I turn on my side and see that they're still awake too.

'OK, that's it.' I throw off my covers and stand up. 'I've gotta shake off this anxiety.'

My hand hovers over my song box and music quietly fills the room. When I was little, dancing always helped me when I was anxious. My eyes close for a moment and instantly I'm a puppet, with the music as the strings.

My arms flow with the changing melody and my legs carry me around the room in leaps and pirouettes. Light and freeing. The music guides me with the beat and the speed of my turns quickens with the rise of the tempo and slows when it calms. Gradually, I begin to feel at peace with my mind and body. A warmth glows in my heart and spreads along my arms and legs. It swirls like energy in my palms and I can't help smiling.

*'Young one, your hands.'*

I look down and see my palms glowing purple. The glow pulses like little waves in a river and travels up my arms. Lux and Nox's golden eyes widen in surprise but before they can comment further there are two swift knocks on the door. I turn around as it clicks open and the light vanishes.

'Are you OK, honey?' Mum asks, peeking her head inside.

'Yeah?' I say, slightly confused. *What just happened?*

I wave my hand over my music box, bringing my room to silence again. Then I notice something tucked under Mum's arm.

She walks into my room and takes the thing into her hands. It's a small dark-blue journal with stars decorating the border. She sits down on my bed, patting the space beside her. I join her and she passes me the book.

'I know you've been having nightmares, sweetheart,' she says.

She chuckles as my jaw drops and my eyes immediately look at Lux and Nox.

*'Don't even think about blaming us. We didn't tell her anything,'* Lux protests.

'They really didn't,' Mum says. 'The past few nights,

I've been hearing you awake in your room. You've not been sleeping well.'

I can't believe she's known all along.

'Do you keep having the same nightmare or is it a different one each time?' she asks, running her hand down my cheek.

'It's different dreams about the same thing …' I murmur. One way or another, it always comes back to the Reaper King.

'Do you want to tell me about them?' she asks.

I hear the slight pressure in her voice, but she doesn't push. I want to, so much, but if I do she might confirm the fear I have that these dreams *do* mean something, and I'm not ready for that possibility yet. I don't wanna know.

Accepting my hesitation, Mum squeezes me in a hug.

'It's OK. That's why I brought this,' she says, putting the book in my hands. 'It's a nightmare journal. Write down all your nightmares in here. You'll feel better getting them out of your head and on to a piece of paper. If you lock them away in this book, I'm sure they'll eventually stop.'

I cross my legs and grab a pen from my bedside table. Mum kisses my head and whispers, 'If you can't go back to sleep and want to talk, you know where to find me,' then quietly leaves.

I write down the nightmare from last night. Remembering Lucas's eyes and Mum and Dad trapped in a cage again strikes fear in my gut, but I do feel a bit better. I scribble down the night before that, and the earlier ones, and by the time I'm finished, ten pages are filled. I close the book shut, locking the nightmares away.

*'Feel better?'* Nox asks.

'Yeah,' I say, yawning. I slowly lie back down and stare at the ceiling. 'Guys, can you sleep on my bed tonight ... please?'

*'Of course, young one,'* Nox says.

*'Those foolish nightmares can't harm you with us around,'* Lux snorts.

They both jump on to the bed. Nox rests beside me. I kiss their heads and cuddle Nox close. His cool shadow fur gently caresses my arms, making me feel warm and safe. *Thanks guys ...*

And for the first time in a long time, I sleep without any nightmares.

# CHAPTER FOUR

I sit on the steps of the city hall. Elbows on my knees. Chin in my hands. Beside me, Margaux sighs. She throws a rock across the pavement, equally bored. We've been waiting for almost half an hour. My fingers drum against the side of my face. *I wonder what's taking Riley and Myla so long.*

On the other side of me, Aaron leans against the wall with his hands in his pockets. His eyes constantly flicker to his holowatch. Slightly away from the group, Elijah and the clown Abigail quietly talk to each other. Elijah's eye twitches in annoyance but before I can try and listen in, Clara's gasp catches my attention.

I follow her gaze and my eyes widen. I stand up and wave. Dad casually waves back as he walks towards us. The moonlight reflects the shiny armour plates attached to his tamer jacket as it flaps in the wind, and I find myself grinning goofily. *Dad's so cool.*

Blending in and out of the dark spaces between the light of the glow bugs and lamp posts, Bolt walks beside him. A panther-like shadow with a snake tail that swings back and forth.

'Sorry for being so late. There was a last-minute switch since Riley is sorting out a minor public incident,' Dad says.

I try to fight my smile, but Dad catches it. He smiles back then shifts his attention to everyone else. He stands with his hands behind his back, proud. Elijah is the first to step forward. He connects his hands and bows. The others all bow too. Even stink Abigail does. *At least we won't have to worry about her bullying today.*

*'True. Although, I'm pretty sure she will not be bothering you for a long time after the last class,'* Nox says.

*'That's a shame. I was looking forward to fighting her and that rat of an umbra she has as a partner,'* Lux snorts.

Dad clears his throat and my focus quickly goes back to him. He eyes me, knowing full well I wasn't paying attention. *Oops.* We're not gonna be able to get away with *anything* today. As if to prove my point,

Bolt's golden eyes linger on me a second longer than the others.

'So, as I was saying. Today I'll be covering the basics of what it means to be a tamer,' Dad says. 'Not the most exciting lesson compared to your physical training, but just as important. It's a reminder why you're doing this training and to always remain humble as tamers are protectors of our society.'

*'Follow us,'* Bolt orders and we silently follow them through the city.

'It goes without saying that tamers are important to the people of Nubis. We are keepers of peace within the walls and protectors from forces outside the walls,' Dad explains.

Every step he takes is full of purpose. He slows down as we pass an old travel-pod station and my eyes flicker to the travelling machines.

*'As you know, we maintain order within the city, and we're always ready to go on rescue missions at any moment for any city in the kingdom. Hence the travel pods.'* Pride echoes from Bolt's voice too. He stares lovingly at Dad before looking at us.

We carry on walking and divert through an alley. Margaux, Clara and Aaron listen closely to every word, but behind them Abigail and Elijah trail back. From the furrowed eyebrows and angry hushed whispers, Elijah seems extra agitated today. He suddenly nods to me as he whispers, and it throws me off.

'As for the hierarchy of the tamers, we try to keep it as equal as possible,' Dad continues, coming to a stop back at the city hall. 'We tend to vote on all decisions made. However, in the event that an urgent decision needs to be made, then the lead tamer decides.'

He turns to face us and brings a hand to his chest. 'And as you all already know, that position currently belongs to me.'

The fiery passion behind his eyes is only a small bit of how much Dad loves his job. A warm smile spreads across my face.

'And eventually someone will take my position as head tamer.'

He makes it a point to stare at me and my smile falters. I don't want to be leader of the tamers. I barely want to be a tamer at all. I'm only doing the training because I've come this far and I want to learn more about my connection with Lux and Nox. I wanna be a martial arts teacher first and foremost.

I chew the inside of my lip and avoid Dad's eyes. If

anything, I wanna be like Mum and do two things. Be a tamer *and* a martial arts teacher. You don't get that choice if you're the leader. But how am I supposed to tell all of this to Dad?

'How is the leader chosen?' Elijah pipes up.

'A vote,' Dad answers. 'You put yourself forward if you want the role and the other tamers vote.'

We walk through the purple grassy field near the martial arts dojo next and cross the East River Bridge, making our way to Mum's lab.

*'The tamers work closely with the scientists. The scientists are always working on different ways to help both tamers and umbra. It was due to their work that we figured out that there was even a third form,'* Bolt explains. *'When tamer and umbra become one ultimate being.'*

'Wow, I didn't know that,' Margaux murmurs to me.

Dad orders us to stand in line by the door. He steps in front of the scanner first, and the light flashes him up and down.

'Hey,' Margaux nudges me. 'Earlier on, Eli was basically telling Abigail to leave you alone from now.'

I raise an eyebrow and Margaux grins.

'I saw you looking at them,' she says. My lips part, baffled by her words. He was backing me up?

'*Seems like you did prove yourself to your classmates,*' Nox acknowledges. A warm fuzzy feeling washes through me.

Margaux stares up at the lab with a smile and there's even a twinkle of curiosity in Elijah's eyes. *Maybe we can be friends after all.*

'Welcome, Daniel McKenna,' a robotic voice greets my father.

The light flashes green and the doors slide open. Dad waves us over. We all go inside and Abigail gasps. The bright white walls stretch up to a domed ceiling high above us. Hologram umbra run and jump around us. I'm so used to going to the lab now because of Mum, but the lab is usually closed off to anyone who isn't a tamer, scientist or child of a scientist.

Our shoes squeak against the shiny white floor and my nose stings from the strong smell of antibacterial spray and disinfectant. I fall back with Lux and Nox, taking in the different rooms we pass. Scientists examine shadow matter and others check over the crystal fragments.

'Mia, you don't have to stay for this section,' Dad calls back to me, and I nod.

\*

I wander off from the group and I find myself stopping in front of a room with a blue door. My chest tightens, knowing what's on the other side, or more specifically *who's* on the other side. Through the blinds beside the door, I spot him lying unconscious in the bed. Samuel Walker. He hasn't woken up since attempting to do a spirit calling. He lies there with his messy blond hair and cosy blue pyjamas. Mum and the other scientists wanted him to be as comfy as possible.

Something flickers past the blinds but when I look back through the window, nothing's there.

'That's weird,' I murmur.

The door clicks open and I quickly stumble back.

'Hey honey, is the lab tour happening already?' Mum asks. She has a clipboard in hand and quirks an eyebrow at *my* hand that hovers over my staff.

'Sorry,' I say sheepishly, lowering my hand, and Mum laughs.

'Who'd you think would be in this room?' she asks.

I shrug. 'Better to be safe than sorry.'

'True,' she replies, 'although I don't imagine there'd be anyone you'd need to fight in a laboratory. Anyway, you can come in. I was just checking over Samuel.'

She opens the door wider and I walk inside with

Lux and Nox. Mum's umbra, Spike, nuzzles my hand with his fluffy bear head on the way in and I stroke his shadows.

Beeping echoes throughout the room. Wavy lines and numbers flicker on the screens around the bed and a blue light scans Samuel every fifteen seconds, inputting the information on the monitors. My heart skips a bit, seeing his calm face.

'Still no change?' I ask.

'Sadly not,' Mum says, looking at one of the monitors and jotting something down on her clipboard. 'Spike has been to the Spirit Plain multiple times to try and find him. Recently we tried bringing the lightcaster crystal fragments to see if anything would happen, but still nothing.'

The lost tone in Mum's voice makes my stomach lurch.

*'We won't give up though,'* Spike adds.

An idea buzzes in my mind but I chew my lip, wondering if I should say it.

'Do you think my powers would work on him? It was something I was thinking about trying with Nan and Grandad,' I murmur. 'Could the light, like, call his soul back to his body?'

Mum's fingers drum against the clipboard. She hums, thinking about it.

'Maybe, but you need a lot more training first, Mia,' she warns me. 'Right now we can't risk you using your powers on Samuel, or anyone. Not until you're sure you can control them.'

I guess she's not wrong.

I open and close my hand. Maybe my powers can be used for good. They *have* helped sometimes, but every time I think about them all I see is the destruction they cause. Still, if I can control them then I can really help people. Like Nan and Grandad, and Samuel. I bite back a small smile that begins to form the more I think about it. Maybe, just maybe, a whole lotta good could come from these powers.

'All right,' I say, coming to a conclusion. 'I won't run away from my powers any more.'

I kiss Mum's cheek, ruffle Spike's shadows and race out the door fuelled with new determination. These powers could actually *help* people. I gotta learn more!

I head straight home and flick through the pages of the *Legends of the Lightcasters* book in the living room. The words are still written in a language I can't understand, but I scan through the pictures and Dad's notes, trying to figure out anything more about the founders – the people who created Lunis. I chew my lip, looking back and forth from the different notes and pictures.

From the little that's been deciphered, we know their names at least: Ria, Rehan, Kikyo, Blaze and Aurora, and the author of this book, the only one whose name we don't know yet. They were the original lightcasters, the first humans to be granted the power of light by two crystals they discovered somewhere in the Nightmare Plains. What happened between them gaining that power and now is still unknown, but putting it together with the city-wall mural, they were the ancestors of my family, the old Queen Lucina, and any other lightcaster who might be out there.

More than once I wondered if the author of this book might be someone in our family since it's been passed down for years on Mum's side, but who? It still blows my mind that me and Lucas are descendants of a founder of Lunis.

'How are you feeling about tomorrow, Baby-girl?' Dad asks, walking into the living room, having returned from the lab.

*Oh yeah, the tamer trials.*

I shrug, closing the book. 'I'm OK. Me, Lux and Nox are a pretty good team. If we can take down the Reaper King we can do anything, right?'

He smiles but I see the pain in his eyes that he can never fully hide.

The front door opens and closes.

'We're home!' Mum calls out from the hallway and Lucas runs inside, hugging Dad and then me.

'Welcome back,' Dad says.

'How about a bit of lightcaster practice?' Mum asks, taking off her lab coat, and I throw my back against the sofa and scrunch up my face. I know I said I'd try, but geez, she only just came in.

'Come on, Lucas, you too,' Mum says, patting his side.

Lucas yawns and stretches his arms in the air. 'OK Mummy.'

He drags his feet to the door. I close my eyes and take a deep breath in and out. *I can do this.*

Mum ushers everyone through the kitchen with a bit too much pep in her step. She doesn't say it, but the scientist part of her is fascinated every time we practise our powers. Whereas Dad's all strict and down to business, going into 'leader of the tamers' mode.

I wave for Lux and Nox to join us. *If I'm being dragged into this, you two gotta come too.*

'*If we must,*' Lux moans. I shake my head at him and we all head outside into the garden.

Pretty blue, pink and yellow rosy-dill flowers and white cloud blossoms decorate the garden with bright colours that glow in the moonlight. All thanks to Dad and Lucas's handiwork, watering them every day.

Dad walks down the steps and Bolt, Spike, Lux and Nox sit by the back door. Their golden eyes watch as I stretch my arms and kick out my legs.

'Ready?' Mum asks.

'Not really,' I mumble. *But it's not like I have a choice.*

Almost like she reads my thoughts, she smiles encouragingly. 'Don't let it stress you out too much, sweetheart. You'll get the hang of it. I know you will.'

'Right now you can do little bursts here and there without the need of Queen Katiya's staff, but let's try and make your powers more visible,' Dad says, getting down to business. 'So, first, wiggle your body. Shake out all the negativity and loosen up.'

*What?* My eyebrows furrow. He shakes his arms and legs and Lucas giggles, copying him. They both look so ridiculous, and I want to laugh.

'Come on, Mia. Loosen up,' Mum chuckles, joining in.

*Oh boy ...* I roll my eyes. Dad jigs his eyebrows up and down, forcing a small smile outta me.

'Fine,' I mumble. *You guys win.*

I shake my arms then my hips, wiggling like a tree worm. Good thing our garden fences are high.

'That's it. There you go, Baby-girl!' Dad cheers. We stop and he stretches out his arms in front of him. 'Now rub your hands together and hold out your palms like this. Focus all of your energy into your hands.'

I do as he says, and so does Lucas. I close my eyes, searching my inner self for the energy. I inhale. A cold breeze shivers down my spine. I exhale and a sense of calm washes through my body. A little flicker of a flame burns in the centre of my chest and I push it towards my hands.

'Found it,' I mutter, keeping my eyes shut.

'Think about what colour it is,' Mum says. 'How does it feel? Is it heavy or light? Imagine pushing it out of your palms.'

My lips press together and I focus on a purple light filling my hands. I don't know if it's really that colour, or it's just because it's my favourite, but it's airy and my palms barely feel anything except *warmth*. Just like it did when I was dancing. I slowly push it out of my hands, feeling it grow bigger and bigger. Someone gasps.

I quickly open my eyes with a smile, but it immediately drops. My hands are still my regular hands. Next to me, Lucas's hands are glowing with a soft blue light.

'I did it! I did it! Look!' He jumps from foot to foot with glee. I look at my empty hands and frown. *Nothing. Again.* I ball my hands into fists.

'Good job, Lucas. Well done!' Mum cheers.

An arm tugs me into a gentle side hug. 'You'll get it,' Dad promises.

*Yeah, right . . .*

The light around Lucas's hands suddenly vanishes and he sticks his bottom lip out.

'It's gone!'

'You done it once, you can do it again,' I mutter. *Unlike me.*

'And so will you,' Mum adds, but I huff.

'Try again. Take your time,' she encourages.

I reluctantly hold up my palms again. This time I keep my eyes open. *Focus . . .*

I find and channel the purple energy once more. It sparks and I hold on to it, pushing it to one concentrated spot in my hands. I feel it swirl in my palms, building up like an invisible hurricane, faster and faster. My hands shake from the pressure and I grit my teeth harder. *Control it. Force it out!* It bubbles and burns beneath my skin like lava.

'Come out already!' I yell. A light bursts from my palms straight up to the sky. It flares like a raging purple flame, and I gasp. My heart almost leaps in my throat.

Mum and Dad stumble back but I stay focused on my hands. I hold my breath. *Keep going! You got this!*

'Mimi!' Lucas yells.

In the corner of my eye I see the umbra rise to their feet and Dad yells. 'That's my girl!'

The warmth of the light that pulses from my palm settles. The flickers greet me with a soft glow, feeling strangely comforting. I gaze into it, drawn in like a magical spell, and for the first time ever . . . I feel at one with my powers.

Fully in control.

*'Her eyes . . .'* Bolt says. *'They're gold, like ours.'*

'I suppose it's because umbra were created partly from lightcasters,' Mum says.

The pressure in my chest builds and my body screams for breath. *Just a little longer.* But I can't last. I gasp, filling my aching lungs, and instantly the light poofs into thin air, leaving behind only emptiness.

'Well done, darling!' Mum claps. She gives me the biggest hug.

*No way . . . I really did it. I flippin' did it!* I grin from ear to ear, unable to hold in the happiness and relief that all come tumbling out.

'Tomorrow after the tamer trials, we'll all go for ice cream to celebrate. I'm so proud of both of you,' Dad announces.

*Yes!*

After dinner I head to my bathroom to get ready for bed. I wash my face, enjoying the cold splash of water against my face.

'Can you guys believe I actually controlled my powers!' I call out to Lux and Nox.

*'The way she's acting, it's like she's conquered the whole kingdom or something,'* Lux muses.

*'Yes, we are proud of you, young one,'* Nox says, ignoring his brother before walking to my bedroom.

I brush my teeth with a cheesy grin. I spit out the toothgel and look in the mirror. But what I see freaks me completely. I jump back and my toothbrush clatters in the sink. Pitch-black eyes stare back at me with black tear-stains running down my cheeks. A devilish shark-tooth grin spreads across my reflected face, and my stomach twists. I want to scream but I can't, and I crash back against the wall. The terrifying reflection is me – but that's *not* my face.

I force myself to look away. *It's OK. Breathe. It's not real.* I snatch another look and my brown eyes stare back at me like normal. With a pounding heart, I gently press my fingers against my cheeks and open my mouth – no shark teeth. My throat's bone dry and I struggle to swallow. *What the flip is going on?*

The door bursts open and I almost jump outta my skin. Lux and Nox stare in a panic.

'*Are you OK, young one? We felt something off,*' Nox asks.

'*You look like you've just been to the Spirit Plain and back,*' Lux adds.

My mouth opens but I struggle to form words. *What do I even say? Did that really just happen?* I realise my hands are shaking.

They are at my side in seconds but I gently wave them away.

'I'm … fine. I just saw something weird but I'm probably just tired,' I tell them, but they continue to stare. 'I was brushing my teeth and I saw this weird reflection of myself in the mirror. I don't know if this is some side effect of my powers but it's gone now.'

They look at each other, obviously having a private conversation, but I'm too rattled to even care. I walk past them into my bedroom.

*'This isn't good, Mouse,'* Lux says. *'Not with the nightmares too. You need to tell Lila and Daniel.'*

'If it happens again, I'll tell them. I promise,' I say. 'I don't want to worry them unless I have to.'

*'All right, but if you don't then we will,'* Nox warns.

'Yes, sir …' I murmur.

I throw myself on my bed and I hear them settle on the carpet. I slip on my purple hair bonnet, trying to forget what happened. I hate having the nightmares while I'm sleeping – but the reflection in the mirror feels like proof I'm living in mine, and I can't wake up from it.

*'I'm waiting …'*

My eyes burst open. The ceiling and walls are

dripping with little red droplets. I reach out my hand and some splash into my palm, staining it. I yank off my sheets, and hop out of bed, my feet squelching on the floor. I look down and see that it's glowing, bathed in red. A sickening metallic smell hits my nose and there's no doubt what it is. Blood.

'Lux! Nox!' I scream, spinning around, but they've gone, and so has the door. The bloodstained walls box me in. My chest tightens as my breathing quickens.

*Wake up. Wake up!* I grip my head, trying to will myself awake. The sickly metallic smell grows stronger. I can't take this! I run across the room and bang my fists against the bloodied walls.

'Let me out!'

*No. Don't move. It's not safe.*

I almost jump out of my skin. A woman's voice. The *same* voice I heard in my last dream. I tremble and cover my ears, trying to tune it out. *Please, just wake up.*

Something glints in the corner of my eye and I turn to look properly. A gold crown rests on the floor several feet away. I squelch over to it, trying not to think about what I'm stepping in. I crouch down and run my fingers over it.

'Mia!'

I jump up and spin around, recognising the voice immediately. 'Dad?'

He's standing there in his tamer clothes. Shadows spurt out of his mouth and I stumble back. He reaches forward and panic fills his eyes. I gasp, stretching my hand towards him.

'Dad!' I try to run to him but skeleton hands shoot out of the bloodied floor, latching on to my arms and legs. I scream, thrashing and jerking against them.

*'He's mine!'*

I scream at the top of my lungs at hearing the Reaper King's voice. *Get outta my head! Get outta my head!* I see dad mouth the words: 'I'm sorry, Mia.'

I try to stretch out to him as bony hands appear from behind and snatch him away.

'Dad! DAD!' I tear and claw at the skeleton hands that trap me. The bones crack and I break free, but it's too late.

More shadows spurt from his mouth as the gruesome limbs pull at him. He reaches out for me but he's yanked back, sucked into the wall, disappearing into the blood.

'NO!' I jump up from my bed, bathed in sweat.

'*Another nightmare?*' Nox asks from the floor.

'*What happened?*' Lux asks. He stands up and taps my head with his horn.

'Dad.' I barely recognise my choked-up voice. 'He was throwing up shadows or something. It was so scary. I couldn't help him. I heard a woman's voice too. She told me it wasn't safe. Then I heard *his* voice.'

'*Young one, what if these nightmares are not just nightmares?*' Nox asks. '*What if the Reaper King is trying to contact you from the Spirit Plain?*'

As much as I hate to admit it, Nox is right. I can't keep running away from this and avoiding the thought of the Reaper King still being out there. I reach for my nightmare journal and write down everything that happened.

'I'm sure I've heard that woman's voice before too,' I say, rubbing my face. 'It's freaking me out.'

'*It was probably just part of the nightmare,*' Lux says.

'I don't know. It felt weird,' I say. They give me a puzzled look. 'Let's just … go back to sleep. Let's get through the tamer trials then we'll decide what to do.'

'*Fine, Mouse. Go to sleep,*' Lux says.

I lie back down, but my eyes are wide open.

'Can you guys tell me a story?' I whisper. Anything

to take my mind off that nightmare.

'Of course. We'll tell you about the time we first met a human,' Nox says.

'It was a foolish one too. Tried to capture us with a rope gun out in the Nightmare Plains when we were minding our own business,' Lux snorts.

'Why would they try and capture you with a rope gun?' I ask with a yawn.

'Who knows? Maybe to eat us,' Lux says.

'Wait, what?'

'Ignore him,' Nox says. 'The human tried to capture us but obviously it was futile and we attacked him, stole his bag and escaped.'

'He tried chasing us but he couldn't keep up. We ended up throwing his bag up a tree somewhere. It's what he deserved,' Lux adds.

I want to ask questions, but instead I fall asleep.

# CHAPTER FIVE

I keep my eyes on my reflection the entire time, but my normal reflection stares back at me. Was I just seeing things yesterday? No, I definitely know what I saw. I just have to try and block it out. After washing my face and brushing my teeth, I moisturise my hair and tie it back into a low ponytail with bangs. *Let's just get these trials over with.*

I throw on a hoodie and put on some shorts with leggings. I smile and pick up the note Dad left me on my desk:

Today's the day, Baby-girl! You got this, but the tamers aren't going to go easy on you. Try your best, I know you can do it. See you outside.
Love Dad xx

*Time to go.*

I click open my door, but this time there's no movement from Lucas's room. He must still be sleeping. Spike is probably in there with him while Mum and Dad prep for the tamer trials at the main gate. I head downstairs with Lux and Nox and grab the big potato pasty from the kitchen that Mum left for me, along with my survival bag that she packed for me.

*'Are you ready, young one?'* Nox asks. I yawn and stretch my arms in the air. It's so early, not even the birds are out.

'Yep. I'm not sweatin' this,' I say. We've faced worse after all.

*'That's right. Your classmates should be more worried,'* Lux says. I high-five their horns and together we head outside. Lux and Nox transform into their adult forms in a flash of bright light.

It's time for the tamer trials.

A long line of tamers stand on either side of the city gate, armour plates and all, with their umbra nobly by their sides. Next to me, Margaux, Elijah, Aaron, Clara and that clown-face Abigail stand across from the gate with their full-sized umbra. Eyes forward, hands firmly behind their backs. We patiently wait to pass through the gate to the Nightmare Plains – the place that haunted me as a little kid and is now my training ground.

'This is it, guys,' Riley says. 'Remember this is all training that you will incorporate when you hopefully become tamers. It should not only improve your danger perception, but the teamwork with your umbra as well.'

Amongst the other tamers, Mum and Jada stand proudly. My eyes briefly connect with my old teacher, and she silently wishes me luck with a smile. Mum gives me a little wink.

Riley steps back and my attention quickly switches to Dad. He paces in front of me and my classmates, his shoulder guards glistening in the moonlight.

'You are all about to take part in the Tamer Trials,' he says. 'For twenty-four hours, you will be individually hunted by almost every tamer in the city, so I hope you packed enough food and supplies. If you get caught, you'll have to return to your class and try again next year.'

Beside him, Bolt swishes his shadowy snake-like tail, addressing us next.

*'You are to stay on the Nightmare Plains at all times.*

*You cannot hide in any of the cities. If something goes wrong, fire your flares.'*

I pat my pocket to make sure my mini flare is in there. *Got it.*

'Sometimes as a tamer you will be in a position where you have to judge whether it's best to run or to fight. This will be a test of that. Weighing the risks. Will you be brave enough to risk getting caught to stop the enemy from following you? Or will you run?' Dad says. *Well, we already got experience with that.*

*'Too much experience,'* Nox adds.

I look up and see it's almost sky connect, the start of a brand-new day. Most of us would normally still be in bed, especially on a weekend, but not today.

'Ready?'

I nod. If someone had told me months ago I'd tame not one, but two umbra, I probably would've fainted from shock or something, but I look back at Lux and Nox, and smile. They nudge me with their noses and I pet their shadowy heads. They're the best thing that's ever happened to me.

I know Mum and Dad are worried that the tamer trials will trigger my emotions after what I've been through escaping the Elite. Constantly being hunted.

But I can only find out by facing the trials. Besides ...
I'm not alone. I have Lux and Nox now.

*'And you always will,'* I hear Nox in my head.

*'You can't get rid of us that easily, Mouse,'* Lux adds,
and I smile.

*You guys are the best.*

'If you're still free at sky connect tomorrow, come
straight back to the gate. Remember, we aren't going
to go easy on you,' Dad says.

Our eyes meet for a second but even without words,
I feel the strong belief and confidence he has in me.

'It's time!' Mum's voice echoes, and all the tamers
clap their hands together, clasping their fingers and
bowing forward. The older teens line up, ready to
depart the city with their umbra. Clara and Aaron look
a little nervous, while Elijah and Margaux seem more
confident. I don't even bother to look at clown-face, but
all of them seem ready for what's next.

I stand at the back and twist my hands in my sleeves,
and suddenly my stomach flutters. One by one, each
of my classmates leaves, racing off into the plains as
quickly as they can on their umbra, not looking back.
When it's my turn, I walk towards the open gates with
Lux and Nox beside me past all the tamers. I gently

gulp and tie my hoodie around my waist. *What if I freeze up when we're out there?*

*'If you do, we will be there to take you far away before any tamer can catch you,'* Nox reassures.

*'We're passing this trial no matter what,'* Lux adds.

*Yeah, that's right. Why the flip am I getting nervous? We got this!*

Jada gives me a sneaky thumbs-up and Ruby bows her head. We reach Dad last. He bows to me with an encouraging smile. I'm about to bow back when something catches my eye. Hiding in the bushes are Mikasa, Thomas and Lincoln, waving a small 'GO MIA, LUX AND NOX' flag.

'Good luck, Mimi!' I hear and I realise Lucas is there too with Spike. I chuckle as the others try to hush him, pulling him back into the silver leaves. Only they would break the tamer-only tradition for me. They're the best. I hear Dad sigh, but he's still smiling. He probably guessed this would happen.

I hop on Nox's back and reach over to pat Lux.

*Ready guys?*

Dad steps aside and the Nightmare Plains await. My fingers tangle with Nox's shadow fur. I barely see the others racing ahead into the moonlit purple land, and my stomach twists in knots. *I got this . . . or at the very least I can go down trying.*

'Let's go,' I mutter.

Nox rises on to his hind legs and we're off, galloping across the plains. We have twenty minutes before the tamers give chase.

The light smell of rosy-dill welcomes us back like an old friend and the wind whips around us, blowing my ponytail back and forth. The skeleton trees wave in the breeze, and the wild carno plants play a game of cat and mouse, snapping at Lux and Nox's shadow hooves.

We pass Mum and Dad's tree where a new safety bag is securely hidden away ready for another emergency should there ever be one. Memories of me, TJ and Lucas racing for it months ago flash in my mind, but Lux and Nox keep running. We leap over logs and boulders and pass the old cabin we stayed in just before me and TJ had to do the Spirit Calling. My heart tightens. It all feels so long ago.

A loud bang forces our eyes up and the sky lights in an explosion of colour. An announcement and a warning all in one, with a single message to all of us in the Nightmare Plains: the tamers are coming; let the challenge begin.

We gallop for hours. The winds die down and the trees are replaced by a grassy lilac field. We finally slow to a stop and I realise that just north of us is the umbra cave we found on our journey to Stella, hidden underground.

I hop off Nox and the plains are quiet with no sign of any tamers or classmates.

*I wonder how all those umbra are doing. I hope they're safe. We never did find that girl who had been with them once. They said the Elite took her, but she wasn't with any of the umbra when she was captured.*

I hear Nox sigh. '*Perhaps she got away from the Elite long ago and got lost, or is living in Stella or Nexus now.*'

'*Or perhaps she's no longer of this world,*' Lux chimes in.

Both me and Nox stare at him, but he just blinks back at us.

'Whilst we're out here, let's work on you being more positive, mate,' I say. He huffs, and walks a little ahead.

My eyes meet Nox's and we burst into laughter. We jog after Lux and I listen for any signs of someone close by. We've come pretty far so we've probably got some time before we'll see anyone.

'Should we practise that umbra-tamer connection thing we've done before? You know, when I can see through your eyes, sense what you sense and stuff? We'd be able to see if any tamers were coming from miles away.'

*It seemed to work when you were riding on my back. Perhaps a physical touch is needed,'* Nox says, lowering to the ground.

'Wait,' I say, stopping him. He stands back up in confusion. If he had eyebrows they would probably be raised and I laugh silently at the thought. 'I wanna practise running and jumping on your back, if that's OK? Similar to our new race formation.'

His eyes shift to Lux.

*'Why would you want to do that?'* he asks.

'Because if we ever needed to get away quick, you guys could run and I could jump on your back and we'd be OFF!' I zoom my hand forward and their echoey laughs fill my head. 'It'd be so cool. Don't even deny it.'

I wiggle my shoulders at him and Lux rolls his golden eyes.

*'Just climb on his back already,'* he says.

'Fine,' I muse.

A gentle breeze blows and my smile fades. Beneath the whistle of the winds, something sounds off.

'*Maybe you're hearing things,*' Lux says, looking around.

'No, I hear something.' I close my eyes, forcing myself not to rely on sight. I focus on the noises around me, blanking out everything else. There's a soft rustle of leaves on the trees, the gentle pitter-patter of Lux's hooves as he walks towards me. The buzz of the tinker bugs that scutter by my feet. The bristles of the grass brushing against each other. All normal sounds, but just beneath those noises a twig cracks and my attention snaps north.

*Someone's coming.*

A rush of energy shoots through my vision. Everything around me intensifies with colour, sound and sight. I feel my connection with Lux and Nox like electric sparks, and dead ahead, someone sitting on their umbra hides behind the hollow trees, highlighted gold in my vision. My hands brush the shadowy bodies of Lux and Nox as we stand connected.

*Do you guys see that?*

The person and their umbra suddenly dashes from the tree towards us and I see his tamer jacket flapping in the wind, and I gasp.

'It's Bently!' I yell, jumping on to Lux's back. 'Let's go! Race formation! Just like we practised!'

We gallop away and Bently gives chase. The wind slices at us from all angles and I glance back at him riding Shiro, his rhinoceros umbra with two long dragon-like tails.

It's now or never.

*Nox, you ready?*

'Of course.'

The biggest smirk spreads across my face. Lux jumps, dodging the rope shot at us. It barely grazes us and we do a swift U-turn, coming face to face with Bently and Shiro. They slow down and we dash towards our pursuers. Bently's eyes widen but he keeps coming.

His arm snaps up, ready to shoot another rope net, when I jump to my feet, crouching on Lux's back. The cold wind fights to push me off, but my fingers grip his shadow fur. Lux swings his head back and sonic screams. The ear-piercing sound pushes Bently and Shiro back.

'NOW!' I yell, backflipping into the air. For a single moment, my body feels completely weightless in the world around me until I land perfectly on Nox. 'YES!'

I punch my fist in the air. Lux keeps Bently and Shiro occupied while me and Nox race around them. I yank the rope gun from Bently's grasp and fire it off, capturing them both.

'Nice, guys!' I shout, slowing down with Nox, and Lux stops his screams.

'All right, I'll give you that one, Mia. That was good,' Bently says, grinning from his ropey prison. *Of course, it was good. We're the best team.*

'*Better luck next time,*' Lux tells them and Shiro growls.

'*Don't get too cocky. The others aren't far behind.*' His voice is smug, just like Bently's face, but it's big talk considering they're stuck under a net. As if we're actually gonna get caught now. This is way easier than I thought.

'See you after sky connect!' We gallop out and Bently yells after us.

'You better hope so, Mia!'


The fields of grass turn to soft swamp the further we gallop. The dewy smell of dirt and damp lingers in the air from the rain yesterday and I wiggle my nose.

'You guys did great,' I say, praising Lux and Nox, and Lux snickers.

We don't slow down until we're through the swamp and almost halfway between Nubis and Stella. My throat burns with thirst but I'm extra paranoid of not having enough water. We should hit the lake soon.

I slide down from Nox's back and drag my feet through the grass, giving the umbra a break from carrying me. Mud and dirt cake my leggings, and the hoodie around my waist is no longer the light purple it was before. As we walk, Lux and Nox come to an abrupt halt. Their noses rise to the air.

A chill runs down my spine. *What's going on, guys?*

'*Look,*' Nox says.

A few metres away stands a black shadowy creature. Its pointy ears flick back as its cat-like face stares right at us and its three fox-like tails bristle. It pins its glowing red eyes on me, and a low growl rumbles from the beast. Sharp teeth glisten in the moonlight. My blood runs cold, just like it did all those years ago when I first met Shade who became Miles's umbra. Those *eyes*.

Lux points his horn dead ahead and Nox steps forward.

The creature's body twitches and it shakes its head wildly, suddenly jumping like it's possessed. It cries out, its eyes shifting from red to gold, back and forth, fighting something we can't see. My breath hitches in my throat as I realise what could be happening.

*Impossible. There's just no way!*

'*Young one, get on,*' Nox says, and I hop on to his back.

'*No ... NO! LEAVE ME ALONE!*' I hear a female voice in my head – the umbra's.

'What's going on? Is someone trying to take control of you?' I yell.

'*What is wrong with—*' Nox breaks off and I gasp, gripping him for dear life as he jumps and leaps all over the place. His screams ring in my ears.

'Nox, what's wrong?'

He cries out again and I'm thrown off his back, smacking to the ground.

'*Brother!*' Lux yells and I quickly stand up, hissing at the pain stabbing my side.

But I forget the agony when I look at my umbra. Nox's eyes are flashing from gold to red and panic grips my heart.

'Nox! What's going on?' I yell. *What's happening?!*

He throws his head back and forth, still screaming so I can barely think. Then the mental connection between us snaps and his thoughts are no longer in my head. 'NOX!'

I grab his shadowy face and press my forehead against his. He growls, baring his teeth and viciously

fights against my grip. I stare into his blood-red eyes and fear bubbles in my chest, but I squeeze my eyes shut and take deep breaths. *No, don't be afraid. It's Nox. Stay strong! He's not like Shade. Don't be afraid. DON'T BE AFRAID!*

My eyes burst open and I stare straight back at Nox. 'I've got you! I'm here. Whatever's going on, fight it!'

*Your powers can help him.*

The woman's voice comes out of nowhere. I look left and right, but no one's there.

I keep hold of Nox as hard as I can, taking every bash and shove. I focus everything on him and my jaw clenches. Something sparks inside me, like a quiet storm brewing. It flows from my heart towards my palms like a river. *Control it . . . Remember what Mum said. Like martial arts . . . And dancing.* I release a breath and relax my hands as a bright light glows from them, shining over Nox's cheeks. *It's OK, Nox.*

A calmness washes through my mind and I push more of the energy towards him, willing my light to flow through him. *It's OK.* After a moment, the light vanishes and Nox catches himself before he falls to the ground. His eyes return to gold, and they stay gold. I sigh in relief but my eyes burn with tears.

Lux nudges him, still concerned for his brother, and I look down at my palms. *Did I actually help him with my powers?* I look up towards the wild umbra but she's already gone. Nox slowly begins to warm, connecting us again, and I hear his thoughts.

'Mia, what happened?' I spin around to see Mum and Spike. I hadn't heard anyone approaching, but as I look at them, all I feel is dread. I open my mouth but no words come out.

*'What is it, Mia?'* Spike asks with a gentle but persistent tone. I look back at Nox, trying to wrap my head around what just happened. The only possible explanation takes over my every thought like loud alarm bells, but I can't think about that now.

Nox is shaking. I hug him tight, but my chest feels heavy and tears run down my cheeks. There's no going back to normal any time soon.

This war is far from over.

# CHAPTER SIX

The tamer trials are called off and we all head back to the city.

It's lunchtime when we reach Nubis, but after what happened I can't eat and instead settle for some mini cookies that were in my backpack for the trials. Mum sends me to pick up Lucas from his playdate at a friend's house while she talks to Dad and the other tamers about what happened. I wanted in on the conversation too, but Mum said she would fill me in later.

I walk down the street followed by Lux and Nox who are both silent. The glow bugs and lanterns softly light our path, blending with the neon street lights that brighten our dark city. I think about Nox's fear and his ear-piercing screams before the connection between us snapped, and feel sick to my stomach. It was as if a part of my soul had been cut, just like that. Cold. I never want to feel that again.

And I now realise that the other voice in my head was the woman from my dreams. But how could she speak to me in real life, or know my powers could help? It's giving me the creeps. I have to find out who she is.

'How are you feeling, Nox?' I ask.

*'Better, but strange,'* he says. *'I had no control of my mind or my actions. I felt like I was being used.'*

I stroke his fluffy shadow cheek, but my other hand balls into a fist, angry.

'We know the Elite's taming techniques turn umbra's eyes red, which means someone else must have been on the plains with us,' I say.

*'If someone was there then they were well hidden. I didn't even catch a scent,'* Lux says. He stamps his shadowy hoof in frustration.

'Either way, this is confirmation that the Elite are still out there. Or at the very least someone is using their taming techniques,' I say with a shudder.

We cross the busy street and pass the hold, where two guards stand in front of the metal doors that lead down to where the Elite are being kept. Including Miles's parents.

I sigh, feeling myself finally allowing the one thought I have been holding off. The one I hope isn't true.

*Could it have been something to do with Miles?*

*'That could very well be the case, young one,'* Nox says. *'But I'm not so sure. We would have sensed Shade.'*

Lux growls, *'We should be in on that meeting.'*

I nod. He's right. If they suspect Miles, Mum might not tell us everything they talk about.

'So let's get in on the meeting first and fetch Lucas afterwards,' I decide. Then I add, 'I heard that woman's voice too. The one from my dreams. She told me that my powers would help Nox, and they did.'

*'So she may not be an enemy,'* Nox muses.

*'But it puts a different slant on things,'* Lux says. *'The fact that she can talk to you outside of your dreams raises all sorts of new questions.'*

'Yeah, we gotta find out who she is,' I say. But first we need to figure out a way into that tamer meeting. My stomach churns at the thought of disobeying Mum and Dad, especially as they've been putting more trust in me and responsibility, but we need to know what they're talking about.

'We'll have to be careful of Riley's umbra, Myla. She has supersonic hearing. If we hurry, we can reach the city hall first, while Mum and Dad are still rounding everyone up. Lucas will be fine staying a bit longer.'

We change course and walk through the market, heading for the city hall. It's usually used for concerts and community events, and is the only place big enough to hold all of the tamers and their umbra in one space.

We reach the central library next door to the city hall. The only building connected to the city hall, and the best way to get in without being seen. Lux and Nox transform into their baby forms and I cautiously enter the main entrance first to scope it out. We slip past the head librarian while her back is turned, and sneak silently between the shelves until we arrive at the white wooden doors that connect with city hall. We walk through the hallway and it's deathly quiet. Thank Lunis there're no mini events going on today, otherwise it'd be packed in here.

When we reach the main auditorium it's dark and silent. The only light glows from Lux's fur. I turn to face the huge stage. Maybe it's because it's dark, but for some reason it feels bigger and creepier than usual. I imagine someone or *something* standing in the shadows watching us, and I shiver.

*'Nothing's there, Mouse.'*

I jump. 'Geez, thanks for scaring me, you clown.' I push Lux and he snickers in my head.

Time to find somewhere to hide. I look around. The pillars along the sides of the room are too obvious. My eyes shift back to the stage. Hiding underneath it would be pretty good, but we might not hear everything.

I glance up and a smile spreads across my face. I point to the lighting rig above the stage. 'I'm gonna climb up there – they won't be using it today. Can you guys make it to the balconies over the floor seats behind us?'

'*Of course,*' they say together. It always cracks me up when they do that.

'Good. Let's hurry. We don't have much time.' I race to the metal scaffold at the side of the stage, while Lux and Nox make for the stairs to the upper seating area. I climb to the top and throw myself into the small balcony box where the tech team would usually be. The spot is perfect. High enough to see and hear everything without being seen. Most times when people enter a room, they don't tend to look up. Nan told me that once. Let's hope she's right.

*'Young one, we are in position,'* Nox says.

*Good job, guys!*

Just in time. The door clicks open and the

auditorium lights come on. I duck as the tamers start filing in. I peek over the railing and spot Mum, Dad and Jada walking in last without a certain phoenix umbra. Thank Lunis, it looks like Jada left Ruby outside.

Just as I think I can relax, Riley's umbra, Myla, enters, sniffing around with her bunny-like nose, big mousey ears twitching. I duck when she looks up, but she doesn't seem to notice anything.

I peek again and see all the tamers standing in a circle just in front of the stage with their umbra beside them. They each clasp their hands together and bow in greeting. Dad steps out into the circle with Bolt and looks at everyone. His face is serious.

'First, I want to thank you all for your quick response in stopping the tamer trials and getting all the students back safely. As to why they were cancelled, it appears we have confirmation that we may not have all of the Elite in custody,' Dad tells them. 'Mia's report that Nox's eyes turned red during the tamer trials, and him losing his sense of self as a result, almost certainly confirms this. If they're still in operation, we cannot rule out the involvement of the Reaper King himself, or Maria and Magnus's son, Miles. His whereabouts are still currently unknown.'

Dad walks around the circle of tamers, each step purposeful as he thinks over his next words. My palms itch and I twist and turn my sleeves with nerves. *What are you planning, Dad?*

'But what if it didn't happen?'

My eyes zip to the speaker – it's Riley!

'You said yourself, Lila, that she's been having nightmares. What if Mia only thought she saw that happen?'

'Riley, that was said to you in confidence,' Mum snipes, shooting him a look.

*What in the flip is this? He thinks we're lying! Mum told him about my nightmares?*

I force myself to calm down and clench my fists, feeling a familiar spark bubbling up.

'Why would Mia lie about something like that?' Jada defends me.

'And Mia's nightmares don't happen when she's awake,' Mum adds. I narrow my eyes.

'Look, we all said that there was a chance Mia wasn't ready for the tamer trials and being out in the plains again ... Maybe it got too much,' Riley says.

'Well, she got me and Shiro good enough,' Bently counters.

Dad's jaw clenches like it usually does when he is frustrated. 'Regardless, Riley, Mia doesn't lie.'

'All I'm saying is that we gotta be open to the possibility that she may not be telling the whole truth,' grumbles Riley.

*Yeah, and all I'm saying is that you should go kick rocks, ya muppet!* My fists shake at my side.

'She did seem nervous when she was waiting by the gates. Maybe she accidently used her own powers on Nox or something,' Rosé says. She's one of the newer tamers. I don't know her too well and I almost throw my hands up at her words. *Why in Lunis is she chiming in now?*

'Mouse.'

*I know, I know! I'm calm.*

'You're both chattin' rubbish. Mia's not seeing things and I doubt it was her powers,' Jada says. 'We've already established that when an umbra's eyes turn red it's the Elite's doing.'

'You don't know that for sure though,' Riley snipes. 'We don't *know* how the Elite tame the umbra.'

'I mean, every Elite umbra has red eyes. Kinda case and point,' Jada bites back. 'Mia helped save the whole city, so how about cuttin' her some slack?'

Before Riley can respond, the door bursts open and I duck for cover. When I peek over the railing, I see Mr Lin, one of my martial arts teachers, standing there, breathless. He must have run here all the way from the gate. He always watches the gate with some of the other martial artists when the tamers are having a meeting.

'Sorry to interrupt, but we've just heard that Queen Katiya is coming to Nubis!' he says.

Everyone erupts in chatter.

'What do you mean, she's coming here?' Mum asks, waving for everyone to keep it down.

'Two of the Queen's Guard just arrived at the gate and announced it,' Mr Lin says. 'She'll be here in a few hours, when the evening star is the highest in the sky.'

Everyone looks as shocked as I feel. Why would the queen be coming here?

'It must be something important for it to be such short notice,' Dad adds.

'Her guard said it was to "mend bridges",' Mr Lin says, and I quirk an eyebrow. *Now* she cares about our city, after all these years?

Mum presses the side of her finger against her lips. 'And where are the two guards now?'

'Still at the gates,' he says.

Dad turns to the rest of the tamers. 'Meeting dismissed. For now.'

They quickly file out of the hall and the moment the door clicks shut, I jump up and climb down from my spot. No longer caring who sees us, we dash out the doors and race down the steps. Already a huge crowd is filling the road, on its way to the main gate.

*Let's get to a rooftop.*

*'Get on my back, young one.'*

I leap on Nox's back. He takes a few steps back and jumps up on to the roof of Ms Dawn's flower shop. There's a clear view of the gate up ahead.

The two men dressed in royal uniform each stand with one arm behind their back and the other on the hilt of their sword. They are talking to Mum and Dad while the crowd looks on in curiosity.

*'They're the Queen's Guard we met back in Stella, are they not?'* Nox asks.

'Yeah – Arto and Castello,' I agree. 'The ones who helped us out of the castle when the Elite came.' And I suddenly wonder if TJ might accompany the queen. I clasp my hands together, buzzing at the possibility.

*'Don't get your hopes up just yet, Mouse. Lisa did say he was in no-contact training,'* Lux says. Yeah, Auntie Lisa

said the queen was strict on no outside contact apart from family for some reason when training under her guard. So, only they could pass on messages.

*'We should get the little one quick before we get caught,'* Nox adds. I gasp.

*Shoot! That's right. I completely forgot about picking up Lucas!* We leap down from the roof.

I almost jump out of my skin when bursts of red light flash up from the pavements and a loud voice booms.

**'Attention. Attention. This is a public announcement. Queen Katiya will be arriving in Nubis this evening. Make any preparations you deem necessary. That is all.'**

One day I'll get used to these new public announcement calls, but I wish they weren't always so loud.

The town erupts in chaos. People scramble in their shops, cleaning and changing things from shelves, probably trying to make their places look extra good in case the queen passes by. This'll be her first ever visit to Nubis so I kinda get why everyone is excited, but I can only scrunch up my nose.

'Can you believe the queen is actually coming?' a woman says to Mr and Mrs Davies at their bakery. 'It's all thanks to our amazing tamers, and little Mia and Lucas with those powers of theirs.'

My heart flutters. *Someone actually said something nice about my powers . . .*

'Yes! What are they called again? Lightcasters?' Mrs Davies says. 'Mia is good friends with the twins actually.'

I stop in my tracks, listen in and watch.

'Yeah, that's the name of it. She has the same powers as the queen herself,' the woman says. She clasps her hands together with a weird dreamy look in her eyes.

I hunch my shoulders and hasten my pace again, wondering what they'd say if they knew the queen didn't actually have any powers.

Robocleaners sweep the roads and pavements and we dodge out of the way of people who are running around with flowers. Some are already dressed up with dangly bracelets and celebration necklaces.

We cross the river and cut through an alleyway lit with hanging lanterns and fairy lights. At the other end, we take a sharp left, and I see Mrs Avery's house.

I knock on her door and moments later she opens up with a look of surprise. 'Oh, hello, Mia. Have the tamer trials finished already?'

I connect my hands and bow. 'Yeah, we finished, so I'm here to pick up Lucas.'

Mrs Avery steps back with a warm smile that wrinkles the edges of her eyes. She brushes her greying hair behind her ear and looks past me at all the people rushing around.

'What in Lunis is going on?' she asks. 'I thought I heard a public announcement, but I was in the basement, sorting out Landon's playroom.'

'The queen is coming to Nubis,' I say. 'Apparently.'

Her eyes widen. 'Really? That's incredible.'

'Yeah, I have no idea why,' I say with a shrug.

'Well, whatever the reason, she's most definitely welcome. Would you like to come in and have a cup of tea, dear? Or maybe a hot chocolate?'

'No thanks, Mrs Avery. I'm gonna have dinner when I get home.'

'OK, dear, next time.' She opens the door wider, inviting me in with Lux and Nox and she goes to get Lucas. A sweet smell of honey wafts from further down the hallway and I smile. She must have been making some to sell at her stall. I don't know how she handles all those whomper bees in her garden. They're tiny, but their big fuzzy bodies and two monster stingers are flippin' scary.

'Lucas, Mia's here!' Mrs Avery calls out and a loud cheer follows. I hear Lucas's little feet thud down the stairs and he stumbles into the hallway with Landon close behind.

'Mimi!'

I catch him in my arms and kiss the top of his head. 'Hey Lu-Lu. You good?'

He gives me a big cheeky grin. 'Yep. Me and Landon were building a *really* big city with dragons and hover pods in it. The city was bigger than me!' He stretches out his arms to show just how big it was.

'That's cool,' I say as he goes to give Lux and Nox a hug too. I turn to Mrs Avery. 'We'll be off now. See ya, Mrs Avery! Bye, Landon.'

'Have a good day. I'll give your mum a call later, but I'm sure I'll see you all at the main gate when the queen arrives,' Mrs Avery says. Lucas gives her and Landon a hug and waves goodbye.

We cross the street while Lucas jabbers on about all the games he played with Landon, his 'bestest friend in the whole kingdom and universe'.

'I'm glad you had fun, Lu-Lu,' I say, holding his hand. Some umbra run by with their tamers and we cross the road again.

'Me too. Do you think Mummy and Daddy will let me have a sleepover soon?' he asks.

'I don't see why not,' I say.

*'Mia, Lucas!'*

I turn around and Bolt runs towards us from across the street.

'Hi Bolt! Where's Daddy?' Lucas asks.

*'At the main gate. Your parents wished for me to inform you that the queen is arriving soon and want you with them to greet her,'* he says.

'Can we go home first? I'm kinda hungry,' I say.

'Me too!' Lucas adds, and Bolt nods.

*'Of course. They'll meet you there,'* Bolt says, and I stroke his panther-like head in thanks.


Back home, Lucas kicks off his shoes and runs inside to play with his toys in the living room. Lux and Nox join him and I glance up at the holoclock on the wall.

'I don't have to change my clothes, do I?' I ask Bolt, slipping off my shoes and walking into the living room.

He looks me up and down. *'I believe you should. You are very muddy.'*

'I'm gonna wear some really nice clothes because she saw me in grubby ones, and I don't want her to think

I'm smelly,' Lucas says, smashing his umbra figurine into a tower of building blocks.

'I'm pretty sure she doesn't think you're smelly,' I say, rolling my eyes.

'You don't know that, Mimi. You have to be nice to the queen. She won't help us again if we're mean and smelly.'

I go upstairs and change into a clean shirt, leggings and shorts. I wrap a new dark blue hoodie around my waist and re-tie my hair. I check myself in the mirror and make my way back downstairs.

*'Lila and Daniel are on their way,'* Bolt announces.

He turns to look back at me from the window and his golden eyes watch me intensely. It makes me feel anxious. My eyes shift to him and awkwardly look away.

*'So, what did you think of the meeting today?'*

I freeze, then sigh.

'When? How?' I ask.

*'The second I entered the city hall.'*

I cross my arms in protest. 'No way. How did you see me?'

*'Mia. I have been with you from the day you were born. You think I wouldn't be able to pick up your scent in a room?'* he says.

*Guess I didn't think of that.*

'But you didn't say anything to Mum and Dad,' I say, more as a statement than a question.

*'No. It was unnecessary. You were not in danger and you were not causing harm. I understood your intentions, even if they were impatient. Spike hasn't said a word either.'*

'You're the best,' I say, hugging him round the neck. His shadowy snake tail wraps around me and he rubs his head against mine. His whole body vibrates like he's purring, and I giggle.

The stars shift and half an hour later the front door swings open.

'Mia, Lucas, we're back!' Mum calls out in an exhausted voice.

'We're in the living room, Mummy!' Lucas calls back.

'What happened in the meeting?' I ask when she walks in. Bolt gives me an amused look. Mum sits down next to me as Dad takes off his tamer jacket in the hallway.

'The meeting was cut short after finding out the queen is coming. We did manage to talk a bit about the incident with Nox . . .' She brushes a strand of hair from my face, hesitating. 'But things got a bit complicated.'

Dad enters and strokes Bolt's head. He settles in the

armchair and says, 'Not everyone believed your story about Nox's eyes turning red.'

Lux snorts. My blood boils remembering how dismissive Riley was and my fingers dig into the edge of the sofa.

'So, what happens now?' I ask.

'Nothing, for now at least. Remember what I said in class. The tamers are a unit and we have to be unanimous in our decisions. Always. Unless it's an emergency. But figuring out what happened to Nox on the Nightmare Plains has to be put on hold for now because of the queen's visit.'

'But—'

There's a knock at the door and Mum gets up to answer it.

'What will it take for the others to believe me?' I ask, waving away a toy that Lucas tries to shove in my face. 'What proof do I need?'

Dad rubs his hand up and down his stubbled cheek. 'It's not something that's easy to prove.'

Seeing the look in my eyes, Dad sighs and gets up to sit next me. Every time I think about the attack and Nox's screams, one thought appears in my mind.

'Dad. What if . . .'

'... It was someone from the Elite who attacked Nox? Yes. That was my first thought,' Dad says. 'Or at the very least it was someone who has the same taming abilities. It could even be more than one person because it was such a bold move.'

I lean forward. 'Well, there's one place where we may find answers *and* proof that the Elite are still hiding something.'

He presses his lips together, probably guessing what I'm gonna say.

'Astaroth,' I breathe. 'It's the only city the tamers haven't checked. Apart from Nexus, but that's too far away to be a hideout for this person.'

Dad narrows his eyes. Judging by his face, I'm probably not gonna like what he's going to say now, and he knows it.

'That's a whole big mission in itself, Baby-girl,' Dad says.

'And we don't have the time or resources for it right now ...' I sigh. That's always his answer to everything lately.

'*Mouse,*' Lux probes my mind. My shoulders tense. *I know* ... I need to tell them more about my nightmares and about the woman's voice I heard in the Nightmare

Plains. But what if they think I'm imagining things, like Riley said?

*'Or it might encourage them to agree to the plan to search Astaroth,'* Lux adds.

Mum comes back in. 'Jada and the others need help sorting out the security measures for the gate. The queen is almost here.'

'Mum, Dad. There's something I need to tell you,' I murmur.

My heart pounds in my ears and I scrunch up the bottom of my hoodie. Lux and Nox's eyes urge me to spill the beans.

Mum raises an eyebrow. 'What is it, honey?'

I take a breath and look down into my lap. It's now or never I guess.

'Every time I've had a nightmare, it's been about the Reaper King,' I tell them. 'It feels like he's in my mind. I know it's a nightmare but it just seems so real. I've . . . I've seen things when I'm awake too.'

'Like what, honey?' Mum asks, resting a hand on my shoulder.

'Like in the bathroom the other night. My reflection suddenly looked all scary,' I explain, clamping my hands between my knees. I try to read the expression on her face, but it's impossible to know what's going on behind those strangely calm eyes.

'And what does he say in the dreams?' Dad asks, rubbing my back. Lucas climbs on the sofa next to me and hugs me.

'Different things. Like, he's going to get me. That we're alike. All sorts. Sometimes he even appears to look like Miles, but . . . It's just nightmares, right?'

'I sometimes have scary dreams, too, Mimi,' Lucas whispers. 'But not *all* the time, and my teddies pre-tect me.'

'What are your nightmares about, sweetheart?' Mum asks.

'A lotta stuff,' he says. 'But it's mostly good dreams.'

'Do you hear a woman's voice too?' I ask him.

He shakes his head.

'I've been hearing this woman's voice lately too,' I tell Mum and Dad, 'but I don't know who she is. She seems to be trying to help. I . . . I heard her on the plains, too, when Nox was being attacked.'

They both fall silent and the worry I was trying to hide comes crashing in. *Please say something.* They look at each other again, as if deciding who should speak. In the end, it's Dad.

'It's possible these are more than nightmares. We don't know for sure, but we must be honest with you, Baby-girl. We haven't begun to comprehend the Reaper King's powers, even in banishment,' he says.

'We've been trying to find out the powers he shares with the Elite, but they're not giving us anything,' Mum says. 'We're hoping Miles will be able to help us with that, when he returns.'

'As for this woman, I have no idea who she could be. Perhaps she's also linked to the Reaper King,' Dad muses.

'Either way, I don't feel comfortable with someone communicating telepathically with you,' Mum adds, 'even if she has been helping you.'

'I wish you'd told us sooner, Mia,' Dad sighs, rubbing his forehead.

'But you've told us now. That's what's important,' Mum adds, bringing me closer to kiss my head.

'W-What can we do? How do I stop it?' My fingers dig into my knees and Lucas hugs me tighter.

'Right now, the Reaper King knows you have the potential to be so powerful, maybe even more than him, and he's scared. That's why he's in your dreams. But when you have full control of your powers, you might be able to force him out of your mind and this woman too,' Mum says. 'After the queen has gone, we'll up your training, and Lucas's too.'

A thought strikes me. 'What if I try and communicate with the woman?' I suggest. 'Get in *her* head. I could find out who she is.'

Dad scratches his stubbly beard. 'That's not a bad idea,' he says to Mum.

'Going to Astaroth might lead to some answers too,' I throw in. 'Something has to be there. It was the Elite's home and maybe I—'

'Baby-girl...' Dad warns and I fight the urge to huff.

*'One step at a time, Mia. Harness your powers first,'* Spike says.

'We should really get going. The queen could be here any minute,' Mum says, looking at the holoclock.

'Is it all right if I visit Nan and Grandad after Queen Katiya's visit? Maybe tomorrow?' I ask.

I haven't been for a while and I always feel so guilty about it. And something tells me that there must be something I can do to help. Nan always told me to trust my instincts.

'Of course, honey,' Mum says. 'We'll go together.'

'I wanna see Nanny and Grandad too!' Lucas chirps.

'And I know you said I may not be ready yet, but after saving Nox, maybe my powers will work on Nan and Grandad now,' I say.

Mum hums and presses a finger to her lips. 'OK, we'll see, but I'm still not completely comfortable with the idea yet.'

'All right, let's eat some dinner, then we've really got to go,' Dad says, taking Lucas's hand and leading him to the kitchen.

That's right, first things first. It's time to come face to face with Queen Katiya again. Can't say I'm particularly excited, but my heart tingles at the thought of possibly seeing TJ.

# Chapter Seven

The evening star twinkles at its highest point when we head to the main gate for the arrival of Queen Katiya. Behind me, Lucas is now holding Mum's hand while Dad walks next to me with our umbra. Crowds of people are gathered by the gate. A loud hum of voices, all eagerly waiting for the queen's arrival. At the front, the tamers make sure to keep everyone in check behind the barriers.

'Mia!' Someone shouts and I see Mikasa with her parents, all dressed up with ribbons and bows in her hair. I smile and wave. I spot Thomas and Lincoln with their parents too.

Riley lets us through the crowd-control barriers and I fight the urge to give him a dirty look. *I know what you said, Jerkface.* To the right, construction workers ensure a small portable stage is secure and perfectly decorated with blue and gold flower crystals. My eyes light up when I see Jada. She notices me just as my arms wrap around her in the tightest hug. Her long arms hug me back and she faintly chuckles.

'Hey, best student. I've missed you too,' she says.

'I wish I could hang out with you more,' I say. I'll never forget how she defended me against Riley and Rosé. My sister for life.

'I know, I'm sorry,' she says.

*'It's good to see you, Mia,'* Ruby says, flying down to join us.

I pet her head, and smile. 'It's good to see you too, Ruby.'

'She's here! Make way for the queen!' Bently yells.

The giant city gate creaks open. A little girl sneaks under the barrier and runs out from the crowd. She throws rose petals on to the path before quickly being guided back by a tamer. She giggles and spins on her heel, gasping.

I follow her gaze to the entrance, and a long white hover car outlined in sparkly gold gemstones drives in. It stops and Castello opens the door. Dressed in shimmering jewels and a long dark blue gown, the queen steps out and stands before us. Her brown wavy hair is adorned with a golden crown that shines in the moonlight.

Arto bows with one fist on his chest and the other behind his back. She nods at him and walks forward. Each step is delicate yet calculated, and her hands knit gracefully together in front of her.

A sickly pleasant smile spreads across her lips the moment her eyes meet mine, but I don't return it. Beside her, a black shadowy fox-like creature follows with eight long bushy shadow tails that swing back and forth. Constell, Queen Katiya's umbra.

They stop just in front of the crowd, unwavering under the gaze of the hundreds of eyes that watch her every move and every breath. Dad guides her to the small stage. Her eyes flicker to me for a moment and I could swear I saw her smile at me again. She steps on to the stage and takes in the crowd before her. Everyone bows, but as I do so, my stomach drops at one single thought. It's painfully clear that TJ isn't here.

'Citizens of Nubis, I would like to thank you for having me at such short notice,' she begins. 'I felt compelled to come personally as I'd like to rebuild the bridges between Nubis, Stella and Nexus.'

Mum's hand squeezes my shoulders. She stares hard

at the queen. Dad's eyes harden too, and my eyes trail along the line of tamers. They all remain completely silent and emotionless.

'It makes me proud that all of you brave souls continue to fight and live in the darkness, and the rest of us who still live in the light can truly learn so much from you.'

I arch an eyebrow.

'As queen of this kingdom, I *will* protect and help you all. That first step was sharing Stella technology. Next will be starting a Queen's Guard programme here in Nubis. Teaching children and adults how to fight without the need of umbra as well. But also . . .'

She turns to look behind her and gasps erupt amongst the crowd. Travel pod after travel pod drive through the gates, showcasing crates of fruit, vegetables, diamonds and *weapons*.

'Most importantly, I want to thank in person the brave heroes behind the fall of the Reaper King. Mia and Lucas McKenna, who saved not only Nubis, but the entire kingdom from a far worse fate.'

All eyes snap to me as Queen Katiya offers me and Lucas another smile. Then she bows and the whole crowd gasps as one. My jaw drops.

'Thank you,' she says again, her eyes locking with mine.

I don't know how to feel. I look up at Mum and Dad. They're just as surprised as everyone else.

The queen raises her hands and the diamond bracelets on her wrists jingle.

'Please, everyone. Enjoy the gifts,' she says, then turns to us again. 'Lila, Daniel, may I speak with you and your children?'

My eyebrows furrow in suspicion. For a wild moment I wonder if she's going to ask for her staff back. I hold it protectively against my thigh strap, but she just smiles. Maybe I shouldn't judge her so harshly.

Mum and Dad agree to talk, and I see the queen gesture to Arto and Castello, telling them to leave her alone with us. They nod, then smile brightly and bow their heads to me.

Arto lets out a small chuckle, seeing my face, and butterflies well up in my stomach. As they leave, Castello leans over and whispers, 'Don't worry, TJ's fine.'

I relax a bit and grin at him. *Good.*

I grab Lucas's hand and tug him along behind Mum and Dad, very much ready to be in on this conversation.

'Mimi, too tight,' Lucas whispers.

'Sorry,' I say, loosening my grip.

'Perhaps we should speak at one of the constellation towers. It would be more private,' Mum suggests.

'The tower sounds like a brilliant idea,' Queen Katiya says.

As we pass the medicentre, the queen asks, 'How are your parents, Lila?'

Mum sighs. 'No different, but their vitals are all fine. We still don't know what happened to them.'

'That's a shame, I hope you find answers soon,' she says, glancing once more at the building.

We climb the constellation tower and walk through the sliding doors. The lights glow a soft dark blue and Mum rotates the roof control dial. The glass dome ceiling zooms in on the stars above and Queen Katiya glances up in wonder.

'Fascinating . . .' she whispers, staring up at the sky.

'What did you want to talk about, Your Majesty?' Mum asks. The queen's eyes fall back to her.

'I wanted to tell you that I plan on having more of an open communication between myself, you and the tamers,' she says.

'No disrespect, Your Majesty, but getting the tamers

on your side is going to be a challenge. As you can understand, it's been just us for the longest time,' Dad says, making a point to remind her just how well we've managed so far.

She nods and gently paces the room. Constell follows close behind her.

Beside me, Lucas yawns.

'Spike, could you take Lucas home? He's a little tired,' Mum asks.

'But I wanna stay longer, Mummy,' Lucas says, even as he yawns again.

'You, mister, need to go to your bed,' Mum says, and he yawns again, proving her point. He climbs on to Spike and lies down on the bear-like umbra's back. I ruffle his hair and wish him a good sleep, and Mum kisses his head.

'Your Majesty, what can you tell us about the Reaper King?' Dad asks the moment Spike and Lucas leave. My ears perk up and I glance at Lux and Nox.

The queen's smile drops. 'Not much, but I can tell you how his powers come through into our world from the Spirit Plain. You're aware of the crystals of the founders, am I correct?'

'Yes. The crystals are believed to be both a link to the

Spirit Plain and the original source of the lightcaster power,' Mum answers in full scientist mode.

'Well, think of the crystals like conductors of the most potent light and darkness in the world, with enough power to rip through the door between this world and the Spirit Plain. Through touching one, you can unlock the door for yourself and go through,' the queen explains. 'So, if one crystal is destroyed . . .'

'One of the locks on the door is broken,' I say, and the queen nods.

'Leaving the door less secure and as a result . . .' she continues.

'. . . His powers can always leak through into our world,' I finish.

'Exactly, but since he's still weak from the battle with Queen Lucina, he's not powerful enough to force his full corporeal form into this world. That's why he needs Mia or Lucas,' Queen Katiya says.

'*Because of the damaged crystal, with the help of the umbra to lead the way, you can go in and out of the Spirit Plain without touching a crystal, but it also means the Reaper King can come out in small doses,*' Constell adds.

'But then who broke one of the crystals in the first place?' Mum interjects, and the queen stops walking.

'That we do not know. However, I believe it must have happened during the battle between the Reaper King and Queen Lucina,' Queen Katiya says.

*It's highly likely that is the case,'* Constell follows up.

'I had my guards look all over Astaroth and Lunavale, but we found nothing,' Queen Katiya says.

'We banished the Reaper King with the crystal you gave us, though,' I say. 'It stopped the portal from opening up, so he'll never be able to return to full power, right? He'll stay in the Spirit Plain?'

'I don't believe he'll ever give up on trying to come into our world,' she says.

*She knows why.*

*That voice! It's that woman again!* My heart pounds in my ears and I hope no one saw me startle.

'And why's that?' I ask Queen Katiya. Lux and Nox look at me, sensing something off.

'I don't know,' is her reply.

*Lies.*

'But Mia, if you ever have any questions about your powers, you're more than welcome to talk to me about them,' she says with a small smile. The glint in her eye makes my stomach churn.

'I'm good, thanks,' I say.

'Mia . . .' Mum's tone warns me to choose my next words carefully and not be rude.

I gulp and scratch my arm. 'Mum and Dad help me out a lot so I'm sure I'll get the hang of it. Your staff has helped though,' I say, plastering a fake smile on my face.

'I'm glad to hear that,' Queen Katiya says. 'But I hope you'll at least consider the new Queen's Guard programme I plan to open up in the city. Of course, my offer for you to train with me in Stella is still on the table. But I'm glad you're making good use of my staff.'

I force a smile again. 'It's been really helpful.'

'Good. Always keep it close to you,' she says.

I raise a slight eyebrow, but nod. 'Sure.'

'Thank you, Your Majesty. We appreciate your insights on lightcasters,' Dad says.

'Of course,' Queen Katiya replies, and Mum looks at the sky.

'All right, well, it's getting late. I'm going to take Mia home and check on Lucas,' she says, bowing her head. 'It was lovely seeing you, Your Majesty.'

'I'd like to discuss this new Queen's Guard programme with you, if you have time now,' Dad says.

'Of course,' the queen says, glancing at her umbra. 'But Lila, Mia, just know that you have my royal line as well, so do call me whenever you wish. If I do not answer, one of my guard always will.'

'Goodbye, Your Majesty,' I say, giving her a quick curtsy. *Well that definitely felt weird.*

'Goodbye, Mia. I'm sure we'll see each other again soon.' She nods to Lux and Nox.

We walk out the door and head down the stairs.

When we're outside, I take Mum's arm and whisper, 'That woman spoke to me again while we were in there.'

I know Mum is shocked, but she hides it well. 'What did she say?'

'That the queen knows why the Reaper King keeps coming back.'

# CHAPTER EIGHT

The next morning we go to the medicentre, as Mum promised. Memories of Nan and Grandad in Stella flash in my mind like a movie. Maybe if I had made it there sooner, they would've been OK.

An arm wraps around me and I almost jump out of my skin. Mum gives me an apologetic look. *Geez, I need to stop being on edge.*

'It'll be all right, young one,' Nox says.

'Remember, they are just having a long sleep,' Lux adds.

'Yeah, so is Samuel Walker. He's been "asleep" in the lab for years now. That could've been me, or TJ.'

'*But it wasn't,*' Lux says. '*And now you have us. You're lucky to have the best umbra in the kingdom.*'

I roll my eyes, but smile. *Yeah, yeah.*

He bumps me with his curved horn. '*Say it then.*'

I quirk an eyebrow. 'Say what?'

'*Say we're the best umbra in the kingdom,*' he demands. Mum chuckles but stays out of it and I pull a face at Lux.

'You're the best umbra in the kingdom,' I repeat.

'*Louder.*'

*You've gotta be kidding me.* He looks at me and I take a deep breath. *Fine.*

'You're the best umbra in the kingdom!' I yell at the top of my lungs. A few people passing by give us strange looks. I narrow my eyes in embarrassment.

'*Much better,*' Lux muses.

'*Shame it's not true though,*' Spike says.

'*What'd you say, polar bear?*' Lux snaps back.

'All right, you two, break it up,' Mum playfully scolds before glancing at me. 'Has that woman tried to speak to you again since yesterday?'

I shake my head. 'I've tried reaching out to her, but there's been nothing.'

I felt like a clown, sitting on my bed, calling out in my head to some woman I've never even met. I tried and tried to contact her, but there was no response.

Soon we arrive at the medicentre and stand before the huge white building with big blue windows and sliding doors.

'Ready?' Mum asks.

I struggle to swallow the lump in my throat, but manage a 'yeah' and we walk inside.

My trainers squeak against the shiny white-tiled floor. Two silver cleaner bots hover around, spraying, drying and sweeping it with their bristly feet and heat fans. The strong smell of cleaning solution burns my nostrils. Mum wraps her arm around my shoulders and squeezes me close.

'Are you ready, sweetheart?' she asks again, and I inhale a deep breath. I can do this.

'I'm ready.'

The five of us walk through the reception hall and step through the glass door into the decontamination zone. Mum's visited so many times she must know the way like the back of her hand.

The door seals shut behind us and we're engulfed in a freezing power-jet of antibacterial mist. Lux and Nox whine and shake their bodies, not liking the feel against their shadow fur.

A beep marks the end of the decontamination process. The excess mist is extracted and the doors slide open with a heavy wheeze. I follow Mum out the other side with the umbra.

The hallway is quiet. We see a few doctors and visitors in the hall as we walk past door after door. I get flashbacks of Nan and Grandad in those beds in Stella and my stomach churns. What if they never wake up?

Finally we reach their room. Mum gives me a small smile and hovers her hand over the steel handprint on the wall. It flicks from red to green, and the door slowly slides open.

I step inside and, one foot in front of the other, I cautiously make my way over to the two beds. Nan and Grandad lie with their eyes closed. The gentle rise and fall of their chests give me a sense of relief. I look back at my grandparents but I can't bring myself to smile. Their brown skin almost glows in the moonlight shining through the window. They look . . . so normal.

'*See? They're just sleeping,*' Lux reassures.

'Just sleeping . . .' I repeat, letting my fingers brush against the bed rails.

Mum checks the health monitor then sits down by Grandad.

'Hey Nan, hey Grandad. It's me, Mia,' I say. 'I'm sorry I haven't visited you much, but . . . I'm here now.'

They don't even twitch in response. I look over at Mum. 'Do you really think they can hear me?'

'I'd like to think so,' Mum says. 'But honestly, I've never seen anything like this before.'

I look down at my hands. Maybe . . .

I gulp, then hesitantly hover my palms over Nan. I close my eyes and focus on the light inside me. It flicks like a soft flame in my chest and in my mind I see it warp into a purple colour. I push it along my arms and my eyes burst open. My hands are engulfed in a bright light and I will the light to flow towards Nan, just like it had for Nox. Come on . . . Come on!

Mum gasps and my hands start to shake. *No! No! NO!* My chest tightens as if an invisible rope grips my heart, and a sharp pain stabs through me. I gasp. The light zaps away and I stumble back, completely drained. Mum and Spike rush to Nan's side and I rest my hand against Nox.

*'Are you OK, young one?'* he asks, but I'm focused on Nan. Her chest rises and falls the same as before, like nothing happened.

Mum sighs and turns to me with a look that rattles my heart. Pain. 'Thank you for trying, sweetheart.'

I fall back against Lux. I don't know what I expected to happen but I had hoped for something more than this.

We silently watch Nan and Grandad again. None of us feels like speaking.

Eventually, Mum stands up. 'Come on, let's head ho—'

She never finishes. There's a big gasp for air and Nan suddenly sits bolt upright. She looks at us with urgent, shock-filled eyes.

'Nan!?' I yell. Mum grips her hand.

'She attacked us. Lila, Mia, you have to get away!'

'Who attacked you?' Mum's voice is strained, but she doesn't get an answer. Nan breathes erratically and her eyes close.

'No! Nan! Wake up!' I shout.

Her head falls back and Mum catches her and gently lays her back down on to the pillow. Nan's breathing returns to a slow, gentle rhythm again, exactly as before.

'She woke up! Was it my powers?' I ask Mum. I feel lightheaded but Lux steadies me with his body.

Mum stares at Nan and taps a finger frantically against her lips. 'It must have been. Do you think you can you do it again? Perhaps if you could sustain it for a little longer . . .' She trails off, looking at me. 'Are you all right, sweetheart?'

'I'm OK. I think I can give it another shot,' I say, trying to shake away the dizziness.

Nerves prickle the back of my neck and I swallow down a lump in my throat. I can't mess this up. I rub my hands together until they're warm and try to focus, but my brain feels woozy. I close my eyes, fill my lungs and hold my breath. I . . . got this. I hover shaky hands over Nan again and try to find my light. It flickers inside me but I can't keep it lit. I squeeze my eyes harder. *Come on. Come on . . .*

The light refuses to spark. I push and push, trying to force my powers out. My fingers and palms burn in protest and I sway on my feet.

'Mia, stop!' Mum grabs my arms and shakes me. My eyes burst open and I gasp for air. I stumble back with a hand on my beating chest.

'Why didn't it work?' I ask, panting.

'You're pushing yourself too hard. It's OK. We'll try again another day,' Mum says. Her arm rests comfortingly over my shoulders but I glare down at my hands. Why does it never work when I want it to? Oh yeah, because that'd be too flippin' easy and convenient, wouldn't it?

'Besides, we've now learned something important,'

Mum adds, guiding me to the door. 'Now we know that the person behind their attack is a woman.'

We make it back home a few hours later after deciding to grab something to eat. While Mum fills Dad in on what happened, I drag my feet upstairs and into my room. It feels like heavy weights are hanging from my body. The second the door clicks shut, I clench my fist and kick my chair. It clatters against the wall and I yell in frustration.

*'Focus on the fact that we are closer to the truth, and use this knowledge to fuel your drive to get stronger and better,'* Nox says, jumping out of the way when I throw my pillows at the wall.

I take a deep breath and hurl myself on my bed. Yeah, so Nan mentioned a woman – but who is it? Someone from the Elite? The woman I've been hearing in my nightmares? It could be anyone.

'I can't stand these powers. What's actually the point?' I shout.

*'What kind of question is that?'* Lux asks, and I throw my last pillow at him.

'Thanks for making me feel better, you jerk.'

*'Pleasure, Mouse!'* He hoofs the pillow back and it

smacks me square in the face. I huff and slam it down on my bed, then bury my face in my hands.

'It's just starting to feel like our enemies are building up more and more by the day,' I say into my hands.

'*True. Perhaps you should think about where best to focus your energy next,*' Nox says.

'Yeah, Astaroth,' I say, getting up. I lean on the windowsill and stare up at the stars and moon outside. 'It's where it all began with the Elite. The first city to be taken by the Darkness. There's got to be something there.'

'*You didn't believe Katiya when she said her guards found nothing there?*' Nox asks.

I shake my head. 'It's not as simple as that. It's just that I don't think they looked in all the right places. Mum and Dad think the same deep down too, I know it. You're telling me that's where the Elite have been staying but there's no clues?'

'*True.*' Lux says. '*When do we leave?*'

I pick up my staff, twirl it with my fingers and attach it back to my thigh strap. 'Later tonight.'

Before I lose my nerve.

'*What about the kid?*' Lux adds, and I smile sadly at him.

'Lucas stays here. Safe,' I say. 'He's not gonna like it but I won't put him in danger, and Mum and Dad are refusing to go there. So it's down to us.'

*'Wise decision, young one,'* Nox says.

'We might even find Miles,' I say, which is a stretch, but I can't help being hopeful. I really want to see him again.

I dig into my backpack and pull out the map from Mum and Dad's old survival pack. Astaroth is way nearer than Stella – only a couple of hours away. We should be able to make it there and back well within a day.

*'What about your parents?'* Nox asks.

'Don't worry, I'm gonna tell them – just not in person,' I say, grabbing some paper from my desk. 'I'll leave a note on my bed just in case something goes wrong.'

*'And we're going together,'* Lux says, but it's more of a statement than a question and I smile back at him.

'Of course,' I say. 'We're the best when we're together.'

Nox nuzzles his shadowy snout against my cheek and I stroke his and Lux's heads. They're the only reason my hands don't shake any more at the thought of going out in the Nightmare Plains. They're the reason I can be brave. Them and Lucas.

I stare out at the sky again and sigh.

'This might be dangerous,' I say, 'but we got this.'

I clench my hand into a fist. We're going into the monster's lair. Worst case scenario, I can try and use my powers to protect us, but let's hope we don't have to rely on that.

As the night star shines in the sky, our plan kicks into action. We walk out of my room and I tiptoe across the landing to the stairs. Muffled snores fill the halls. Mum and Dad must have gone to bed early too. We make it downstairs to the front door and I place my hand on the door handle.

'Mimi?'

I jump. Behind me Lucas blinks and rubs his eyes. 'Where you going, Mimi?'

'Shh, what are you doing up? Go to bed,' I whisper, trying to shoo him back to his room. He whines and I snap a finger to my lips.

'Where you going?' He asks again. I roll my eyes and look at Lux and Nox for help. They give me a look that only means they ain't gonna do a thing and I sigh.

'All right, fine, but you gotta keep this a secret. I'm going to Astaroth, but I won't be gone for long. I need you to be a big boy and look after Mum and Dad while I'm gone,' I tell him.

'No—' I clap my hand over his mouth and zip my attention upstairs. Apart from the snores, all remains silent.

Lucas's bottom lip trembles and he reaches out to hold my hand.

'It'll be OK,' I say, wiping his wet cheeks. 'Do you still have your whistle?'

He nods and blinks back the tears.

'I'll be back before you know it. We're made of strong stuff, ya know,' I say, flexing my muscles. He giggles, but it quickly fades and his eyes well up again.

'I don't want you to go to the scary place. What if you get trapped?' His grip on my hand tightens and panic fills his eyes.

'I'm not going alone. I'll have Lux and Nox with me,' I say. 'And don't forget, most of the Elite are locked up too. But I need you to look after Mum and Dad while I'm gone. You're strong. With and without your powers.'

He sniffles and wipes his eyes with his pyjama sleeves.

'Lu-Lu, look at me,' I say, softly. He hiccups and

lowers his arms to look at me with sad glossy brown eyes. 'I *will* come back. I promise.'

'OK,' he whispers. He opens his arms and I pull him into a big hug. 'But I'm coming too.'

'Wait, what?' I pull away and he frowns.

'I'm coming too, Mimi. I'll pretect you, and you'll pretect me,' he whispers.

It looks like I have no choice. 'All right. Deal,' I say, and he beams at me.

'I'm gonna get changed!' he whisper-shouts.

'OK, but you gotta be quick,' I whisper back.

*'Lila and Daniel will notice quicker with both of you gone,'* Lux warns as Lucas runs upstairs.

*'Are you sure this is wise, young one? As you said, it will be dangerous,'* Nox adds.

I know, but as much as the big sister side of me wants him to stay, I won't let anything happen to him. It doesn't matter if it's in the Nightmare Plains, Astaroth or home. Lucas is always safe with me and he's strong in his own right. And we're stronger together.

I grab some snacks and water from the kitchen and in no time Lucas is back with his little bag and a hoodie tied around his waist.

'See? I'm just like you, Mimi,' he whispers, swinging his waist left and right. 'I got my boomerang too.'

I give him a thumbs-up. 'Yep. Now let's skedaddle.'

Outside, it's like a ghost town. The buzz of the queen's visit has died down and while fireworks still blast the sky with colour it's strangely peaceful. I wonder how long the queen is going to stay here. The tamers apparently set up a room for her at a glamourous guest homestead in the west part of the city.

The soft hum of glow bugs keeps us company in the quiet and I'm mindful not to step on the flowers that were planted in the cracks of the pavements. Normally there's at least one tamer who patrols the streets when most people are asleep, but I can't see a sign of them.

We near the city entrance and I carefully peek behind a corner.

*Great, it's Bently and Shiro guarding the gate.*

The brown-haired man stands at the very top of the wall with his rhinoceros-like umbra beside him spying out into the Nightmare Plains.

*How we gonna do this, guys?*

*'Could we say we're doing a perimeter run outside the city?'* Nox suggests, but I shake my head.

'I don't think so. They'd know Mum and Dad would tell them if we were gonna be doing that. Plus Lucas is with us.'

'I'll distract them. You and Lux can leap up on to the watch ledges and jump over the other side,' Nox says. 'I'll catch up with you after.'

*Decision, decisions.* I chew on my lip, weighing up the risks.

*OK, let's do it. Game faces on.*

Nox nods and slinks into the shadows. I jump on Lux's back and we watch him until he disappears completely. A few moments later there's a loud splash by the bridge.

We see Bently and Shiro turn their attention toward the bridge and my heart pounds. *Go Bently . . . Skedaddle already!*

The tamer climbs down the ladder from the top of the wall and Shiro leaps down the different ledges after him. They stop just in front of the gate and look at each other.

'Maybe it was nothing,' Bently says. They're about to climb back up when there's another big splash and their attention snaps back to the bridge.

They run off to investigate and I grin. *Good job, Nox!*

'*Hold on,*' Lux says. I settle Lucas firmly in front of me and clutch Lux's shadow fur. He leaps up effortlessly from ledge to ledge until we reach the top of the wall. Lucas chuckles. At the very top, a lump comes to my throat at the sight of the death drop below us. *That's a long way down.* The wind blows colder as if it's threatening to push us off.

'*Will you relax? You're perfectly safe. Aren't you the same girl who jumps from roofs?*' Lux teases.

*This is triple the height of a house, mate. If I drop off, I'm a goner.*

'*Then make sure you don't let go.*'

'Lucas, hold on tight and close your eyes.'

Before he can ask why, Lux leaps. I hug Lucas in a vice grip while grasping Lux's shadow fur with both hands. I bite down on my lip and squeeze my eyes shut, keeping in the scream that's bubbling in my throat. We land with a gentle thud. I slowly peek through one eye and then pat my body. *Definitely alive.*

When I look at Lucas, he's grinning from ear to ear.

'That was so much fun!' he says.

'Shh, not too loud, remember?' I say, but my stomach drops, realising something. 'You know one thing I didn't think of?'

'*What?*' Lux asks, glancing back at me.

'I didn't think of how we're gonna get back unnoticed. We can't exactly climb back up,' I say, staring at the huge stone wall.

'*We'll cross that bridge later. For now, we focus on finding proof that the Elite are hiding something in Astaroth and maybe something that leads to finding Nox's attacker,*' Lux says.

We're about to set off into the plains when a black mass appears at the top of the wall. A grin spreads across my face as Nox leaps off and lands perfectly beside us.

'*Mission Astaroth is on! Let's goooo!*'

We gallop off, far from the gate. The air is surprisingly warm against my skin. The crooked trees welcome us back with a wave. Various creatures scatter at the sight of us, but the wild umbra run with us.

Determination swells in my gut. The fear that once bubbled at the memories of the Nightmare Plains vanishes. Maybe it's because this time we're chasing after something rather than being chased ourselves.

I pull out the map and rest it on Lux's back in front of Lucas.

'Mimi, how far away is Astaroth?' Lucas asks.

'It's not as far as Stella. We need to keep going straight until we reach Mum and Dad's tree then take a right towards some hills. We should see Astaroth once we get atop the hills after passing the forest near Lunavale,' I say.

*'Are you nervous, young one?'* Nox suddenly asks, galloping beside us. I raise an eyebrow.

'Nervous?'

*'About what we may encounter in Astaroth.'*

I clear my throat. Am I nervous? I feel something, but 'nervous' doesn't really sit right. Maybe 'cautious' is the better word. Cautious, but determined, because we *need* to find something. We can't afford to go home empty-handed.

'We just don't know what to expect, ya know? So I'm a little on edge,' I answer. 'I'd feel worse if I was alone though.'

'Me too,' Lucas says. I nuzzle my face in his curly locks. I'm actually kinda glad he came.

The warm air turns colder as we gallop closer to Astaroth, and the landscape around us morphs. Broken trees block our path, cracked right through the middle like someone tore each of them apart. The rosy-dills and carno plants that sprinkle the plains change to prickly bluebell cactuses that stick out across the purple grass like sore thumbs. Just as unwelcoming, red thorny terror-bell plants poke from bushes, but they're nothing under Lux and Nox's shadowy hooves.

'Perhaps I can speed up our journey. I could try and use the staff like last time,' I say, glancing at the sky. 'Who knows how long it'll take before Mum and Dad see my note. We don't want them coming after us before we've even reached Astaroth. I've no idea if it'll work though.'

*Doesn't hurt to try,'* Nox says.

I pull the staff from my thigh strap. It glows purple in my grasp. A thousand electric sparks shiver up my arms and through my body. Like a bubbling volcano I feel my powers ready to burst from my chest. *Lux, Nox, you ready?*

*Ready,'* they say in unison.

'Hold on tight, Lucas,' I warn.

My eyes close and I focus. *Don't be afraid. Control it.* The energy boils inside me, ready to explode. *Everything's gonna be OK.* I suck in a huge breath and scream, releasing a burst of energy. Wild flames of light engulf Lux and Nox, and suddenly we're off like a bolt towards the mountains.

'WOAH!' Lucas screams, glowing too.

Adrenaline pumps through my veins. We tear through the air like lightning itself. The wind whips against our bodies but I barely feel a thing, just light. Powerful, like nothing can touch us. I feel free!

The stars twinkle above yet the world around us darkens the closer we run to the mountains and Astaroth. We leap and gallop up one of the hills at sonic speed, and my fingers tighten around Lux's fur.

'OK, you can slow down!' I call out, hanging on with all my might.

*'We can't!'* they yell.

We race to the top, galloping at a speed so fast I can barely hold on. The edge of the mountain gets closer and my heart leaps in my chest.

'No! No! NO!' Lucas yells.

'We're gonna go off the edge!' I shout.

*'Only you can stop it!'* Lux yells at me.

I squeeze my eyes shut and try to force my powers down. *STOP, STOP, STOP!*

The light suddenly zaps away from us, snapping back like a rubber band. Lux stumbles, narrowly avoiding flying off the edge.

'You guys good?' I yell.

Lux shakes his body and Nox glances over the edge of the mountain. Lucas shivers against me. I hug him and kiss the top of his head.

*'Yes, we're good, but let's not do that again for a while,'* Nox says.

*'You got that right,'* Lux agrees.

'You OK, Lu-Lu?' I ask. He nods shakily.

'That was scary,' he whispers, and the words dagger my heart.

'Sorry,' I apologise. Maybe I shouldn't have brought him here. Did I make a big mistake?

*'Mouse, we're here,'* Lux says.

The smell of rot and damp fills my nose. I look up and my lips part in shock. The cold air sticks in my throat and the wind pushes us forward. My fingers grip Lux's shadow fur a little harder.

A creepy mist hangs ahead, but out of it rises a tall grim castle. Astaroth – once the home of the Elite.

'Let's go,' I mutter, and we leap down the hill and race towards the city of nightmares. The very first city the Reaper King attacked.

# Chapter Nine

Like Nubis, Astaroth is a city of darkness – but that's where the comparison ends. Chills run down my spine looking around. Green and white glowing vines grow along windows and walls. There are houses and shops, cafes and other places, but each building is topped with weird spikes, like they're trying to keep something out. Every door is made from titanium steel and the whole street is cobbled. The odd patches of grass are a gloomy grey, like the trees. Dull and lacking life. The whole place raises goosebumps on my arms, reeking of death and creatures meant to live only in the Nightmare Plains. Did Miles really live here for so many years?

After the adrenaline-fuelled journey, Lucas has fallen asleep against me. I gaze up at the abandoned buildings and streets. It feels so strange being here.

'*Stay alert, young one,*' Nox warns.

'A hundred per cent.'

We turn down an alleyway and what we find there brings a smile to my face. Bright neon inks decorate the walls in pretty drawings for as far as the eye can see. I pat Lux to stop and slide off his back, first making sure Lucas is secure. Images of different umbra are depicted running across the walls. I stare at the art in awe, my fingers brushing against the rough brick as we walk along it.

I reach a new drawing that stops me in my tracks, and I'm frozen on the spot. *Wait, what?*

On the wall a huge drawing of a girl with a low ponytail and bangs, along with a star necklace hanging from her neck, smiles at us. There's absolutely no doubt who it's meant to be.

'It's me,' I murmur, reaching out. My fingers shakily trace along the purple curls of the girl's hair and a strange warmth nestles inside in my chest. *Miles . . .*

'*It appears that he never forgot about you either,*' Nox says solemnly. I nod. Miles has always been a talented drawer. I'm kinda glad that never changed, but . . . A dull pain aches in my heart. *What was his life like here? Was he the only kid here?* So many questions and not a single answer.

'Come on guys. Let's get going,' I mutter, letting my fingers fall from the pretty drawing. *We'll see each other again soon, I just know it.*

Lucas yawns and sits up. 'Is it sky connect?'

'Not yet,' I say, hopping on Nox's back. 'You gonna be OK on Lux's back by yourself?'

'Yep.' He rubs his eyes and gives me a sleepy smile. 'I love Luxy.'

*'You're not too bad yourself, tiny human,'* Lux replies. I raise my eyebrows.

*Wow, he actually said something nice.*

*'Don't get used to it,'* he retorts.

We exit the other end of the alleyway and I hear the swift pitter-patters of feet scuttle behind us. We spin around, my hand ready on my staff, but I clap a hand over my mouth to stop myself screaming.

Huge red horned spiders the size of Lux and Nox skitter across the road. Glowing red webs are left in their wake on the street and between buildings. *Hell flipping no. Guys, we gotta go. Like now!*

*'Don't worry. I will not let them touch you,'* Nox says.

I squeeze his shadow fur so hard my knuckles turn white. Their beady eyes twitch in all different directions and their gangly prickly legs move at lightning speed.

One of the spiders stops and my breath hitches. It turns to us. A scream bubbles in the back of my throat. *Don't. Move.*

'Nox . . .'

It taps two of its front legs, then sprints towards us. I scream my lungs out, almost falling off Nox. He growls at the eight-legged monster and so does Lux.

'No! Leave Mimi alone!' Lucas shouts.

A boomerang whizzes through the air, expanding to double its size with spiked edges. It slashes the spider. A monstrous roar blares from the nightmare beast and it skitters away. The boomerang spins back to Lucas. He catches it with both hands as the spikes retract and it returns to its small size again.

'Well done, Lu-Lu!' I cheer. *He actually used it right!* He grins.

'Don't worry, Mimi. Spiders don't scare me!'

At the sound, the other spiders snap their attention in our direction and I yelp as they charge at us.

*'Hold on, young one! We have to do something unexpected.'*

We gallop off as fast as we can – TOWARDS the

oncoming creatures. I press my body against Nox's back and Lucas clings tight to Lux. We leap over the spiders and dash off before they can turn around. My eyes stay glued ahead, refusing to even peek behind as we race into the darkness, far away from those monsters.

When we finally slow down, we are in a deserted street littered with the glass from shattered street lamps. There's not one sign of a glow bug or working light. Thankfully there's not a spider either, but I jump at the smallest skitter of a rat across the street.

'Thanks for protecting me, Lu-Lu,' I say, feeling clammy all over.

Lucas pats his chest and puffs it out a bit. 'I'm always here, Mimi!'

It's pitch black here. Not even the moonlight touches this part of the city. To take my mind off feeling scared, I start trying to refocus on our reasons for coming here.

'Hey Lux, Nox, do you guys really think you were created from the battle between old Queen Lucina and the Reaper King?' I ask.

*'Yes, it is how every umbra was created,'* Nox says.

'But obviously we were the best of the bunch,' Lux adds. I can hear the smirk in his voice and I chuckle.

'But *how* do you know that?' I ask.

'*Because most of us remember the day we were created,*' Lux says.

*What?* His answer throws me completely. He remembers the day he was created? Did Mum know this already? Guess she probably did.

'Can you tell me about it?' I ask, ducking my head under a broken signpost.

'*There was a bright light, and then a woman, who appears to be your Queen Lucina, was dying and the Reaper King was being sealed away,*' Nox says.

'Woah …' I mutter. I don't know if I'd *want* to remember the day I was born.

Each pavement and road we walk on is chipped and cracked. The giant red spiderwebs that cling to the walls and buildings are a scary reminder of the demon arachnids we left behind.

I'm about to ask another question when a new sound catches my attention. Nox stops in his tracks.

It's a voice. Muffled, but I can make out the words. 'What do you mean, someone's here? Who is it?'

*Did you guys hear that?*

'*Yes,*' Nox says.

We walk towards where it came from and a shiver runs down my spine.

'Is it one of *them?*' The voice comes again, louder and clearer. It's a girl, and she sounds about the same age as me. Maybe younger?

We peek around the corner where there's a huge black fountain with benches around it and decorated with gargoyles. Nearby is what looks like a row of abandoned shops. Water trickles out from the fountain, surprisingly pretty in the limited starlight.

I press my finger against my lips to remind Lucas to stay quiet, and we step out into the opening, but stop abruptly. A girl with wild messy black hair is crouched by the fountain. Her eyes are hidden behind her bangs.

She doesn't move. Frozen in her long black, bell-sleeved dress. She reminds me of a doll except she's obviously a person, going by all the muck on her shoes and scrapes on her arms. Battle scars as Dad likes to call them.

Beside her, a small bear-like umbra with small horns on its head and spikes for tails stares at us with bright golden eyes. The girl cocks her head to the side in our direction, finally noticing us. Her bangs fall away from her face and I see her pale skin, almost luminous in the dark. Her big hazel eyes connect with mine. I jerk my head back. *Who is this girl?*

She jerks her head back too. I tilt my head left and she does the same. *Is she copying me?*

A creepy grin spreads across the girl's face.

'So, it's *you*,' she says.

Her face is frozen in a smile and her voice is filled with curiosity. Shivers tickle down my spine but I keep a straight face. I'm comforted by the presence of Lux and Nox, but this girl is weirding me out. *Why is she smiling like that?*

There's something about the way she's looking at me that puts my instincts on high alert. The twinkle in her eye . . . It's like she *knows* me or something. *Lux, keep Lucas close.*

'*Of course,*' Lux replies.

'Was that you talking just now?' I ask the girl, mindful of the distance between us.

'Yep. Timi was telling me you were all here,' she says, petting the bear umbra's head.

'You're a tamer?' Lucas asks, but the girl shakes her head.

'Nope. Never. Timi is a wild umbra.'

I raise an eyebrow and look from her to the umbra.

*'What's your name, human?'* Lux asks.

'And are you here alone?' I add right after.

Her head tilts to the other side and her smile falters, as if debating whether to answer or not.

'Layla.' Her voice is as quiet as a three-eared mouse. I've heard that name before . . . I scratch my head, trying to remember, but suddenly her grin grows again. She looks me dead in the eye. 'You're Mia.'

My heart skips a beat and the hairs on the back of my neck stand on end. A hundred questions fill my head and I fight the urge to step back. *How the . . . ?*

*'Keep calm, young one,'* Nox whispers to me.

I take a silent breath. *He's right.*

'How do you know my name?' I ask.

'Miles told me,' she says.

Her answer comes like a punch in the stomach. She knows Miles. Of course she does if she's been staying here in Astaroth. But it doesn't make me feel any better.

'Is he here?' I ask with a little too much hope in my voice.

'Nope. I did see him a few days ago though. He told me he was heading to Nubis soon.'

My heart jumps and I can't help but smile inside.

'I don't know your name, though,' she says, looking at Lucas.

*'Are you really here alone?'* Nox says before he can reply.

Layla jumps up to her feet and I clutch my weapon on instinct. She sways playfully side to side with her hands behind her back, looking at my hand in amusement. *Could she be the one who attacked Nox?* That golden-eyed umbra with her suggests otherwise though.

'Besides the umbra and the creatures, I'm here alone. I didn't want to be a part of the ritual. I knew they'd lose anyway. The umbra told me, so I hid. The Elite wasn't going to be able to release the Reaper King that easily because of a girl and boy with powers of light, they said,' she explains.

*OK . . . I guess that meant me and Lucas.*

'Where are your parents?' I ask.

'I don't know. I barely remember what they look like now,' Layla shrugs.

'Are you lost then?' Lucas pipes up.

She skips away and stares up at the huge fountain, so close the water splashes over her hair. 'Nope. I'm exactly where I want to be,' she tells him.

I stand up straighter and try to channel Dad in tamer mode. 'I have one more question.'

She glances over her shoulder at me, ignoring the fact she's getting wet.

'Have you ever heard of an umbra's eyes turning red?'

Immediately her smile drops. She stumbles away from the fountain and a grave look crosses her face.

I take my own step back and alarm bells ring in my head as she closes the gap between us in seconds.

'Why you asking?' The intensity of her eyes raises the hairs on the back of my neck again, and my grip on the staff tightens. I take a fighting stance. Just in case.

'I know it's linked to how the Elite tame their umbra, and someone tried to do it to my umbra,' I explain, nodding at Nox.

She studies my face, mulling over my response, then takes a breath and relaxes her shoulders.

'Taming is the worst thing you can do to an umbra. Especially how *they* do it,' she says. Beside her, the small bear umbra snorts in agreement.

'What do you mean?' I ask. My relationship with Lux and Nox is everything. How could it be bad?

She turns back and crouches down to stroke the bear

umbra's head. 'I know what it feels like. I've been hit by the same power the Elite use against them.'

My mouth falls open. I stare at her with wide eyes but she refuses to look away from the umbra. *How is that even possible?*

She sits on the edge of the fountain. 'I tried saving one of my friends from being tamed years ago, but the powers of the Elite somehow went through me before they got to her,' she explains. 'They get into your head with their shadow powers. It feels like you're a puppet and they're controlling the strings.'

She raises her hands up and down like invisible strings are connected to her wrists. *Just like what Nox said.*

'I don't know what happens afterwards,' Layla continues. 'That was the first and only time they tamed in front of me. None of my umbra friends will tell me what happens after they get control. They say it's too scary and that it was like the Elite were running some sort of tests on them at the time.'

'Sorry, Luxy. Sorry, Noxy,' I hear Lucas whisper, and Nox licks his cheek.

*'As if tamers would scare us,'* Lux snorts. *'But what those foolish Elite do is unforgivable.'*

'So, why are you here?' I ask Layla, gesturing all around us. 'Why stay here after that's happened?'

A cat-like smile spreads across her face again. She leans forward and playfully twirls her finger around a single strand of her hair.

'To get revenge, of course.'

I cross my arms and smirk. Well, I didn't see that coming. 'Looks like we got a common enemy then. It would be a big help if you came with me back to my city and told everyone about what happened to you,' I say. Mum and Dad are gonna flip but Layla's my best and only proof so far about Nox being attacked. It'll be worth it. 'Someone tried to attack Nox in the Nightmare Plains and I'm trying to find out who it was.'

Of course, this is a risky move, but maybe Layla could be a big help.

'The only way an umbra's eyes turn red is if they're being tamed by a member of the Elite,' she says, confirming my original thoughts. 'One of my umbra friends told me they were attacked along with someone else yesterday, too. But for some reason they were released again afterwards and ran away.' Perhaps because that umbra wasn't the actual target. Maybe the attacker *was* after Lux and Nox.

'Wait, so, you just randomly talk to different umbra even though you're not a tamer?' I ask, trying to wrap my head around it.

Layla jumps back up on her feet. Her arms rest behind her back. 'You got that right. Taming is wrong no matter how you do it. If you just talk to the umbra, nine times out of ten they'll help you with whatever you want.'

I look back at Lux and Nox, but they have the same questioning look in their golden eyes.

'So, will you come with me?' I ask.

She walks over and snatches my hand, which startles me. I yank out my bo staff and I thrust it against her neck with my free hand. Layla's eyes twinkle with mischief.

'Will it be fun? That's all I care about to be honest. That, and getting revenge.' She presses her neck into the staff without an ounce of fear.

'It will be interesting, I guess,' I say, lowering the weapon. Layla lets go of my hand.

'All right then, deal,' she says, looking at Lux and Nox. 'Can I ride on one of your backs? What's your names, Mr and Mr Umbra? I know one is Nox.'

He wrinkles his shadowy snout.

'I'm guessing that's you,' she says.

*Yes, and my brother is Lux,*' he replies.

'And you're riding with me on Nox,' I add, answering her first question. There's no way she's riding with Lucas.

'Mimi. What about the big castle?' Lucas asks, pointing to the huge building we haven't yet reached.

Layla climbs on to Nox's back and I climb on behind her.

'You can't go in there. The door won't open unless you have the Reaper King's powers, which I don't have,' she says, glancing back at me. 'Pretty sure you don't either.'

'No harm in checking though,' I say, glancing up at the night sky. *We've still got time.*

We gallop through the city towards the giant castle and stop by the stone steps. From far away, the giant castle walls look grey, dull and haunted, but up close the walls look very much *alive*. I go to press my palm against the rough brick but stop myself. There are so many bugs crawling in and out of the cracks that it looks like the walls themselves are breathing. Yet the stones look strong enough to keep anyone and anything out, or *in*.

I slide off Nox and walk up the cracked stairs. I reach

the top of the steps and stop in front of the huge metal doors. There're no visible handles and I can't figure out another way to open it.

'Guess I'm just gonna have to push,' I mutter. I roll up my sleeves and shove against the metal doors as hard as I can.

'You're not gonna be able to open the door,' Layla sings.

'I'll help, Mimi!' Lucas slides off Lux's back and pushes the door with me.

Layla giggles, but I ignore her and push again.

*'Let us help, young one,'* Nox says.

'All right. All together then. Three, two, one!' The four of us throw our bodies against the metal doors, but they refuse to budge.

'Told you so!' Layla shouts. I look back at her with a scrunched-up nose.

'Whatever. Let's go.'

I take Lucas's hand and walk back down the stairs. I help him get back on Lux and I jump on Nox's back. A dull ache swells in my shoulder from banging against the door but I ignore it.

'You gonna be OK on Lux by yourself again?' I ask Lucas.

He nods and pats his chest. 'I got this, Mimi!'

Together we head out of the city but a tiny bit of fear settles in my stomach. I fight back the urge to focus on the girl in front of me. Layla might have the answers to what happened to Nox, but I can't help feeling we're about to open a whole new bucket of worms. Either way, I need to ready myself for possibly the biggest telling off of my life, and I hope it'll be worth it. But at least we found someone else who could back up my story that Nox was attacked by the Elite's powers, and her name is Layla.

# CHAPTER TEN

I keep my eye on Layla the whole way home. While I'm hoping she's going to lead us to some answers, it'd be silly to underestimate her. There's more to her story than she's telling.

Nerves tingle in the pit of my stomach the closer we get to Nubis. *We're gonna be in so much trouble.*

And then I freeze. What feels like thousands of tiny spiders skitter up my arms and the back of my neck. Numbness takes over my body and the world turns black. Everything falls to silence apart from one woman's voice, whispering two words:

*'Go back …'*

The words whisper over and over again.

*'Go back. Go back.'*

Over and over and over again.

*'Mouse?'* Lux's voice echoes faintly, then gets louder.

*'Mouse!'*

I blink, finding myself back in reality. The soft glow of lights reveal the city ahead. Nox and Lux are staring at me, worried.

'Are you OK, Mimi?' Lucas asks.

'I'm OK,' I tell them, rubbing my stiff shoulder. I know I didn't just imagine that. That voice didn't belong to me, Lux or Nox, and it wasn't Layla either. It was *her* again.

*I'm fine,* I reaffirm, feeling them checking my thoughts. Too scared to even think about the fear bubbling in my gut. *I gotta find out who this woman is.*

We reach the gate and it creaks open automatically. In the entrance Mum, Dad and every single tamer in Nubis is ready to ride out into the Nightmare Plains with their umbra. Mum's furious eyes shoot to me and I gulp.

'Mia Alison McKenna. You have one minute to explain yourself.' Her voice is steeped in anger and I swallow hard.

I jump off Nox's back and almost stumble. I rub my neck, awkwardly giving everyone a smile. But no one returns it.

'Hi, Mummy,' Lucas says, breaking the silence.

Even he decides to stay safe on Lux's back. Dad's jaw is clenched so hard I can see the veins jutting out of his neck. I rack my brain for the best explanation, but I can't come up with anything! I feel the sweat build on my forehead. Every tamer is staring at us but when my eyes connect with Rosé and Riley, my hand balls into a fist. No, I don't regret what I did.

'We found proof that I was telling the truth about what happened to Nox during the tamer trials,' I say. Riley awkwardly clears his throat and I give him a pointed glare.

'She's my proof.' I jerk my thumb back at Layla and Nox. 'Her name is Layla and she lives in Astaroth.'

There are gasps and curious mutters amongst the tamers, and Mum's face softens ever so slightly as she takes in the girl. 'You've been living in Astaroth all this time? Where are your parents?' she asks.

Layla jumps off Nox and giggles. 'Don't know. They're not part of the Elite though, if that's what you're thinking. Maria found me in the Nightmare Plains and took me to Astaroth,' Layla explains, but her smile waivers. 'You're not like the Elite. Are you?'

'No, we're not,' Dad interjects, still stern. 'We've captured the Elite and stopped them from bringing back the Reaper King.'

At his words, a wide grin spreads across Layla's face again.

'You think you've stopped them?' she laughs, and everyone's attention turns to her. A mischievous glint lights her brown eyes and she cocks her head to the side.

'We *have* stopped them. They're all locked away in the hold,' Riley counters.

'Not the one who attacked Nox and one of my friends out in the Nightmare Plains. You know those people never ever give up, right?' she retorts.

There's a moment of complete silence.

'Layla, what do you know about the Elite?' Jada asks.

'Pretty much all what I just said. They never told me much. They mainly wanted to use me for all the stuff I know about umbra. Like I said to Mia, taming them is wrong,' she says.

Mum looks back at Dad with the same confusion I originally had. They have a silent conversation between themselves then look to the other tamers. *I seriously gotta learn how to do that, or at least understand what they're saying.*

*'Well, technically you have silent conversations with us all the time,'* Nox muses.

*Fair enough, but theirs are different. They can't actually read each other's minds.* Well, I don't think so anyway.

'If you don't mind, Layla, we need to discuss something in private,' Mum announces.

She gathers the tamers at a distance, and after a moment Dad walks back to us with Bolt. I arch an eyebrow at him but his face gives away nothing.

'For now, Layla, you can stay with Jada. It'll only be for a while. As you can probably guess, since you spent time with the Elite, we can't allow you to roam the city alone just yet,' he says with a kind smile that almost makes me smile too. There's a reason behind everything Dad does. Our eyes connect, confirming it. They've got a plan.

Jada comes over. 'Hey, Layla, I'll show you my place,' she says, jerking her chin for them to leave.

Layla nods and her eyes shift to me with a cheeky smile. *Seriously, what's up with this girl?*

'See you later, Mia!' she says.

I wait until she and Jada are out of sight, then ask Dad, 'You don't really trust her, do you?'

'No, I don't, but her experience of the Elite could be important,' he says.

Mum walks up to us with her arms crossed. 'It's good she's here with us now. She may open up to Jada, rather than an adult. But don't think you're not in trouble still, missy. Not only did you sneak out of the city, you put Lucas in danger too. Mia, you promised me!'

I look down at my feet. The weight of the promise I broke feels ready to crush and swallow me.

'I'm really sorry, Mum. I mean it. I wasn't even going to take him but he convinced me,' I say, looking up at her. 'He wanted to come.'

Mum sighs and presses her fingers against her head. 'Let's go home.'

Dad walks over to Nox and scoops Lucas up in his arms. Lucas nuzzles his head into Dad's neck and closes his eyes.

'Sorry, Daddy,' Lucas whispers. 'I just wanted to pretect Mimi.'

'It's OK. Come on,' Dad says, and we head home together.

*

At home, the smell of honey-toffee cookies wafts into the living room from the kitchen. Dad managed to convince Lucas to help him after he insisted he wasn't tired. I'm stroking Nox's head when Mum walks in with a book tucked in her arm. A much calmer expression on her face compared to earlier. She sits on the sofa next to me and I fidget with the bottom of my sleeves. I keep my eyes down.

'So, Mia, after everything that's happened, tell me what made you do this,' Mum asks.

I stumble over what words to say. It's *because* of everything that's happened.

'I . . . I needed to find proof that Nox was attacked during the tamer trials,' I begin, still searching for the right words. 'The tamers don't take action unless everyone's on board, and I didn't want you or Dad to get hurt or captured again because we waited too long to act. I couldn't just sit here and wait.'

Mum doesn't utter a word and when I finally brave it and look up, to my surprise there's a soft smile on her face, but her eyes look the exact opposite. Sad. She takes my hand and brushes against the back of it with her thumb.

'Mia, I'm sorry every day that you and Lucas had to go through everything with the Reaper King. You should have never been put in that position in the first place. I know you're strong. You've proven it, but you can't put yourself at risk like that.'

I avoid her eyes and hold back a sigh. 'I didn't mean to break your trust. I'm sorry.'

Her arms wrap around me in a tender hug. I bury my face into her and the sweet rosy-dill perfume overwhelms my senses.

'You scared us,' she whispers, holding me closer. 'But at least you were sensible enough to leave us a note. However, if you sneak out again to leave the city, you'll be in serious trouble. Do you hear me? You're lucky you only have one short class tomorrow.'

'Yes, Mum.'

We pull apart and Mum smiles. 'I've got something to show you.'

She lifts the book in her hands. A small photo album with a blue cover and white border. 'Look what I found.'

She opens it, revealing the first page of moving photos. I smile at each picture of Mum in her teens. There's one with her, Nan and Grandad in a sky tower restaurant toasting to something. My smile falters, thinking about Nan and Grandad.

As if reading my thoughts, Mum nudges me with her shoulder. 'We'll go again tomorrow and you can have another try. If it doesn't work, it just means you're not quite ready yet. It'll be OK.'

'Yeah ...' I mumble, glancing at another photo. Teenage Mum shoots her arrow into the distance with the sunset behind her. Her strong purple bow in her grip. *She was so cool. She still is now.*

'And your father and I will be holding another tamer meeting tomorrow to talk about the search for Nox's attacker,' Mum says, turning the page. 'But we really need to practise your powers more to stop this woman from talking to you.'

The last thing she said was 'Go back'... There has to be something still in Astaroth, but I keep that to myself for now.

'Yeah. I'm ready to work on it,' I promise, and my eyes shift to another picture.

'Is that you and Miles's dad?' I ask. It looks like Mum is playfully sparring with a dark-haired boy. If I didn't know better, I'd think it was somehow a picture of Miles in the future.

'Believe it or not, Magnus was my best friend back when I lived in Stella. I knew him way before I met your dad. Our families were close.' I hear the smile in her voice. I take a peek at her and her eyes seem far away, lost in a memory.

'So, like you and Auntie Carly?' I ask. I wonder how

she's doing with TJ right now in Stella?

'Yep, she may not be your auntie by blood, but we were close too before she moved to Lunavale and met Auntie Lisa, but I knew Magnus first.'

She closes the album and kisses my head. 'It was your Dad who stole my heart though,' she whispers, and I smirk. Good thing too, or I wouldn't be here.

'What are my beautiful ladies talking about?' Dad asks from the doorway with a big grin.

'We were talking about you, handsome,' Mum laughs. I roll my eyes and yawn.

'Looks like you're ready for bed,' she says and before I can protest, another yawn slips from my lips.

'I just put Lucas to bed too,' Dad says. It wouldn't hurt to get a little bit of sleep.

I head to my room after saying goodnight and close the door behind me. Rolling my shoulders backwards and forwards, I fill my lungs with two deep breaths. Lately it's been nice to stretch and dance a before bed. The soft plush carpet presses against my feet. Like the current in a river, I bring my arms up and down. I push left on my heels, then right, feeling the stretch in my legs. Then I pirouette, letting my body take full control.

Every rhythmic movement carried by a silent song in my head. I dance away in the small space of my room, allowing my mind to melt in the movement. All the worries fade from my mind, floating away.

Something click-clacks near my window and I jump. I open my eyes and notice a purple glow fading from my hands. *Did you guys see that?*

*'Yes, your whole body glowed for a second,'* Nox says. *'It's been doing that a lot lately. It seems to be triggered by dancing.'*

*Maybe that's how I can control my powers.* Something taps the window again, and I grab my bo staff from the floor. It taps one more time. I yank back the curtains. A small robot bird pecks at the glass. I open my window and it flies inside. It lands in the middle of my room and a blue light flashes from its eyes. It scans me up and down twice, almost blinding me, before opening its beak. *Wait, I know what that is—*

'Mia McKenna. You have a video call from Tyler-James Johnson. Do you wish to receive it?' Its loud robotic voice echoes in my room and my jaw drops.

'Yes!' I gasp, jumping on my bed. Buzzing at the thought of seeing that goofball, I can barely contain myself. A bright beam of light flashes from the bird's beak and then a holographic image of TJ, waving with a cheesy grin on his face, appears in the middle of my room.

'What's up?' he says casually. His voice is as clear as night, though the hologram flickers a little. *I can't believe it!*

'Was you actually given your own holocommunicator bot or are you just borrowing it?' I ask, gobsmacked. It's so unfair! First Miles, now TJ has one.

He sits on what looks like his bed and leans against an invisible wall with his hands behind his head. An oh-so smug look on his face. 'Perks of the job.'

*Yeah, right.* I smirk, crossing my arms. 'You're just a trainee, mate. Quit lying.'

I do my best to resist a cheesy smile of my own and lean against my wall too. It's been so long since we've talked. Literally months, and for the first time in ages I feel normal, despite all the craziness happening.

'I'm not lying, you moosefoot. That bot literally travels at the speed of light to the person receiving it. It's so cool,' TJ says.

'Yeah-Yeah. Whatever, you *goofball*.'

He grins and scratches the back of his head. Yeah,

he's definitely lying all right. I don't even think they make ones that go at the speed of light. I've been saving up for AGES to get one, but they're so flippin' expensive. Only the rich have them in Nexus and Stella.

'Hey Lux. Hey Nox. How are you guys too? It's been a while.'

*'We are good. It's nice to see you are too,'* Nox says, bowing his head, and resting on the carpet.

'So, how you been, Superstar?'

'I'm all right too,' I say. *Sorta . . .*

He frowns, seeing straight through my extra big smile.

'Who's the one lying now.'

'I'm honestly fine. I mean it.' I don't want him worrying about me too.

He rubs his chin. 'Oh, I get it.' He leans forward with a weird smile that makes me lean back a bit more. 'You miss me, right? It's OK, you don't have to be sad. Just a few more months and I'll be back home to visit. Can you survive until then?'

My eyes widen and I feel my face go hot with embarrassment. *What is this guy even saying?!*

'Shut up, ya clown. I don't miss you!' I throw a pillow right through his hologram. He chuckles and leans back again.

'Yeah-yeah, sure you don't. So, is that weird red-cloak friend of yours back yet? You know, the one who helped capture our parents and then chased after us with his Elite friends.'

'All right, sunshine. Relax, and no. Miles isn't back yet.'

'Good.'

I raise an eyebrow. 'Good?'

'I still don't trust him.'

I get where TJ is coming from. A lot's happened these past few months but none of us can deny the fact that Miles helped us in the end. That's what matters.

'It's not him that I'm worried about anyway. Right now, I'm trying to find out who attacked Nox during the tamer trials,' I say.

'Wait, what? What happened?' TJ says.

Lux grunts, laying his head back down and Nox growls at the memory.

'We believe a member of the Elite tried to tame Nox,' I say.

*'Some of the tamers didn't believe I was attacked, so we went to get proof. We found a girl in Astaroth called*

*Layla who is friends with the other umbra that was also targeted,'* Nox answers.

TJ frowns. 'Wait. Layla? Isn't that the name of the girl those cave umbra mentioned? Or am I buggin'?'

That's where I recognised the name! I jump up from my seat. Memories of the kangaroo-like umbra we met on our journey to Stella replay like an old movie in my head. The makeshift bed and the doll. The fear and anger the umbra first felt when we came into their home. The last thing they asked was for us to look out for a girl. Could they have been talking about *this* Layla?

'I knew I recognised that name before! I can't believe it. We might've actually found her!' I yell. I clap a hand over my mouth.

I'd have to ask her to be sure, but it all adds up. Her having umbra friends, not knowing where her parents are, being with the Elite. It lines up with what the cave umbra said too.

*'Well, that's a plot twist I never expected,'* Lux says bluntly.

'This is nuts. I can't believe it,' TJ says.

'Right?' I say, still in shock.

'But who do you think attacked Nox?' he asks.

'No idea,' I say. 'The only thing I really know about

183

Layla is that she has a strange connection with the umbra, which would make sense if she's the girl the cave umbra were talking about, but it could have been anyone out there in the plains who attacked Nox.'

'Well, I guess it's down to you, Lux and Nox to find out, but . . . Be careful, Mia.'

'I will. But there's something else,' I say, and TJ sits up as I tell him a bit about my nightmares and the woman's voice.

He whistles. 'You think it's got something to do with the Reaper King?'

'Maybe. I don't know. It's like she keeps sending me these little messages, helping me, but I can't work out who she is, and I have no idea where to start,' I say.

'Well, maybe when you hear her voice again, you can just ask her who she is,' TJ suggests. 'And what about that lightcaster book your dad has?'

'It's been tricky to translate. All we know is that there were six founders, who were the original lightcasters, and their power came from two crystals. One of which is destroyed, of course. The queen pretty much confirmed that story.'

'So weird.'

'Yep . . . When are you really coming back anyway?

Is it seriously months?' I ask, and my heart sinks when he narrows his eyes with a sigh. I'm not gonna like the answer and he knows it.

'Yeah, this training is seriously no joke. I've still got a lot of work to do.'

I hug my knees to my chest, trying my hardest to hide my disappointment. Things just aren't the same without him.

'How's lightcaster training?' he asks.

I scrunch up my face. 'Sucks, but not terrible, I guess. I'm trying. Sometimes, I feel like my powers have a life of their own or something, but when I dance I seem to be more in control.'

He smiles. 'You can do it. I know you can—'

A voice calls his name, cutting him off.

TJ sighs. 'Ah, geez. Looks like I've gotta go do a bit of training now.'

'Isn't it night-time in Stella?' I ask.

'Yep, we often train at night. It's actually when I'm the most awake, so it's all good. I'm still not fully used to the whole sunlight thing here yet.' He gets up from his bed and playfully salutes me.

'See ya, Mia. We'll chat soon! Bye Lux! Bye Nox!'

'See ya later, TJ.' I wave back.

He gives me a thumbs-up and the hologram cuts off, leaving my room silent. I get up and push the button on the robot bird's head, sending it flying off back to TJ. I fall back against my bed and sigh.

*'Relax Mouse, he'll be back soon. It seems like he wanted to check in on you too,'* Lux muses. He gets up and I watch him carefully as he walks over. *'Now sleep.'*

His curved horn taps against my head. I wince, chuckling.

'All right. All right,' I say, rubbing the top of my head. He throws my night bonnet to me from my bedside cabinet. I catch it and slip it on before settling into bed.

*'You can't escape ...'*

I jump up and rub my eyes. My eyes slowly adjust to the darkness of a room that's not my own. Black posters of red eyes hang on the walls. I freeze. In the middle of the room someone stands with their back to me, facing the wall. My heart skips a beat, frantically searching for Lux and Nox, but they're not here.

The person doesn't move. My eyes adjust to the darkness and I can just about make out that the person is a little taller than me. Wait ... I shuffle forward.

'Miles? Is that you ...?' I trail off as the figure slowly

turns around.

His skin is paler than usual, almost glowing in the darkness. His red eyes slowly bleed to black. His mouth spreads into a shark-like smile and my heart skips a beat as he speaks.

'You can save me. You can save everyone. Just help me set him free.'

*'Don't listen to him.'*

I cup my ears, trying to block out the voices. 'Get out of my head!'

He steps forward and I shuffle backwards until my back hits the wall. With each slow step he grows taller, his arms stretching longer. His hands turn to claws, his eyes sparking back to red. My mouth opens but the scream won't come out.

He dashes forward, grabbing my shoulders, and I find my voice.

'GET AWAY!'

# CHAPTER ELEVEN

'Mia! Mia, wake up, honey!'

I'm screaming at the top of my lungs, thrashing my arms uncontrollably. I jump up and gasp. Something glints in the corner of my eye, and I throw myself back against the wall.

'It's OK, it's just Lux,' Mum says.

I blink multiple times and clear my scratchy throat. My eyes shift to Mum and Dad's worried faces and I launch myself into Mum's arms. Sweat drips down my face and my eyes sting, fighting back the tears. I bury my face into her chest, trying to forget the nightmare.

'It's OK, honey.' Mum's gentle voice and the soft motion of her rubbing my back calms my racing heart.

'Mimi...' Lucas calls out from the door, but my head stays pressed against Mum.

'She's OK,' Dad says.

'How about you write it down in your nightmare journal?' she suggests, and I nod. The quicker I get it written down and locked away in the book, the better.

Mum's cheek rests on the top of my head and I close my eyes, still scared. Dad gets up and goes to Lucas.

'Come on little man, let's get you to bed and let Mia get some sleep,' he says, and I'm quietly grateful. I just want to hug Mum a little longer.

'Night night, Mimi,' Lucas whispers as Dad takes him to his room. The door clicks shut and Mum gently pulls back to look at me.

Mum lets go and gets my journal from the drawer. I cross my legs and flick through it. Pages and pages of dreams are written down and I frown.

'What's the matter, sweetheart?' Mum asks.

'Nothing … It's just I don't remember writing so much,' I mutter. Almost half the book is filled.

I write down this last dream and close the book.

'Have you written all your old dreams down too?' she asks.

'Yeah. I'm probably just buggin'. I feel better anyway. I'm gonna try and sleep now,' I mutter, but I stop Mum when she gets up. 'After sky connect, can we do some lightcaster training?'

Her eyes widen but a bright smile spreads across her face. 'Of course, sweetheart.'

She leans down and kisses my head. I'm still a bundle of nerves, but I can't keep trying to run away from these powers. I'm facing them head on before they consume me.

I wake up with a throbbing headache. Moonlight shines through my curtains and the silver line connecting the stars begins to fade. Lux and Nox get up and jump down from my bed.

'Did you have a better sleep?' Nox asks.

'Yeah, much better,' I say, scratching the back of my head. My legs swing off the bed and I hear Lux clear his throat. I roll my eyes.

'Yeah-yeah, I'm not backing out of training,' I tell him.

*'Good. Get dressed then.'*

*Geez, can't I even eat breakfast first?*

There's movement in the corridor and soft thuds of someone walking downstairs. Everyone must be up now. I glance over at my desk and spot a new butterfly note. I pick it up and smile.

After breakfast, Mum and Dad take me and Lucas

out into the garden. On more than one occasion I catch Mum looking at me to see if I'm OK, and each time I just give her a smile. Lucas playfully chases after Bolt without a care in the world.

Our garden isn't huge like Mrs Avery's, but it's big enough to hold a swing set and our mini assault course. A silver apple tree sits in the middle with small yellow apples slowly starting to grow again thanks to Mum's special garden lamp. One day she wants to make a humongous one that could grow hundreds of fruit and vegetable crops for the entire city.

Dad calls Lucas over and we all turn to face each other. A cold breeze blows between us, leaving goosebumps prickling up my arms. I roll my shoulders back. Time to do this.

'OK, sweethearts. We're going to try something different this time,' Mum says. 'First, we'll test your powers mentally.'

'Mental-ly?' Lucas asks.

Mum nods, tapping her temple. 'It means in your mind,' she explains. 'Spike and Bolt will talk to you and all you have to do is try and block out their voices.'

'OK, but I've already done that before,' I shrug. Mum and Dad look at me in shock.

'When?' Dad asks.

'Years ago. Back when me and Miles first saw Shade out in the Nightmare Plains. She tried talking to me but I managed to block it out.'

'Do you think you could do it again?' he asks, and I nod. I'm sure I can.

'I'll give it a go,' I say.

Spike walks closer to me and my attention turns to him. His golden eyes look me up and down, sizing me up. I close my eyes and wait.

*'Can you hear . . . ?'*

I imagine a door between me and Spike and seal it shut. I focus on keeping it closed, and slowly open my eyes to a completrely shocked look on Spike's face.

'You really can't hear him?' Mum's voice is filled with intrigue.

'Not a thing,' I say, looking back at Spike. I reopen the door I had mentally closed and Spike's voice comes back.

*'I could feel you blocking me. How strange. I've never experienced that before,'* Spike says, just as bewildered as Mum and Dad.

'I just imagined a door between us and closed it,' I explain. 'I have to concentrate, but it isn't too hard.'

'So, you can do it easily against the umbra. Maybe give it a go every night before you go to sleep. Imagine closing the door to this woman and the Reaper King and see if that helps with your nightmares,' Mum says.

For some reason this feels different to shutting out an umbra. I can't imagine it would be so easy.

'Lucas, how about you give it a go?' Dad encourages, crouching down to his level. 'Bolt will talk to you and you try to block it out. Try not to hear his voice.'

'OK, Daddy!' Lucas says, jumping from foot to foot. He stops and squeezes his eyes shut.

*'Raise your hand if you can hear me,'* Bolt says and Lucas raises his right hand. *'Now lower it.'*

He lowers it.

'Lucas, you're supposed to block him out,' I call out.

'I'm trying, Mimi!' he whines.

*'Now stand on one leg,'* Bolt says. Lucas whines again, clapping his hands over his ears.

'I guess it's not so easy for Lucas,' Mum says. Lucas opens his eyes with an over-the-top sigh.

'It's too hard,' Lucas complains. He sticks out his bottom lip and I ruffle his hair.

'You have to imagine closing a door between you and Bolt,' I say.

'I did,' he says, pushing out his lip. *Maybe he just has a hard time concentrating.*

'It's OK, sweetie. That's why we practise,' Mum says. He then chuckles, chasing a blue butterfly.

Dad looks at his holowatch and I realise it's almost time for me to go to class.

'Tamer meeting. We're going to discuss our next actions now that we know there's another member of the Elite at large,' Dad says. 'I'll fill you in on the details later tonight.'

'Are you sure you're going to be all right today, honey?' Mum asks. It takes me a second to realise she's still worried about my recent nightmare.

'Yeah. Today's my special class with Jada so I wanna go,' I say. Plus, I wanna keep an eye on that Layla girl and find out if she's really the one the cave umbra were talking about.

'All right, have a good day,' Mum says. I give her and everyone else a kiss goodbye and race back inside.

'Mia!'

My hand's on the front door handle ready to leave, but I turn around to see Dad jogging over to me. He crouches down and looks up at me. The oddly serious look in his eyes make me a little nervous.

'Are you sure you're OK, Baby-girl?'

'Yeah, don't worry, Dad. Mum gave me this good idea a while ago to help me forget about my nightmares,' I tell him. I hug him tightly. I don't want him to worry, but at the same time I can't blame him. I'm scared too.

'OK then,' Dad says. 'And how about I quickly do your hair before you leave.'

His eyes wander up and I jerk my head back, touching my hair. He chuckles when I wince at how dry it is.

'Fine,' I mumble. I hate having my hair done. Especially when there's pesky knots all tangled in my ponytail.

I drag my feet into the living room while he goes upstairs to get my hair stuff. I plonk my butt on the floor and when he returns, Dad sits on the sofa behind me.

He gets to work parting my hair and moisturising it with butterseed oil. I wince at each tug of the comb. At least the sweet buttery smell takes my mind off the pain, and the nightmare I had last night.

When Dad's done, he pulls my hair back into a low ponytail with bangs.

'There, wasn't so bad was it?' he jokes and I roll away with a grin.

'Thanks, Dad. I'll see ya later.'

'All right, Baby-girl. I love you.'

'Love ya too!'

I race out the front door with Lux and Nox close behind me, all of us filled with renewed determination. If I practise the technique of blocking different umbra voices out of my mind, then maybe it *will* work on my dreams and get me closer to finding out if this woman is a friend or an enemy. It's a little ray of hope.

I hop over the gate and race across the field in time for the Kay star to align with the Ursa Minor constellation. I quickly stand in line with everyone, high-fiving Mikasa as the sound of Jada's combat boots approach from behind.

I turn around and my smile falters.

'Mia! Hey, Mia!' Layla yells from across the field. She waves frantically, hanging off Jada's arm, and I roll my eyes. 'This is going to be so much fun. We're classmates!'

'Yeah, fun …' I mutter, suddenly feeling the complete opposite.

Layla lets go of Jada and runs over with a confident smile. I clasp my hands and bow. Jada does the same, and so does everyone else except Layla, who swings back and forth on her heels.

She tilts her head to the side with a raised eyebrow. 'What are you guys doing? They did that a lot in Astaroth too.'

'It's how you greet someone. How can you not know that?' I ask, raising an eyebrow back.

She shrugs. 'Never asked.'

Jada claps for us to line up and Layla shimmies herself beside me, bumping Thomas out of the way. He grumbles and she grins, making kissy noises at him. 'Love you too.'

Whether she's really up to no good or not, she's definitely annoying.

'Hey, Layla, I have something I wanna ask you—'

Jada claps her hands again, interrupting me. 'OK everyone, today's gonna be a busy day. Layla's joining us since my house is being prepped,' Jada says, which means the tamers haven't made it escape-proof yet. 'Let's start off with a quick sprint around the field, back handspring halfway, and end with a round-off!'

'Me too?' Layla asks.

'That'd be interesting,' Mikasa chimes in.

I blink at her, confused, but then I understand.

'Yeah, maybe we should see what you're made of,' I say. Is she just an average kid or has she had training? I'll have to ask her about the cave umbra later.

'All right, let's do it. Now go-go-go!' Jada yells and blows her whistle.

Lincoln and Mikasa rush past, leaving a cold breeze behind them, and a smirk spreads across my face. Big mistake. I keep my pace steady and, copying me, so does Thomas. For some reason Layla lags behind, beaming like a scarecrow cat.

'She's a bit weird, ain't she?' Thomas speaks up, following my glance backwards. 'What's her deal anyway?'

'Don't really know,' I reply. 'She says she wants to get revenge on the Elite for hurting her umbra friends.'

We round the first curve of the field and Layla maintains her distance behind us. Ahead, Mikasa and Lincoln huff and puff, readying themselves to do a back handspring, but the realisation that they've peaked too soon is clear as night in every little stumble.

We reach halfway and my legs are still sturdy and pumping iron. I'm in a much better state than the muppets in front of us.

'Wait, what? So, she might actually be on our side then,' Thomas says.

I spin around and spring off my feet into an easy back handspring. I land perfectly and start jogging again. 'Could be.'

Thomas does a back handspring too and moments later, so does Layla. Flawlessly. Not a toe outta line. So, she's flexible and athletic too.

The end goal comes in sight and it's finally time to pick up speed.

Mikasa glances back as I close in on her.

'No, no!' she yells, but even her voice sounds knackered.

Lincoln slows dramatically too, and I pass them both with ease, releasing all my saved-up energy in one sprinting burst. Thomas is right on my heels like an annoying little spiked-tooth rabbit. The end is dead ahead. I raise my hands to finish when someone zips past, springing into a round-off and snatching first place. I stumble forward with a gasp. My chest heaves and I cough.

'Layla wins,' Jada announces, clapping.

Layla jumps up and down, cheering, and I clench my fist in annoyance.

'Anyway, follow me inside. Today's class is actually going to be star studies,' Jada says.

'Huh? How comes you had us running around then?' Lincoln asks.

Jada looks back at him with a smirk. 'Because I think that physical training should be included in every lesson. You know that.'

The door swings open to the west-constellation tower. Plush seats and tall walls greet us. Moonlight flows into the room from the glass dome ceiling above, bathing the walls in a light blue just like it did when we brought Queen Katiya here. Lincoln crashes down in the comfy seat beside me and Layla takes the other side, earning a huff from Mikasa. Jada stands at a silver podium at the front of the room.

'As you can see, the sky is above us, but what else do you see?' Jada asks.

She slips on a gold glove and raises her hand. With a click of her fingers a black screen closes off the sky above our heads, encasing us in darkness except for the glow of Lux's white fur and Jada's golden glove. Jada's wrist twists and little stars dot the ceiling and walls around us. She twinkles her fingers and on command the stars shift, morphing into pictures on the ceiling. 'The answer isn't stars.'

'I see stars,' Lincoln states bluntly.

*'Yes, they are stars, but that's not the answer Jada is looking for,'* Ruby says, flying across the ceiling. *'Look again.'*

'Thomas, what do you see?' Jada asks, point blank ignoring the clown next to me. Thomas hums and rubs his chin.

I throw my head back and stare at the stars above. All I see are the usual constellations. The Ursa Minor is just above the Kay star. The Capricorn constellation. I squint my eyes. What am I missing? Miles would know, that's for sure. My stomach twists. I really hope he comes back soon.

'I see the moon?' Thomas says, although it sounds more like a question. He isn't so sure himself.

'Close,' Jada says with a smile. 'It's a solar-sellation. In other words, a sun among the stars. A cluster of stars so close together it looks like a moon. When this constellation appears, it usually means a story is being told by the stars.'

'Oh, so you mean, like how there's like a constellation the shape of clouds?'

'Exactly. Except, this cluster of stars often tell the same stories. Weather constellations change all the time, the cloud shape meaning it's going to be cloudy, and the cloud shape with a bunch of little stars below it meaning it'll rain,' Jada says.

'*When it comes to solar-stellations some stars shine brighter than others. Those are the ones you need to pay attention to and imagine a line connecting them to understand the story being told,*' Ruby says.

'Yeah, it's easy,' Layla says. 'I've seen this one a thousand times. It tells the story of a girl and boy. See those stars that look like a crown? It means, like, royalty, so I always believed it meant the Reaper King. The girl and the boy fight the Reaper King and free the kingdom. That's what that sun symbol means.'

'Who taught you how to read the stars?' Jada asks, surprised. 'Only experienced star readers have been able to read that prophecy directly from the stars.'

'My umbra friends mainly, but people did this in Astaroth too,' Layla answers. 'If you look closely, towards the end of the constellation, you'll see more children with what looks like light around them. I never really knew what that meant.'

As my eyes follow her story, my heart flutters.

It reminds me of the pictures in the *Legends of the Lightcasters* book. A boy and a girl, me and Lucas, saving everyone from the Reaper King.

'Being able to read the stars is important, but always remember that the reading is also down to a person's perception,' Jada explains. 'The symbols could mean different things to different people, but we won't know until the prophecies come true, or we find proof of the stories from the past.'

What feels like a vice grip tightens around my heart. So, the story of the lightcasters really is in the stars after all. My fate ... Lucas's ... It's still unchanged. I grit my teeth and glance down at my hand, squeezing it into a fist. But I'm more in control of my powers now and if that story is down to interpretation then I wonder how else it could be different. Either way, I feel more prepared to face this fate.

After class, me, Mikasa, Lincoln and Thomas head down the steps when Layla calls after me. 'Hey, Mia. Can we talk? Pretty please?'

'Want us to wait for you?' Mikasa asks.

'It's OK. I'll catch up,' I say. The others head off and I fall back to talk to Layla.

'I wanna be friends, so we should hang out! Are you free to today?' she asks, pushing her face into mine.

'I don't think you can,' I say, nodding behind her at Jada who is waiting to take Layla back home.

'Hang out with me at Jada's then!'

She grabs my arm, and I snatch it back and push her away. 'Don't do that!'

'Sorry, I just want to be friends,' she grins.

'Look, you being able to read the stars is pretty cool, but I still gotta get to know you first,' I explain.

'Then play with me! We'll get to know each other if we hang out!'

I sigh. 'Fine, I'll meet you at Jada's house later today, but you gotta promise to always be honest, and I'll do the same. You won't be locked up forever; it's just until Jada and the tamers are ready to trust you.'

'Cool!' She beams at me. I wave goodbye and turn to find the others, but I'm caught up short when someone grabs my arm. Instinctively I spin around, automatically snapping out my bo staff. I find myself face to face with Layla, a huge grin plastered across her face despite my weapon pressed against her neck.

'What are you doing? I said, don't touch me,' I warn. 'I could've really hurt you!'

She grins even wider, unshaken. Almost daring me to do something.

'I knew it'd be fun here. You're just like an umbra.'

*What's that supposed to mean?* I lower my staff and attach it back to my thigh strap. She doesn't look fazed and carries on smiling.

'Maybe we can have a sparring match or something at Jada's house,' I mutter. 'No promises though.'

'Yay! Thanks, Mia!' She goes to hug me, but I shake my head and she stops herself. 'Although I wouldn't spar me if I were you. You're gonna regret it,' she sings, tapping her nose.

'Sure,' I laugh.

All of a sudden, her face turns serious. 'You don't want to fight me, Mia.' The confidence in her voice sends a chill down my spine. She's deadly serious. She actually believes she can beat me. *Yeah, right.*

'Do you even know martial arts?' I ask.

'All you need to know is that I can fight,' she replies. 'See ya, Mia! Don't forget about later! You can bring the others if you like.' She whispers the last part and I sigh.

'Whatever you're planning you can forget about it. Remember, Layla, right now you're not allowed to leave the house without permission,' Jada calls out, eyeing us suspiciously. She ushers Layla along and the girl glances back at me and winks. Well, I guess we'll see how this goes.

Later I walk to Jada's house with Mikasa, Thomas and Lincoln. Lux and Nox decided to head home.

'You sure Jada won't mind?' Thomas asks. 'She said Layla isn't allowed to leave the house.'

'She's out. There's a tamer meeting right now,' I say.

The streets are mainly empty except for people heading home from work and kids running to the park to play. It's like Queen Katiya's presence has completely relaxed everyone. I don't even feel the stares as much.

We walk around the back of the house in the small grassy alleyway and the smell of sweet tulips fills my nose.

'How are we gonna get in? The house is locked,' Lincoln asks, climbing over the fence and landing on the grass last. I glance up at the windows but there's no sign of Layla. Not that she'd be able to let us in anyway since the escape-proofing.

'Jada has a back door override switch for emergencies. I overheard her tell Mum.'

I crouch by a cherry bush and find the button. **'Override activated.'**

The back door swings open. We run into the house and enter the kitchen. Silence greets us. It's been a while since I've been in Jada's house. Little coffee granules are scattered by the sink where she must have been in a rush to make her caramel coffee and the smell of it lingers in the air. Her mug is in the sink but the rest of the kitchen is clean. The floor doesn't have a crumb in sight and her counters are filled with many different types of coffee.

'Layla? You ready for the sparring match?' I call out into the hallway, smiling at the long collection of combat boots all lined up perfectly by the front door.

Something creaks behind me and I turn back to the kitchen and gasp: 'Don't let the garden door shut! It'll go back on autolock and we won't be able to get out!' I yell. Lincoln catches the door with his foot. Thomas grabs a chair from the table and wedges it in the doorway.

Feet stampede down the stairs and there's Layla.

'You guys came!' she beams.

I cross my arms and raise an eyebrow. 'We said we would. You ready to spar?'

'Of course. We'll even make it interesting. You win and I'll tell you something secret about the Elite,' she teases.

My eyes flicker to the others and a grin spreads across my face. 'Deal.'

'BUT ... if I win, you gotta do something for me,' she says.

'What?'

'You gotta save me from the boredom of being locked in this house all day,' she says.

'We can't let you out,' Mikasa chimes in.

'Then visit. It's all I'm asking,' she says, raising her hands.

'Fine,' I say, glancing at the holoclock on the wall. 'Come on, Jada's gonna be back soon.'

We head outside. Lincoln, Mikasa and Thomas stand back in silence, their eyes glued to me and Layla. On standby in case she tries to leg it and escape.

Cold air blows between us but the tension is almost stifling. I grind my feet into the dirt and take a deep breath. *I've got this.* I've been doing martial arts for years. I'm not gonna lose.

Layla stands there swaying with a confident smirk. Her hands rest behind her back as if she hasn't a care in the world. Does she have a trick up her sleeve? I push the thought away, not wanting it to distract me.

'OK, guys, this will be a standard sparring match. The person with the most points after five minutes wins. Get ready,' Mikasa calls out. She stands between us as ref. She's a pro at sparring so it's only right. I bow to Layla and she copies me.

'Face punching is not allowed. No dirty moves either. I will call the point each round and when I do, you break and reset, got it?' Mikasa explains, but those words aren't for me. She gives Layla a hard stare before stepping back.

I take my stance, fists up and jump lightly on my feet. Ready.

Mikasa whistles and in the blink of an eye Layla is right in front of me. I jump back and block a punch straight to the face. She goes for my legs next with a swivel kick and I jump over it. *What kind of martial arts is this?*

'Oi! Below the head only!' Mikasa yells, but whether Layla hears her is a completely different story. I counter her kick with my own and gain space from the girl and her relentless attacks. My chest heaves and I reposition my stance with my fists back up in case she tries anything else.

'What the flip are you doing? This is martial arts, not random street fighting!' I yell, but her smirk grows.

'That's Mia's point! Reset!' Mikasa says.

We separate but I turn back to face Layla. A wildness flickers in her eyes. Before I'm ready, she dashes forward again without warning. Mikasa and Lincoln yell out. I dodge left as Layla dives at me. She catches herself from crashing to the floor and races for me again.

My mind frantically ticks, trying to think of ways to take her down without hurting her. She pushes off her feet, springing to attack. I spin into a roundhouse kick, and she stops still and, without flinching, she flat out catches my leg. Everyone gasps.

My back slaps against the hard ground. Pain shoots up my spine and Layla pins me down. I struggle against her grip, fighting the urge to kick her in the stomach and headbutt her.

'I won!' she cheers. She lets go and jumps for joy. I slam my fist against the dirt. My back is throbbing but I'm more embarrassed than anything. I get up, fuming.

'What was that? You cheated!' I yell, but she just laughs her head off.

'You think it's funny?' Mikasa yells and she runs at Layla, throwing Thomas off when he tries to stop her.

Lincoln manages to grab her before she reaches Layla, but my own anger boils more.

'She done Mia dirty. Let me at her!' Mikasa yells, struggling.

'It's OK, Kas,' I say, rubbing my back. I glare at Layla. It wasn't worth it. After all, we aren't really supposed to be here, and we're not allowed to spar or fight outside of class unless it's life or death. The last thing we need is to get caught.

Layla stops jumping and looks at us, confused.

'I don't get it? I won – why is she so mad?' she asks.

'You only got a point and you cheated,' I say, brushing my clothes. 'There's no respect here for cheaters.'

'I learned to fight from umbra. I tried to warn ya,' she shrugs.

'*Umbra* taught you?' I ask. How does an umbra teach you to fight?

'Yep, I used to play fight with wild ones all the time.' The more she speaks, the more confused I get. Then I suddenly remember what I was gonna ask.

'Did you used to live in a cave with lots of umbra?' I ask.

Layla blinks and tilts her head to the side. 'Yeah, I did. Why? How did you even know?'

'I met them a few months ago!' I say. Her eyes widen and she grabs my hands before I can even think.

'How are they? Are they safe?'

'Woah-woah-woah. We're not changing the subject now. You cheated,' Mikasa interrupts.

'Why does it matter how I did it? In a real fight no one's gonna care how you do it,' Layla says, letting go of my hands.

'The umbra were safe and yeah, you're right about fighting, but that's not the point. We were sparring, not in a real fight. You're supposed to follow the rules and not actually injure your opponent,' I explain, trying to ignore the throbbing of my back.

'Cheater …' Lincoln mutters, barging past Layla. Mikasa shoots her the dirtiest look and walks over to check on me.

'Sorry?' Layla says with a slight laugh in her tone.

'You know, if you really do want to be friends like you say you do, you gotta … I don't know, be more thoughtful in your actions,' I say.

'I mean, you're not wrong, but seeing all of your faces so mad is a bit funny though. Just a little bit.' Layla chuckles and I roll my eyes.

'You're too much.'

'But you like me. I know you do, or you wouldn't be trying to make me feel better.'

'Whatever, Layla . . . But we're done now. Just please go back in the house,' I say.

'See I knew it!' she calls after me. 'And thanks for checking on my cave friends.'

I stare at her as she heads back to the house and my heart tugs. Those umbra were really worried about her. I wonder if we could reunite her with them after we find out who attacked Nox.

I walk to the fence with Mikasa and the others. My back twinges but I turn to look at Layla and give her a small smile.

'See you later, Layla.' But I stand there while the others go ahead to check she goes into the house and shuts the door properly.

Before she does, she calls out, 'Hey! As a way to make it up to you, I'll tell you this. Remember when we first met, I told you one of my umbra friends was attacked in the Nightmare Plains along with Nox. Well, she saw a person wearing a uniform *very* similar to the tamers' one before her vision was blinded by their shadow powers.'

'Wait, what?' I ask, frozen to the spot.

'You heard me. Bye, best friend! Sorry I beat your butt!' Layla heads into the house and the door clicks to a close. **`House locks activated.`**

I join the others on the street outside to find Lux and Nox galloping towards us with worried looks in their eyes.

'*What happened, young one?*' Nox asks.

'*It was that Elite brat. Where is she?*' Lux says, and for once I'm not even mad he's rummaging in my mind.

'Mia, what did she just say?' Mikasa asks, but I'm too stunned to reply.

'Am I buggin' or did I just hear Layla suggest Nox's attacker is a tamer?' Thomas asks.

'I … I have to go and tell Mum and Dad,' I say urgently.

'Want us to come with you?' Lincoln asks, but I shake my head.

'Nah, it's all good. I'll catch you guys later.'

My mind races over Layla's words. Do the Elite have a spy amongst the tamers? Could there be a traitor right here, in Nubis?

# CHAPTER TWELVE

I race back to the main streets. Apparently the queen had left earlier in the day but the roads are still decorated with crystal roses and banners.

'Mum and Dad are probably still in the tamer meeting,' I say to Lux and Nox, crossing the road. I don't know whether to go home and wait for them or interrupt the gathering.

Layla's words buzz around in my mind. Surely there's no way one of the tamers could be involved. After all, she only said the person was wearing something similar.

I slow to a stop and clench my jaw as another terrible thought strikes me. What about Miles? He could have had access to tamer gear. But surely it couldn't be . . .

A shadow flies overhead and I look up, squinting my eyes. 'Isn't that Ruby?'

*'Yes, with Jada on her back. Looks like they're heading*

*for the gate,'* Nox confirms. *'Aren't they supposed to be in the tamer meeting?'*

'Maybe we should see where they're going,' I say.

*'Perhaps your parents are there too,'* Nox adds.

I break out into a sprint and chase after them. I skip the bridge and jump on the stones across the river instead. We reach the gate in time to watch it slowly open up and my heart squeezes in my chest.

Mum, Rosé and Bently are standing at the entrance, but my eyes are fixed on one person alone. Miles walks through the gate with his bunny-eared hellhound umbra, Shade. His usually short dark hair is a little longer and messier than before, but his black jacket and trousers look fresh. Has he come from Astaroth?

His brown eyes carefully scan everyone and Shade sticks close to his side. *It's really him.*

I go to step out from around the corner but Lux tugs me back.

*'Wait. We should see what happens first,'* Lux suggests.

Most of the tamers arrived now, except for Dad, but all I can think about is the boy in front of me. The air feels thick, almost stifling. Miles comes to a stop and glances over in my direction. For a single moment, our eyes meet. My heart pounds loudly in my chest and I just want to run to him. A hint of a smile ghosts his lips but he follows Mum and the other tamers. He gives me one last look before turning away.

'Let's go after them, guys,' I say, hopping on Nox.

We catch up with them at city hall just as Miles, Mum and the other tamers walk inside. *Flip! There's no sneaking in this time.*

*'Looks like we're going to have to wait then,'* Nox says.

An hour later I'm still sitting on the steps outside watching Lux and Nox tussle with their horns. I rest my elbows on my knees and sigh.

I wish I knew what Miles has been doing all this time. I have so many questions. In my heart I want to trust him, but I can't forget that he was a part of the Elite raid on Nubis.

The door finally opens and I leap to my feet, scooting over to the side to make space for everyone to leave. I wonder if I should have hidden, but it's too late now. The tamers file out the hall, each one giving me a nod of acknowledgement. I can't read anything on their faces other than surprise.

Mum comes out and shakes her head, the only one not surprised to see me there. 'I'm heading to the lab.

Miles will be out in a minute but he's going to be under Riley's supervision for a while and will be staying at his house for the time being,' she tells me. 'I'll fill you in properly when I get home, OK? Trust your instincts.'

She whispers the last bit and pats my shoulder. 'I will— Wait, Mum, there's something important I have to tell you!'

I take her hand and tug her to the side.

'What is it, darling?'

'It's about Layla,' I say. 'Don't get mad, but we sparred at Jada's house. Jada didn't know, but something Layla said makes me wonder if one of the tamers is a secret member of the Elite, or maybe a spy.'

There's visible shock in Mum's face, her lip trembles ever so slightly and a grave look dominates her hazel eyes. 'Tell me?'

I gulp, feeling my throat dry. 'I found out that Layla is the girl who used to live in a cave with a bunch of umbra I met, and one of her umbra friends was the one who was attacked at the same time as Nox and told her that the attacker looked like he was wearing a tamer uniform.'

Spike steps forward, looking as worried as Mum. *'And the only other people on the Nightmare Plains at the time—'*

'Were tamers,' Mum finishes.

I just can't wrap my head around it. To have Mum confirm that it's a possibility makes it all horribly real.

*'Who else knows about this?'* Spike asks.

'Erm . . . Just me, Mikasa, Thomas and Lincoln. Lux and Nox too, of course. Do you really think one of the tamers is a traitor?'

'Mia, darling, focus.' Mum's hands are like a cool compress against my cheeks. My breath heaves in my chest but I slowly blink back to reality and focus on her again. 'We need to keep this between us and I need to talk to your father,' she says. I nod. She lets go of my face, then asks. 'How did you even spar in Jada's garden? The house should have been locked.'

'Huh?'

'How did you get Layla out of the house?' Mum repeats.

I chew the inside of my cheek, realising the game is up. 'I heard Jada tell you about the override lock,' I confess.

Mum frowns. 'And does Layla know about the lock?'

'She was indoors. She didn't see me work it,' I say. 'And I made sure she was locked in again before we left.'

'Good, but Mia, listen to me.' I look at Mum. She

pushes her fingers against her forehead and sighs. 'I know you're trying to help, and you are, but you're becoming reckless. You need to be more careful, sweetheart. OK?' From the strain in her voice, I can tell how much she's holding back her frustration with me.

'I know, and I will,' I say. 'I mean it.'

'All right, are you sure you're OK? That was a lot to take in,' she says.

'I-I'm fine,' I say.

'Promise?'

'Promise.'

Mum smiles softly and runs a hand gently down my cheek. 'Remember what I said.' She jerks her chin behind me. I don't have to look to know she means Miles. Her message is loud and clear. Be alert and keep what we discussed private. Mum stands up and kisses my head before rushing off with Spike.

I watch them until they disappear and hear soft footsteps approaching behind me. There's a hesitation in the final step and I glance over my shoulder.

'Hey, Miles . . .'

'Hey, Supernova.'

He stands there awkwardly with his hands in his pockets. I gesture to the steps and we both sit down in silence. I clamp my hands between my knees and look at the buildings ahead, very much aware of the boy sitting next to me. Each time our eyes meet neither one of us says a word, but I could swear his ears are slightly red ... Weird. If it was TJ, he would probably say a really bad joke to make us laugh and break the ice. But he isn't ... It's just me and Miles together again, and it doesn't feel like old times at all.

He runs his hand through his hair like he's searching for the words, and my hands stay sandwiched between my knees. His eyebrows are glued in a constant frown, like one of the moody boys you see in those cheesy teen shows on holoTV. The ones filmed in Nexus.

'So—' We both start and cut each other off, and I stifle a laugh. A ghost of a smile flutters against his lips. His eyes meet mine and he suddenly bursts into laughter. I scrunch up my face.

'You're so goofy,' he chuckles and I glare at him.

'*I'm* goofy?' I say, pressing an offended hand to my chest. 'Have you seen yourself, mate? Those trainers are not the ones, my guy. Switch it up.'

His eyes snap down to his shoes and my cheeks puff out, barely holding back the laugh.

'What are you talking about? I'm the coolest guy

you've ever met.' He playfully pops his collar and smirks. 'I taught you everything you know about fighting too.'

*Oh really?* His eyes are deadly serious, but I arch an eyebrow at him. 'I think you're confused, mate. I've always beaten you in a sparring match.' Every. Single. Time.

'Nope. You're wrong.' He pokes my forehead with two fingers and I wince. 'You was really cute and short back then, so I couldn't beat you all the time. That wouldn't have been fair. Besides, I had to train you so no one could mess you about when you got older.'

I roll my eyes. 'Oh, please. Did you leave a part of your memory somewhere? I won those matches fair and square. Don't try and cover it up with lies.' I mean, it's true. I was cute when I was little, and still kinda am, but Miles only taught me a few moves. I'm a whole different beast now. 'Besides, I trained a whole bunch myself when you went off with your parents.'

He falls silent and instant regret floods through me. Awkwardness hangs in the air, and once again it feels like an invisible glass wall separates us. I scrunch up the hoodie sleeves and chew the inside of my lip. There's so many things I wanna know. But more than anything

I want to smash this wall between us. I want my best friend back.

'Hey. So, what happened after you left Nubis?' I have to know. 'I heard you went to Astaroth.'

He stands up abruptly and I sense Lux and Nox, who are keeping their distance, preparing to move in. *It's OK, guys. I got this.* Miles's fist visibly shakes at his side. He looks ahead and my stomach lurches.

'I don't want to talk about it.' His voice sends a shiver down my spine. Cold and emotionless. Guilt wells up in me for asking, but the pained look in his eyes hurts worse. I reach up and wrap my fingers slowly around his wrist.

'Sorry.'

His dark eyes flicker back at me and we both stare at each other. He makes no move to take back his wrist and the imaginary glass wall between us shatters. His wrist feels warm against my palm and suddenly the corner of his lips curve up into a lopsided smile, causing butterflies in my stomach.

'What?' I ask, tilting my head.

'You still do that face when you're frustrated. You scrunch up your nose like this.' He scrunches up his nose and raises his fist like he's gonna poop himself. My jaw drops and I let go of his wrist.

'I do *not* make that face,' I say, crossing my arms.

'Yeah, ya do. You're like a baby!'

'You're a baby!'

He quirks an eyebrow. 'I'm taller *and* older than you.'

'Yeah, and I'm smarter,' I shoot back, and he smirks.

He looks me up and down and runs his hand coolly through his hair. 'I don't think so . . .'

His lopsided smile turns into a toothy grin and my heart flutters again. *Clown.*

He crashes back down on the step beside me, lazily observing the passers-by. I gaze up at the stars and lean back on my hands.

'I've missed this.' His voice is so gentle I almost don't hear it. I spot a redness in his cheeks and warmth fills my heart. I let myself lean against him, just for a single quiet moment. I missed him too, so much, and yet, for some reason, I can't say it out loud. His cheek suddenly presses against the top of my head, like he knows anyway.

'Miles, let's go.'

I jump, hearing Riley's voice behind us. He and Myla are walking down the steps of city hall and I wonder how much of our reunion they witnessed. Behind them, in the darkness of the hall, I spot an oh-so familiar hellhound. Her blood-red eyes lock onto mine, but I clench my fist, holding my nerve.

'Can't we have a bit more time? He's only just got back,' I say.

Riley crosses his arms and I copy him, wishing I could tell Riley to kick rocks. Surely they can't put Miles on complete house arrest like Layla? That's not fair.

Riley mulls it over and I stand up to plead my case.

'No,' he says bluntly. I chew back the bad words I wanna say and roll my eyes. *Jerk.*

He turns around to leave and behind his back, Miles silently mouths for me to come see him later but before I can slyly nod back, Riley ushers him and Shade away.

'What was all that about?' I ask Lux and Nox.

*'It was a bit strange,'* Nox says.

*'Maybe he's upset he has babysitting duties now. I know the feeling,'* Lux says and I give him the side eye.

'I made you babysit Lucas once. Let it go.'

*'Never.'*

'Well, what do you guys wanna do now?' I ask. 'I've got time to drag before I see Miles again.' Honestly, now that he's back I feel better knowing he's safe.

'*Let's head home. We should talk with Lila and see what updates she has,*' Nox says. I agree and we turn around to head home.

'*Astaroth.*'

The voice comes out of nowhere and takes me by surprise.

'*Are you all right, young one?*' Nox asks.

'I heard that woman again,' I say, closing my eyes. *Who are you?*

I wait … and wait … and wait, but there's no response. *So much for that idea.* My mind's completely silent but the message stays with me. The single message is clear enough now. There's something in Astaroth that she wants me to find and I bet it's in that castle. The question is – should we go or is it a trap?

# Chapter Thirteen

Music softly plays from the boombox in the living room after we finish dinner, and I slip off my shoes and walk inside. Lucas yawns on the sofa and snuggles against Mum. His head bobs, trying to fight the sleep.

'Hey. Where's Dad and Bolt?' I ask, crashing on the floor beside Spike.

'Welcome back, sweetheart. Dad's out on a perimeter run with Peter,' Mum says, but the look in her eyes tells me otherwise. I'm guessing he's trying to work out if there's a traitor among the tamers and she wants to keep this from Lucas.

'Mimi,' Lucas mumbles.

'What's up, pipsqueak?' I ask, looking out the window.

'I practised my powers today. I did good. I can pretect you and Mummy more.' His words slur in a yawn and I kiss his head.

'Good job, Lu-Lu.'

He sleepily nods and settles back against Mum. Her fingers soothingly comb through his hair and it eventually sends him to sleep. Seeing his eyes closed and hearing his gentle snores, she shifts her attention back to me.

'Right now, every tamer is a suspect,' she says quietly, rubbing Lucas's back. 'We can't trust anyone. Not even Jada.'

'What!' I slap a hand over my mouth, but luckily my squeak hasn't woken Lucas. 'What do you mean Jada? There's no way she's working with the Elite.'

Not after everything she's done for me. For the city. I wouldn't even be here if it wasn't for her and Ruby.

Mum narrows her eyes. 'I don't want to suspect her either, Mia, but at the end of the day, the only people on the plains during the trials were the tamers. Someone would have noticed a stranger out there. Their scent alone would have alerted our umbra.'

*'It's true. I do not remember any new scents. I was just focused on Nox though,'* Lux says.

*'But you would have sensed a stranger immediately,'* Spike says. *'A tamer's scent wouldn't have stood out in the chaos.'*

'But Jada . . .' I refuse to suspect her. She wouldn't betray us.

'Just be cautious, that's all I'm asking. Was Bently the only tamer you three saw out there?' Mum asks.

*'Yes, Mia trapped him with his rope gun,'* Nox answers.

'So, he was the closest to you that we know of. The only one that can be accounted for is Peter as he was close to capturing Clara when we called off the trials. He was nowhere near you,' Mum says thoughtfully.

*'That leaves a lot of suspects still. Even Bently could have easily got out of the net trap,'* Spike adds.

*'But why would they attack my brother?'* Lux asks. I've thought about that a lot too.

Mum hums. 'Perhaps it was an attempt to kidnap Mia. Even that wild umbra may have not been the actual target. Maybe the attacker was after both you and Nox.'

True. But why would anyone be after me still?

'Anyway, I must get this one to bed,' Mum says, lifting up Lucas. He wraps his arms around her neck and snuggles into her, still asleep. I get up from the sofa and stretch my arms.

'Was everything OK with Miles?' Mum asks.

'Yeah. We couldn't really talk for long because of Riley being around, but I'm working on it,' I say.

'Just remember what I said and be careful, sweetheart,' Mum warns.

'I know, Mum. I will,' I promise, and I wonder if she's guessed my plan to sneak out later to see Miles. If it was Dad who guessed, there'd be no way in Lunis he'd let me.

'Come on, let's get some sleep. Your dad won't be home till much later,' she whispers. As if on cue, a yawn slips from my lips. I could do with a nap before I leave tonight.

I slip on my sleep bonnet and settle into bed. Lux and Nox rest on the floor, and another yawn slips from my lips. Could it actually be a tamer behind Nox's attack?

I'm still working my way through all the tamers when I'm woken by the buzzing of my alarm. I groan and wave my hand over it. With blurry vision I look at the time. *Geez, it's only been an hour.*

I throw off my covers and stare at the ceiling. *Is this a dream?* My eyes take a moment to adjust. I make out Lux and Nox on the floor. They raise their heads.

*'Have any weird dreams, Mouse?'*

'Nope, but for a second I thought this was one,' I say, rubbing my eyes.

'*Well, Daniel and Bolt came in just after you fell asleep so you're safe to leave,*' Nox says. I gaze out of the window, feeling the nerves shiver through my body.

It's time to see Miles.

I listen out for Spike and Bolt but I don't hear them roaming the house. Probably resting in Mum and Dad's room.

'Guys, when Dad comes in to leave me notes, does he check on me or does he just write the note and leave?' I whisper.

'*Sometimes he checks on you, sometimes he doesn't. There's no pattern,*' Nox says.

'*He probably would have left one already if he was going to do it,*' Lux adds. *True, but . . .*

I roll over and reach under the bed for my trainers. Then I grab some extra pillows from my wardrobe and stuff them under the covers to make it look like I'm still in there.

'*THAT'S supposed to look like you sleeping in bed?*' Lux asks, nudging the pillow mound with his snout.

I roll my eyes and swat him. 'You're a big help, mate . . .'

'At least put your bonnet on top of it,' he says, whacking me back with his big fluffy shadowy tail. *Good point though.*

'Hey Lux, can you sleep on the bed so it looks like I'm hidden by you? Like, make it look as if you're resting your head on me?' I ask, puffing up the shape with more pillows.

Surprisingly, without a snarky comment back, he does as I ask. In the dark it looks exactly like I'm sleeping. I give him a thumbs-up. *Perfect.*

*'Are you sure you don't want one of us to come with you, young one. It could be dangerous,'* Nox says, following me to my desk.

'I know,' I say, picking up my bo staff, 'but I'll be OK.'

I twirl the weapon and attach it to my thigh strap. 'Besides, Dad will be suspicious if you and Lux aren't both in my room. We'll keep comms the whole time through our thoughts.'

I gently bring their faces forward and press my forehead against theirs. Their shadows lightly tickle my cheeks and a smile spreads across my lips. 'If I don't respond to you instantly, then you know something's wrong.'

'*Be careful, Mouse.*' Concern flashes in Lux's eyes and I gently stroke his cheek.

'I will. I promise.' I head to the window and push it open. A cold gust of wind blows the curtains and I glance back at Lux and Nox. They bow their heads and a feeling of calm washes over me. *I got this. See you guys later. Love you.*

I swing my legs over and slide down, gripping on to the window ledge. My trainers graze the brick wall and I look down. The kitchen window ledge isn't too far. *Three … Two … One.* I let my fingers slip from the ledge and drop, first to the window ledge and then to solid ground. *Easy!*

I look up and see Lux and Nox at the window. I wave at them and then head into town.


There's always a different vibe when the midnight star fades in my forever-night city. Everyone is mostly asleep and the bustling city turns deathly quiet. Only the faint buzz of colourful glow bugs keeps me company in the dark. The roads and houses are illuminated in bright lights – orange, blue and green – guiding my path, but there's not a human soul in sight.

I cross the street and hop over the river on the

floating stones, careful not to slip. It feels . . . eerie and the giddiness in my heart at seeing Miles again fades ever so slightly.

*Can you guys still hear me?*

'*Of course, young one,*' Nox answers, almost immediately.

'*Did you forget we can always hear you through your thoughts, Mouse? And here I thought you were actually smart.*'

I reach the other side of the river and break off into a sprint. *Ha ha, very funny, mate. I'm just double checking . . . It's kinda creepy out here.*

'*Do you want us to come?*' Nox asks.

*No, it's OK. I'm almost there. I just wanted someone to talk to.*

I skid to a stop, hearing quiet voices around the corner. *What the flip?* I press my shoulder against the wall and slowly peek around. Up ahead Bently is talking to Riley. They must be on sleep-time street patrol . . . Or is this a secret meeting?

I narrow my eyes to Shiro and Myla, but they don't seem to notice me. I strain my ears to listen.

'Rough couple of days, huh? You would've thought things would have calmed down now the queen's gone.'

Bently yawns. 'Daniel's been really focused on upping security around the city too.'

'I think Daniel's just worried about that member of the Elite still out there. If that's even true. Even if it is, what can they do anyway?' Riley replies with a snort. 'One person can't take all the tamers down.'

'Well, hopefully we catch whoever it is,' Bently replies.

They start walking and I keep back in the shadows until they're out of sight. The fact that Riley still has doubts about a rogue Elite leaves a bad taste in my mouth. The gutterslug.

I take the back street to Riley's house. It's a good thing I know this city like the back of my hand. It'll be easier to talk to Miles if Riley is out too.

At last I reach my destination. A single light is on upstairs at the front of the house and I grimace. I stare up at the window, resting my hands on my hips. *This is gonna be risky.*

'Miles!' I whisper-shout, looking left and right down the empty street. *Open the window, you muppet.*

I pick up a small rock and throw it at the window. *Hurry up, Miles!* I'm not about to climb up there for no flippin' reason, but someone's gonna spot me soon enough if this fool doesn't look out his window.

I ready another rock but I don't need it because the curtains twitch and the window opens. Miles pokes his head out.

'Yo, what's up?' I say, waving at him.

'You just can't stay away, can ya?' he teases, and I roll my eyes. Joker.

'You're the one who invited me. Don't act like you ain't happy to see me, mate. Now come downstairs and let me in,' I say.

He raises an eyebrow. 'You gotta climb up. Riley triple locked his door so I can't open it.'

Triple lock a door? What does that even mean?

'You're kidding, right? Just come down and unlock it then.'

He shakes his head. 'Can't. Don't know how, Supernova.'

I sigh. 'Fine, then stand back, I'm climbing up.'

He steps back and I run up the pipe and swing on to the ledge. He offers his hand and I happily grasp it, climbing inside. 'Thanks.'

'No worries, Supernova. But there wasn't really a triple lock.' He winks and I playfully push him with a goofy smile.

'You jerk. You made me do that for no reason!' I laugh, shoving him again.

'It was funny though,' he muses. 'And I'm happy you still have your climbing skills.'

I playfully huff and cross my arms, looking around his room. There's a blue plush rug over a grey carpet that matches kinda nice with the cream-painted walls. Across the room, a small desk is pressed against the wall with a sketchbook laid on it.

His bed is next to us by the window and a large wardrobe stands opposite it. To be fair, it's a big cosy room considering Riley didn't exactly look like he wanted to supervise Miles in the first place. It could definitely be worse.

I walk over to the desk and scoop up the sketchbook, but the book's snatched from my fingers the second I touch it.

'Nope!' He raises the sketchbook above his head.

'Why not?' I jump to grab it, but he swivels and pushes me back with his foot. 'Oi!'

He catches my leg mid-kick and quirks an eyebrow at me. 'Nice try.'

'All right, you jerk,' I mutter and he lets go.

'My sketchbook is off limits for now. I'm working on something,' he says. My eyes trail after him as he walks to the corner of the room. He twirls his finger for me to turn around. 'No looking, I know how slippery you are.'

I huff and spin on my heel in the opposite direction with my arms crossed. He rustles behind me and I chew the inside of my cheek, fighting the urge to peek. *One look won't hurt.*

'OK, Supernova, you can turn around.' I jump and turn back around.

The room is completely spotless as before. *Where did he hide it?*

'You're not gonna be able to figure it out,' Miles muses and I shoot him a look. He shoves his hands in his pockets and crashes on the bed.

'You better show me what's in it,' I say. 'I bet it's me.'

'You wish it was you,' he says, patting the space beside him.

'Says the guy who drew a big picture of me in Astaroth.'

He jerks up into a sitting position. 'I don't know what you're talking about,' he stammers, and it's my turn to smirk.

'Yeah, right. But if you drew me as a reaper in your sketchbook, I'll kick your butt,' I say, taking a seat beside him.

'Sure you would,' he says. His hearty laugh fills the room and the fuzzy feeling returns. He lies back against the bed and peaceful silence fills the space between us. I clamp my hands between my legs and glance at him. The light bounces off his dark eyes and his messy black hair covers them slightly. If he notices me staring, he doesn't make it obvious. His signature half-smile is on his face and I find myself smiling too. *He's really back to stay.*

'So, did Riley set any extra rules?' I ask, finally breaking the silence.

He sighs and throws his hands behind his head. 'I basically can't leave this house without the guard dog.'

'Hey, Myla is actually nice,' I say, defending the umbra.

'I wasn't talking about Myla,' he muses, giving me a playful side eye. I shake my head at him and swallow a chuckle.

'Riley is kinda annoying. He's my teacher now too,' I say.

'Well, I can't leave the house without him so I guess I'll be tagging along for your classes. He's put a tracker on my wrist that's connected to his holophone and he can check it anytime. Shade has a collar version.'

My eyes cast around the room and it's the first time I actually notice the shadowy hellhound. Under the darkness of Miles's desk, her body blends with the shadows and her red eyes stare out at me. They must have been closed when I first walked in. There's no way I woulda missed *those* red eyes. Tucked away below her spiked neck is a dark blue collar.

'Look, I get it. No one here trusts me, but I don't know how long I can stand being cooped up in this house,' Miles says.

'Can't lie, I don't know how long it'll be like this, but things could be worse,' I say. 'You could be—'

'In the hold like my parents,' he finishes.

He sits up, resting his arm on his knee and tilting his head to look at me. 'So, what about you?' he asks suddenly, and I raise an eyebrow.

'What? Do I trust you?'

'Yeah.'

The intensity of his eyes forces me to look down at my knees. *Do I trust Miles?* The question swirls in my mind with a thousand question marks. Had that been asked a few years ago I would've said yes without any hesitation, but now… I realise I'm not sure.

Catching my hesitation, he narrows his eyes. 'Guess

I don't blame you either.' He sighs. 'But whether you trust me or not doesn't matter anyway.'

'What's that supposed to mean?' I ask.

The front door slams shut downstairs and our attention snaps left to the bedroom door. Riley's returned!

'I better skedaddle!' I jump off the bed and run to the window. Miles runs to the door and listens to Riley walking up the stairs and into his own room.

'Wait up!' he whisper-shouts and I stop with one leg out the window. He flicks off the light and runs over to me. 'I'm coming too.'

'What? No, you gotta stay here. What about the tracker?'

'Come on, Supernova. We've hardly talked yet. Let's have fun and explore the city like the old times.'

Our eyes stay connected and a billion thoughts and emotions race through my mind. What if the tracker is set to alert if Miles leaves the house? What if Riley checks on Miles and finds him not there? All these questions, and yet the smirk on his face and these butterflies fluttering in my stomach make me grin.

'All right. I'm down. Let's go!'

His smirk turns into a grin and I reach out my hand to him. He takes it with a firm grip and climbs halfway out of the window with me. His eyes silently ask if I'm ready, and I nod.

'Shade, can you stay here and cover for me if you need to?' he asks, and the hellhound umbra steps out from under the desk.

'*Yes. The fool won't even know you're gone,*' she says and we drop down, escaping.

Like bandits in the night, we run and do backflips on the rooftops of houses and shops, sprinting off again the second our feet land like we used to when we were younger. Miles jumps into a series of side flips and races after me.

'Come on, mate! Keep up!' I cheer.

I look at him with the biggest smile and Miles grins right back. My heart sings with every step. This is what it was supposed to feel like, meeting again after so many years apart. Happy!

Pretty fairy lights brighten the edges of the roofs and light our bodies in the night, projecting shadow versions of ourselves running alongside us.

'Look out!' I yell, skidding to a stop.

A humongous gap separates us from the final building and I gulp, taking a step back. Miles walks to the edge and turns around to face me. A mischievous glint twinkles in his eyes and puts me nervously on edge. *What are you thinking about?* I arch an eyebrow suspiciously at him. He takes his hands out of his pockets and crouches down with his fingers knitted together like a foothold.

'Do you trust me?' he asks.

That question again but in a completely different context. My hand curls into a fist and my eyes shift from him to the gap that separates us from the other building. I get it now.

Adrenaline pulses through my veins and I dig my feet into the ground and shake my arms and shoulders twice, readying myself. *I got this!*

I break out into a sprint. Miles stiffens his stance, one foot slightly in front of the other.

I leap up and place my right foot into his hands. He throws me up in the air, full force. I fly through the air like long shadowy umbra wings are carrying me forward, and the world around me slows down. The cool light of the moon shines against my face and I take it all in. It's like I'm flying!

I land on the far roof and break my fall with a roll. I turn around and Miles takes a few steps back.

'Woah-woah, wait!' I yell, waving my hands, and he races off the edge. 'Miles!'

I stumble to my feet and watch as his arms stretch out. Black shadows shoot from his hands, boosting him over to me. He lands beside me perfectly, and the shadows that wrap around his arms whisper and pulse. My smile vanishes. I'm no longer smiling and happy but filled with rage and fear.

'What the . . .?' I fall silent and stare hard at the ground. *How could I forget?* Miles still has Elite powers – powers that come from a certain darkness.

'Where are we going?' Miles asks, breaking through my thoughts. He hasn't noticed how fazed I am.

'You'll know it when you see it. It's just past the gym. That way,' I say, pointing absently to the left side of the building we stand on.

I learned long ago that there's a good and a bad side to darkness, but the bad shadows that surround Miles swarm him like a virus.

'Are you OK?' he asks.

I nod, not trusting my voice.

Our trainers peek over the edge of the building and the air blows warm against my skin.

He takes a hold of my hand, with his other hand in his pocket. Black shadows pulse from our connected hands and something sparks inside me in response.

'You ready? This will slow down our fall,' he explains. My heart skips a beat as his shadows crowd over me, grazing my skin like a spiderweb, and we step over the edge. I squeeze my eyes shut but we float down gently and I open my eyes safely on the ground.

'This way,' I whisper, letting go of his hand and batting his shadows off me.

I press my back against the wall and peek around the corner of the alley. *All clear.* We run out into the quiet street and a rabbit races into a bush. We head straight past the gym, where a small path leads to our goal.

'*Young one, are you OK?*' Nox asks, having picked up on my scrambled emotions.

*Yeah, I'm . . . good. We're almost at the secret garden.*

'*Did he bring his mutt?*' Lux asks.

*No. Shade stayed in the room.*

'*But she could be following,*' Nox adds.

*I don't think so.*

'*OK, we're here if you need us. Stay safe, young one.*'

*Always.*

*'And don't do anything foolish, Mouse.'*

*I won't, Lux.*

Me and Miles walk through a bunch of blue-and-silver petal bushes near the park. We break out into a small clearing and glowing white night flowers greet us. Shielded from the world by thick walls of bushes that stretched way above our heads, along with a tall silver hollow tree, we finally return to our secret garden together.

I rest on the soft purple grass and Miles sits down beside me. This place never felt the same once he'd left. The constellations were just stars without him there to name every one and the whole garden felt a lot more lonely.

I look up and find his dark eyes staring into mine with a soft smile I've not seen before. 'What ... what are you staring at me for?' I stutter.

He shifts his eyes to the starry flowers sparkling before us.

'Nothing. Thanks for bringing me here, Supernova.' He runs his hand coolly through his hair. I'm still thrown by the thought of him with the Reaper King's powers, but I cradle my knees to my chest and rest my chin there. *I'm glad you're here Miles.*

He throws himself back against the puffy grass with his hands behind his head. His eyes shimmer amongst the stars and I force my attention up to the sky.

'One day things will be back to normal again, I'm sure.'

He raises his fist and a small smile spreads across my lips. 'Yeah . . .'

My fist slowly presses against his. No matter what happens, no matter how far away we are, we've got each other's backs. Even when it doesn't seem that way at first. I'll always have faith in my best friend, even if the trust isn't completely there yet.

'So, what's been going on with you?' I ask.

'I've not been sleeping since . . . that day. I keep thinking about everything that's happened. The lives lost . . . Or should I say stolen,' he says. 'I just needed to get away from everyone for a bit.'

*Everyone.*

'Relax, Supernova. I didn't mean you.'

My cheeks go warm.

Miles sits up on his hands. 'The main reason I wanted to see you tonight was to say thanks.'

I raise an eyebrow at him. 'Huh?'

He turns to me with a lopsided smile. 'Thanks for never giving up on me, Supernova.'

His eyes meet mine in a way that makes my hands feel all fidgety.

'Well, don't let it get to your head,' I say. 'I still don't fully trust your butt.'

'Yeah, sure.'

'I mean it. I never stopped being your friend, but don't forget you were part of the troop that captured my parents and all the others. You *and* your parents.'

He goes silent and in the corner of my eye I see his eyes narrow. 'You're right.'

'So . . . From now on, just be good,'

'Things aren't as black and white as that, Supernova,' he sighs.

'What's that supposed to mean?'

'I mean, there's a reason behind everyone's actions. What we did was wrong, I get that, but my parents didn't just do it for the sake of it,' he says, ruffling his hair.

'You're right. They did it for their flippin' King and look where that got them,' I say.

'Imma let that one go,' he mutters with a little too much attitude.

I crook my neck at him. Did he really just say that?

He's gazing at the twinkling flowers in front of us. His eyes are vacant, like he's lost in thought. There, but not there.

After a moment, he speaks up again. 'Sometimes you gotta do bad things to protect the people you care about,' he says.

'Not sure I agree with that—'

'But that's the thing though,' he interrupts, tilting his head to the side. 'We want to protect different things.'

'And what do you wanna protect?'

His eyes lock on to mine and the intensity of his stare makes my throat dry. Before I can say anything, his eyes dart away again.

'Hey, I'm gonna ask you something, but I'm not gonna force you to answer if you don't want to,' I say.

'Well, that's ominous. What is it?' he asks, facing me once more.

I fiddle with my sleeve and take a deep breath. 'How . . . How exactly do the Elite tame their umbra? And how did you get your powers?'

I can tell he's shocked by my directness. *Great. Now it's awkward.* The air is thick and the silence between us is almost stifling. But I had to ask.

'You're not gonna like the answer,' Miles says eventually.

'Just tell me the truth,' I say, but I can't ignore the pit of worry in my stomach.

He turns to me. 'You know my powers come from *him*, right?' he says, and I nod. 'Well . . . in order to use his powers, we have to be *like* him.'

'And what does that mean?' I ask carefully.

He hesitates and rubs the back of his head, and I brace myself for the answer. 'The Reaper King eats human souls to fuel his power, so . . .'

Goosebumps rise on my skin and a chill shivers down my spine, taking in what he just said. 'You . . . ate a human soul?'

'No! I didn't! For some reason I can use his powers anyway.'

*Liar.*

'But Mum and Dad and the rest of the Elite did, and that's how the umbra are tamed. We use the Reaper King's powers on their minds and then feed them human souls.'

My heart is pounding so loud I hear it thumping in my eardrums.

'You invade their minds like a virus and force them

to eat human souls? How in Lunis is that OK? It's disgusting and cruel! It's *sick*!' I snap.

He raises his hand, about to protest, but I don't wanna hear it. I dont wanna hear any of it! My hands shake against the dirt. Electric sparks jolt in my chest and down my arms. No wonder Layla thinks that taming umbra is wrong.

'Not all of the umbra are forced – some don't mind it . . .' Miles says.

'How is that *better*? You . . . ate . . . a human . . . soul. A person's essence! I don't . . . I don't understand!'

'I'm telling the truth. I didn't do it,' Miles protests. 'His powers just worked for me! I don't know why.'

I take a moment and close my eyes. My lungs fill and release two calm breaths, and when I'm sure I can keep my voice steady, I speak. 'How is that even possible?'

'I don't exactly know. There's a castle in Astaroth where we keep a piece of a crystal – it's like a mini portal to the Spirit Plain – where the Reaper King's power comes from. That's how his powers leak into the world and that's where he originally gave my mum her power. She was the first. And the shadowy smoke from our hands can suck the soul from animals and people. That's how they . . . But I'm telling you the truth. *I* didn't eat anyone's soul! It's one of the reasons why I had to turn on them! They made me do horrible things but not that. It was all supposed to be in order to keep the kingdom safe!'

Even as my thoughts whirl in confusion, I absorb the fact that the queen was at least telling the truth about the crystals – the source of the original power of the lightcasters.

Miles grabs my hands, but I snatch them back. His dark eyes bore into mine, urgent. Afraid.

'Mia, I'm telling you the truth. I didn't have a choice.'

'Fine,' I say, getting up to my feet. Even if he's telling the truth, what the Elite did is way worse than anything I imagined. 'You know I'm gonna have to tell Mum and Dad, right?'

'I know . . .' he says, looking down. 'It's OK, I'm not trying to stop you.'

I recognise something building within me. My light tingles and burns inside me, threatening to release. I can't hear any more. 'I . . . I gotta go.'

'Mia, wait! There's something else I gotta tell ya about the Reaper King!' he yells, but I turn around and run off. 'Mia! Your dreams. Have they been weird lately?'

I don't stop to hear more. I run as fast as I can through the bushes and out into the empty street. I look around, but everything suddenly looks the same and I grip my hair in a panic. I can't think about where I am or where to go. My mind is a jumbled mess. *Home. I need to go home.*

*'Young one! What's wrong? Your emotions spiked!'* Nox calls out in my mind, but I don't answer and keep running. They would have tried to force Nox to eat human souls! I can't think! I can't . . .

*'Mouse! Calm down. What is going on?'* I hear Lux too.

*They ate people's souls! The Elite! They devoured their souls like the Reaper King. That's how they got his powers!* I blast back in my head. *They would have done the same to Nox!*

I almost jump out of my skin as something jumps out of the shadows at me, but then I realise my two umbra are galloping alongside me. Lux gestures for me to ride and I vault on to his back. I grip his shadow fur and rest my head against his neck, almost sobbing, grateful to have them both here.

*'Miles told you this?'* Nox questions.

*Miles said he didn't do it, but they made him do other stuff.*

*'Do you believe him?'*

*Yeah . . . As mad as that sounds, I do.*

*'Then we will believe him as well. You have good judgement and instincts, Mouse,'* Lux says.

'But that doesn't explain how he can use the Reaper King's powers,' I add.

*'We'll cross that bridge when we get to it – let's get you home for now,'* Nox says.

Safely back in my room, the hideous things Miles told me about the Elite still swirl around my head. I feel sick, and with every emotion I feel the light inside me pulsing and pounding too. As I start to breathe more calmly, his final words come back to me: 'Mia! Your dreams. Have they been weird lately?'

I throw myself on to my bed and press my face into my pillow. I wish I knew why he said that. I shouldn't have run away like a coward.

*'Young one, try to relax your mind,'* Nox says. I roll on to my back and stare at the dark ceiling.

*'Dancing often helps you calm down – why not do that?'* Lux suggests.

I shake my head. 'I should probably tell Mum and Dad what happened. I don't think I should wait till morning. But Dad's gonna be so mad and Miles might get in trouble.'

'*Who cares? The little runt deserves it,*' Lux sneers, bumping my head with the curve of his horn.

'He doesn't. He didn't have to tell me any of that stuff. I don't know . . . I just feel bad for running away like that,' I mutter.

'*What's done is done. If you still feel bad, you can talk to him tomorrow, but your feelings were valid in that moment. It was a lot to take in,*' Nox reassures. He presses his shadow nose against my cheek. '*You've been through an enormous amount of stress and pressure for one so young, but you are strong. That's why you are our tamer.*'

'Thanks.' I stroke his head and kiss his cheek. 'Let's go tell Mum and Dad.'

We slowly crack open my door and darkness greets us. We head across the landing to Mum and Dad's room. Their soft snores sound through the door, and I gulp, slowly pulling the handle down and entering the room. Immediately Spike and Bolt raise their heads from the floor at the end of Mum and Dad's bed. Their golden eyes glow in the dark and my eyes adjust to see the shapes of their heads.

'*Mia, are you all right? Why are you up?*' Spike asks.

'*And why are you not in your pyjamas? Where have you been?*' Bolt questions.

I look down at my clothes. *Shoot*. Well, I guess it doesn't matter now. I rub the back of my head sheepishly.

Before I can answer, Mum stirs in her sleep. 'Spike, what is it . . .?' she asks, sitting up. She rubs her eyes and blinks at me. 'Mia? What is it, honey? Did you have another nightmare?'

She pats Dad awake and he sits up swiftly, ready to fight.

'What's going on?' he asks in a sleepy, yet somehow alert, voice.

'I . . . I have something to tell you guys,' I say, twisting and turning the ends of my sleeves. Mum hovers her hand over her bedside lamp and it luminates the room in a soft yellow glow. Obvious confusion is written all over Dad's face, seeing me fully dressed, but Mum is completely calm. Both of them wait quietly for me to carry on.

'I went out to meet Miles and he told me about the Elite.'

Dad opens his mouth but Mum silences him with a gentle hand on his arm.

I tell them everything and, when I'm done, their faces are a mix of shock and disgust.

'And what about Miles?' Mum asks.

'He says he didn't eat any souls. They didn't make him. But he can use the Reaper King's power. He doesn't know why or how.'

She breathes a sigh of relief and pats the space beside her. Dad shuffles over so there's room for me and I climb on to the bed and sit between them.

'Well, first, well done for finding this out, but you are in trouble for sneaking out of the house,' Dad says, cuddling me with Mum. 'You're lucky I'm still half asleep.'

*Definitely lucky.*

'Please don't punish Miles. We just wanted to hang out without Riley being there. We ... snuck out of the bedroom window.'

'I knew I should have had someone at the house to cover while Riley was on sleep patrol. We won't be making that mistake again,' Dad mutters.

'I'm sorry,' I say, but Mum shakes her head.

'It's OK, sweetheart, you had a pass this time. But that's why I told you to be careful,' she whispers. 'We get it. You saved the city and now you're ten times stronger than you were before, but don't take all of the burden on yourself. Like I said before – you're becoming reckless.' Her eyes flicker to my umbra. 'And that goes for the two of you as well.'

'*We aren't children who need to be scolded,*' Lux snorts.

'*But you do need to respect Lila and Daniel,*' Spike interjects, and Lux rolls his eyes.

'*Our apologies,*' Nox says.

'I know, Mum, and I really am sorry,' I whisper. I am. 'It's just . . . I really missed Miles, and it's worse now that TJ isn't here either . . .'

'We get it,' Dad says, kissing the top of my head. 'But TJ will be back soon. Quicker, before you know it.'

'Did you want to sleep in here tonight, or do you want to go to your room? Lucas is looking forward to your martial arts lesson tomorrow,' Mum says, squeezing me tight, and I bury my head into her neck. 'It's the weekend, so try to relax as well.'

'You probably don't need me to say this, but don't judge Miles too harshly on what he told you. Remember, he was a child back then. And if we had told you to do something, you probably would have done it, right? Even if you thought it was wrong. Like when I told you to leave the city that day.'

'But that was to save you and everyone,' I murmur. 'That was way different.'

'But you don't know how Magnus and Maria worded it to Miles. We still don't know *why* the Elite wanted to bring the Reaper King back,' Dad says.

*That's true I guess.*

I decide to return to my room. The second I shut the door, I grab my nightmare journal and open it up. I flick through the pages, seeing even more entries than before. I randomly stop at one and read it.

Today I dreamed that I was chained by beams of light. The room felt like a prison, but it wasn't a prison. It was like a gigantic container or water tank, without the water inside. Someone was standing just out of my sight, taunting me. I didn't recognise the voice at all. It was weird and distorted, but I'm sure it was a woman. Telling me that I'd never be free and that my powers were needed for the greater good.

I couldn't move no matter how hard I pulled, but I begged for someone to save me. I was so scared. The walls stretched so tall and it felt like all my energy was being drained. I was so confused but there was nothing I could do. At one point I didn't even feel like myself, but I woke up as the person stepped into view.

'Guys,' I murmur, pointing to the page. 'I … didn't write this.'

# CHAPTER FOURTEEN

'OK, Lu-Lu, I know you've only just started martial arts in school, but I'm gonna teach you a few things, all right?' I say, crossing my arms.

Lucas nods eagerly, sitting cross-legged on the grass like the perfect student. Lux and Nox join us with Spike and watch by the silver tree.

Mum had decided to go into the lab a little later after what I told her and Dad last night. The moment I told her about my nightmare journal, she sets to work again trying to translate the lightcaster book. Although I have a feeling she won't come up with anything new.

I chew my lip, trying not to think about my nightmare journal. Those were definitely not my words and I have a strong feeling about who it could be. *Hers.* The woman who I've been hearing all this time, and now she's controlling my body. My stomach lurches.

Mum's technique of trying to block out the woman's voice obviously wasn't working. The woman's last word to me echo in my mind. *Astaroth.*

It's the one thing that's going over and over in my head. That there's still answers we haven't found in Astaroth. And I'm convinced that they're in the castle we couldn't enter. Miles mentioned something about a mini portal leading to the Spirit Plain there too.

I shake my head and focus back on Lucas. I need to calm down.

'OK, Lu-Lu, since the art of the empty hands is your favourite martial arts style, show me your punches first, then your kicks,' I say.

I love being a teacher. The giddy emotion of helping Lucas get stronger and smarter brings me so much happiness and . . . fulfilment. *This* is why I want to be a martial arts teacher rather than a tamer. I can help kids so they'll never be afraid of anything ever again. They'll know how to defend themselves.

Lucas giggles and I pull a face. He stretches up and tries to touch a six-winged butterfly fluttering by. I wave my hand in front of his eyes and he snaps his attention back to me with a goofy grin.

'Did you even hear what I said?' I ask.

'Yes, Mimi! I can do kicks and punches really good. Look, look!' He leaps up and makes a point of jumping over the wild weeds so he doesn't step on them, and his little eyebrows wrinkle into a frowning face of focus. He brings up his tiny fists and punches the air in a flurry of attacks, yelling loudly with every thrust.

I clap a hand over my mouth, stifling my laugh as he drops to the ground and spreads his arms out, completely tuckered out.

'See? I'm really-really good, Mimi,' he puffs. I swallow down my smile and replace it with a semi-serious look.

'That was definitely *something*... Erm... How about we practise with slower punches though. Yours were a little too quick,' I say, clearing my throat. *Like a LOT too quick.* He pushes out his bottom lip and sits back up.

'They're supposed to be super quick,' he says, folding his arms. 'They're ultra-mega power punches.'

'They were cool, but you can do even better if you slow everything down and concentrate, ya know? Take control.'

'I was con-cerrating,' he argues, but I shake my head.

'Concentrating,' I correct him. *And trust me, mate, you weren't.* I hear Lux and Nox snigger.

I raise my fists to demonstrate.

'Watch me, OK?' I say. He nods and sits up, cross-legged. 'Focus on what's in front of you and step into the punch. You gotta use your whole body weight when punching, not just swing your arms all over the place.' That's what Mr Lin taught us.

I throw a sharp one-two punch in front of me and look back at a wide-eyed Lucas. He eagerly claps his hands and cheers. 'Go Mimi!'

'That's how you throw a proper punch,' I say, smiling. 'Focused and powerful. *This* is what you were doin'.' I plant my feet on the ground and pummel the air frantically like he had done. Lucas giggles.

'Remember, you gotta move your body with the punch,' I repeat.

I demonstrate again, leaning into the motion.

'OK. My turn. My turn!' Lucas chirps.

He runs in front of me eagerly and focuses. He digs his feet into the dirt and brings his small fists up. Ready. I recognise that look of determination in his eyes and grin.

'You can do this, Lu. Lean into the punch,' I command.

He takes a big breath and shrugs his shoulders up

and down. His feet spread apart and he throws one strong punch forward.

'YO! That's it, you little legend! Good job!' I cheer, giving him two thumbs up. 'Go again, Lu-Lu. You've got this!'

'I got this!' He yells. He puffs out his chest and raises his hands again. He punches his small fists forward with all his might. One after the other, he punches again and again across from me.

Suddenly a beam of light bursts past me, blasting the tree behind. Hundreds of silver leaves explode into the air and my heart leaps into my throat. *What. The. FLIP?*

The flurry of leaves float to the ground and I see the umbra are all up on their feet, barely having dodged the blast of light. My jaw drops.

*'Did that come from his fist?'* Even Spike's usually calm voice sounds shaken.

'Mimi, look! Did you see it? My superpowers worked! It went POW!' Lucas jumps up and down, excited, but I'm completely lost for words. *You've gotta be kidding me.*

'How did you do that?' I ask him.

The back door swings open and Mum runs down the steps. 'What happened?' she yells, urgently, panic in her voice. She must've heard the bang, or maybe Spike called her.

'Mummy, my powers went whoosh against the tree. I almost knocked it over,' Lucas says, throwing his hands up and I jump back.

'Hey! Be careful in case you do it again!' I tell him and look at Mum. 'It was crazy. It just came out as he was practising his punches.'

Mum's eyes widen at the scattered silver leaves. She crouches down to inspect them.

'And that's all he was doing when it happened?' she asks, twisting a leaf between her fingers.

'I was focusing really hard and it just happened, Mummy,' Lucas says.

'It was so random,' I add.

She presses the side of her finger against her lips. Lost completely in her thoughts, I can almost see the cogs in her mind ticking away, trying to work out what could have triggered his powers.

She stands up. 'Can you try and do it again, sweetheart?'

Lucas grins and playfully spins away from us. He takes a deep breath and does three random shoulder shrugs. I lean in, watching him closely.

He yells and unleashes a flurry of punches all over the place. I tut and shout, 'No, not that way. Slowly, remember?'

He immediately stops. 'I forgot,' he giggles. 'Sorry, Mimi.'

He looks ahead and tries again. That look of determination returns to his eyes and he leans into each punch with more focused energy, yelling with every thrust. A burst of light rockets out of his fist and smacks against the back fence. It cracks from the sheer force and Mum's lips part in shock. Lucas turns back to us. His eyes are flashing gold, making me stumble back and almost trip over my feet. *Is that what happens to my eyes?*

'Interesting . . .' Mum murmurs.

She stares at Lucas with a mix of concern and fascination. 'As your powers grow stronger, your eyes flash for longer and more frequently. I need to add this to my notes. How are you feeling, honey?'

She crouches down to him and he hugs her.

'I'm OK, Mummy. Just a little tired. I'm glad the flowers are OK,' he says, pointing to the pink and white flowers surrounding the tree that was hit.

She looks up at me and her lips press together.

'What's wrong, Mum?' I ask, walking over and ruffling Lucas's curly locks.

'There's just so much we don't know.' She kisses Lucas's head and lets go of him so he can run around and play. 'I'm starting to get a little concerned about what might happen as your powers develop. There's so many anomalies. I wish we could translate that lightcaster book.'

It's like she's voicing all my fears.

I have a sudden wild thought. 'Well, what if you scanned me and Lucas?' I suggest.

'What?' Mum asks, standing back up.

'You want to find out more about the lightcasters, right? So, why don't you scan us like you do the umbra when you check over their health and stuff? Maybe we'll be different from other people.'

She falls silent again while she thinks about it.

'I'm not sure if it would even calculate any readings,' she muses. 'That machine was built to detect shadow matter – it's wired to the biology of umbra, not humans.'

'But the umbra were supposedly made from the powers of old Queen Lucina and the Reaper King, right? So wouldn't that make umbra kinda like half lightcaster creatures too?' I ask. 'Maybe that part would show up in me too?'

*'It's not a bad theory and idea, Lila,'* Spike says, and I grin at him for his support.

Mum comes to a decision. 'OK, we'll give it a try. Let me do some final checks, then I'll come and get you and Lucas when I'm ready, OK?'

'It'll work,' I say, and she kisses my head.

'I hope so, darling. Now, why don't you go and see Miles. Get that apology out of the way. I'll message Riley that you're coming.'

'Thanks, Mum. Can me and Lucas go to the dessert cafe today too?' I ask, checking the tokens in my pocket.

'All right, but straight home after,' she says.

'Deal! Hey Lu-Lu, wanna get some dessert? I've still got some tokens left from helping Ms Mabel at the market last month,' I call out.

Lucas skids to a stop, snapping his head in our direction.

'Yes-yes! I want pancakes and ice cream, Mimi!'

'Come on then.' I hold out my hand and he runs over, and takes it. 'Lux, Nox, do you guys wanna come?'

They nod, standing up from the grass.

*'You can buy us some of this ice cream too,'* Lux says.

'I thought you guys didn't eat human food?' I ask, curiously.

'We don't. We have no need for it but we can still taste it,' Nox says.

'Yay! Luxy, Noxy are coming too!' Lucas cheers.

Mum chuckles and walks up the steps. 'Have fun, sweethearts. I'm going to head to the lab. Do you want me to walk you to the cafe?'

'No thank you, Mummy. We're big kids now!' Lucas says, flexing his little arm.

'Yes, you are, but you're still my babies,' Mum laughs. 'Be safe.'

Me and Lucas leave the house last with Lux and Nox and head straight to Riley's.

'Mimi, is Miles the bad boy who tried to hurt us?' Lucas asks. His small hand clutches mine and I squeeze it back. I keep forgetting that he was so young when Miles was staying with us, and barely remembers him. He can only think of him as the red-cloaked enemy.

'Yeah, but it's not completely his fault. His mum and dad made him do it,' I explain.

'I wanna hurt them back,' Lucas says through gritted teeth. 'Really-really bad.'

'No.' I tug him to stop and crouch down in front of

273

him. His brown eyes darken and he frowns. 'Listen to me, Lu-Lu. This is my problem, Mum's problem, Dad's problem and all of the tamers', but it's not *yours*.'

He shakes his head and I hear his chest rattle as he breathes heavily. 'I won't let him hurt you, Mummy or Daddy!'

My stomach lurches seeing the anger in his eyes.

'Lu-Lu, it's OK. Calm down,' I say. 'What do we do when we're scared?'

'I'm not scared, Mimi. I'm angry!' he snaps.

'OK, what do we do when we're angry then?' I ask, trying to keep calm. My own hands start to shake. *Stay in control.*

'T-Take ... Deep breaths.' Lucas says.

*'Yes, little one,'* Nox affirms.

'So take some with me, OK? In ...' I say, slowly filling my lungs with air. 'Out ... In ... Out.'

After a few moments, our breaths are in sync. The shaking in his hands calms and his eyes soften.

'Remember, it's you.' I point to his chest. 'Me.' My finger switches to me.

'Together, always,' he finishes, holding his hands together.

'Exactly.'

'*Don't forget us,*' Lux says, bonking us both on the head with his horn.

'Yes, Luxy,' Lucas says, giggling a little.

'And Miles is trying to help us,' I say, wiping the corners of Lucas's eyes. 'He did a bad thing and he's trying to fix it, but if you want to hang back with Lux and Nox while I talk to him, that's OK.'

'OK, Mimi.'

I nod at him and stand back up. He reaches for my hand again and I gladly hold it.

The streets are quieter than usual. A few people walk their kids to the park, while others are in shops, but there's an uncomfortable tension in the air. No one's really stopping to chat outside like they normally do. Everyone's keeping to themselves. *What's going on?*

We stop at Riley's house and Lucas hangs back with Lux and Nox. I push the doorbell and step back, allowing the small camera light from the peephole to scan me. The light shuts off and seconds later there's footsteps on the other side of the door.

It clicks open and Miles stands in the door. I blink and look around behind him. 'Where's Riley?'

'He's out on a perimeter walk, apparently. Said you'd be coming.' He shrugs, lazily leaning against the door in his black jeans and shirt. I swear, are black clothes the only thing this guy wears? 'You look nice. You didn't have to dress up just to see me.'

'Yeah, right,' I say, waving my hand at him. 'Joker.'

He glances over my shoulder and I follow his gaze.

'Lucas doesn't feel comfortable seeing you,' I say. He sighs and runs an awkward hand through his hair.

'I get it,' he mutters. He leans his head against the door frame and his messy hair slightly shades his eyes. He studies my face but when his dark eyes meet mine, I clear my throat and look at the ground. He doesn't say a word, but the intensity of his gaze makes me nervous. I wiggle my nose, trying to think of how to apologise. Guess I just gotta spit it out.

'I'm sorry about yesterday,' I mumble and he slightly raises an eyebrow.

'Sorry for what? Ditching me?'

I jerk my head up at him. A smirk rests playfully on his lips. 'I'm kidding, Supernova. You don't have to apologise. It's no big deal. What I told you . . . was a lot,' he says. 'Sorry for scaring you.'

'You don't scare me.'

'Liar.'

'Urgh, shut up.' I playfully push him and he chuckles.

'What was you gonna tell me before anyway? You said something about my dreams?' I ask.

He shoves his hands in his pockets and glances briefly over his shoulder. 'Don't worry about it,' he says. I pull a face.

'You sure?' I ask.

'Yeah,' he answers a little too quickly.

Then I see her. Big red eyes by the living-room door. Shade steps into the hallway and sits by his feet, almost protectively.

'I probably can't leave the house today by the way,' Miles says, shaking the bracelet on his wrist. 'The guard dog is on high alert after last night. I can't go anywhere without him, but hopefully I can convince him to bring me along to your next class.'

My eyes flicker from Shade to him. 'All right, I'll see you soon, Tanaka.'

It's his turn to scrunch up his face and I snigger. Even to this day he still hates it when I call him by his last name. I wave him goodbye and he winks at me, earning an eye roll.

I take hold of Lucas's hand as the front door closes. 'See? Everything's OK. *I'm* OK,' I tell him. 'Come on. Let's get going.'

We start walking again, and I can't help but notice that Lucas is unusually quiet. I'm about to question what's up but he beats me to it.

'Mimi, where do we go when we sleep?' He looks up at me with a serious look on his face.

We cross the road and cut through an empty alleyway. The soft glow of fairy lights hanging along the walls illuminates the frown on his face.

'We don't go anywhere, Lu-Lu,' I tell him. 'We sleep and sometimes we dream. Kinda like your mind playing videos in your head. I think Mum calls it your subconscious mind.'

He nods slowly, taking in my words, but his unreadable expression starts to freak me out a bit. We exit the alley but it's obvious that something's still playing on his mind.

'What is it, Lu-Lu?'

He chews the inside of his lip and his grip on my hand tightens. 'Mimi, I want my head to stop playing videos about the scary man. I don't like those dreams.'

I stop walking. 'The scary man?'

Dread fills me up. Lucas nods. 'He keeps saying that he's gonna get me.'

My feet suddenly freeze. *No . . . It can't be . . .* 'How long has this been happening?'

'A really long time,' he mumbles, wiping his eyes. He shows me his hand. 'Five days. I counted it. I don't want to be taken away, Mimi.'

Lux and Nox glance at each other but I know what they're thinking before I even read their minds. I grit my teeth. This could be bad. But maybe we could be totally wrong. It could be just random dreams, right?

'Mimi?'

My attention snaps down to Lucas's worried face. Immediately I crouch and clamp my hands on his tiny shoulders.

'I'll make sure you don't get taken,' I promise. 'The scary man will have to fight me, Mum and Dad, PLUS all our umbra first.'

He smiles and I hug him close.

'I've been dreaming about a scary man too, and about everything's that happened to us, but don't worry. Your dreams can't hurt you,' I say.

Lucas nods and I stand up and take his hand again, squeezing it. I refuse to let Lucas see me scared or angry. I'm his big sister and I gotta protect him.

'*It could also be nightmares from everything that's happened. He is extremely young,*' Nox says.

'*That's actually most likely the case,*' Lux agrees.

But what if it's not?

We reach the dessert cafe and the bell dings, announcing our arrival.

'Hi, Auntie Lisa,' I say, clasping my fingers together and bowing.

Lucas waves. 'Hi Auntie!'

I nudge him and he quickly remembers to lock his fingers and bow. Auntie Lisa chuckles and bows back at us.

'How are you two today?' she asks, gesturing for us to take a booth. I take my favourite one by the window and the giant music box.

'We're good. We're going over to the lab a bit later to help Mum,' I tell her.

She smiles, putting the menus in front of us. 'That's good to hear.'

'How's Auntie Carly? I spoke to TJ too,' I say, reading down the list of yummy desserts.

'I should've known he'd find a way to talk to you. Auntie Carly is good too. She keeps me updated about TJ,' Auntie Lisa says. 'He's definitely happy that he's getting stronger and wants to show you all the cool things he's learnt when he comes home.'

'Can we put the moonlight song on?' Lucas asks. I stare deadpan at him but he only smiles in return.

'That song's so annoying. No one in the cafe wants to listen to that. I'll pick.'

He jumps up and stands on the plush seat, shoving two fingers in my face.

'I'll give you *two* of my toys if you put it on? Pretty please?'

'Nope.'

He puffs out his cheeks and dramatically falls back in the seat. He crosses his arms and sticks out his bottom lip, as if that's gonna make me change my mind. I lean over the table and flick his forehead. He whines, rubbing his head.

'Mia, let him put on a song.' Auntie Lisa chuckles and I sigh.

'Fine ... Go put it on then,' I tell him. *Only 'cause Auntie Lisa said.*

He jumps out of his seat with a grin and flicks through the list of songs on the touchless jukebox, seeming to feel a lot better after our talk. I secretly hope he doesn't find the song.

No such luck. His finger lands on the song with a huge picture of a smiling moon. The sickly cute song booms out at full blast and I clap my hands over my ears, thankful that the cafe isn't too crowded.

*'It's bright outside . . . when the moon comes out.*
*He lights the dark and brings the spark.*
*La la la, the moon is out.*
*The stars are happy, the town is happy too.'*

Lucas runs back with a smile that looks like butter wouldn't melt.

'Well, I'm glad you're happy,' I say, pressing my finger on the menu picture of the ice cream and pancakes. It sends the order straight through to Auntie Lisa and we sit back and wait.

Lucas bounces in his seat to the music. 'I *am* happy, thank you, Mimi!'

'I was being sarcastic . . .' I mumble.

It's not long before Auntie Lisa comes back with two huge ice-cream bowls and pancakes with lemon juice and sprinkles. We both say thank you and tuck in, and Lux and Nox come over to taste.

Through the window next to us, I watch the passers-by.

A dad tries to tug along his son, who seems way more interested in the toys displayed in the shop window than going anywhere with his dad. Further down the road, a woman gossips with a man by Ms Dawn's flower shop.

My eyes accidently meet the woman's and I awkwardly look away, but in the corner of my eye I catch her nudging the man and nodding at me, which strikes a nerve. I brazenly stare back, but both of their faces are like thunder and I shoot them a glare. *Geez, the queen's speech didn't have a lasting effect then.*

I kiss my teeth and look back at Lucas. More than once I tell him to slow down as he devours his ice cream. When we've finished, I go to pay, but Auntie Lisa waves her hand dismissively.

'Save your money and get yourself some toys or something,' she says.

'Thanks, Auntie.'

'No worries,' she says with a smile.

I go to put my tokens back when they're snatched out of my hand. Next thing I know, Lucas is running off with my money.

'Hey!' I race after him, waving to Auntie Lisa as the cheeky muppet bolts out of the shop. *When did he get so fast?*

I chase after him, my legs pumping, and Lux dashes past me. He closes the gap in seconds and catches Lucas by the back of his shirt. I laugh at the shock on Lucas's face and he squirms around. Lux lifts him slightly off the ground and Lucas whines louder.

'Ha! Gotcha!' I cheer.

'No fair! That's cheating!' he says, crossing his arms. He sticks out his bottom lip again, suspended in the air.

*'That's what you get for being slippery,'* Lux muses.

He puts Lucas down in front of me and nuzzles his cheek, making my little brother laugh.

'I'll be taking that!' I snatch my money from him, triumphantly putting it back in my purse.

'I was just playing,' Lucas says, but that grin tells me otherwise.

'Yeah, sure.'

'Mia!' Someone yells.

I wince, recognising the high-pitched voice. I slowly turn around and see Layla waving frantically from across the road. She runs over in a short flowery dress with new combat boots and her hair in two high ponytails. Jada must've helped her because she almost looks like a completely different person to the girl I met in Astaroth. She stops and crouches in front of Lucas.

'It's so nice seeing your brother again. He's more adorable than I remember.' She ruffles his hair but he bats her hand away.

'What? Did you think he was ugly or something?' I ask, wrapping my arm around Lucas protectively and bringing him closer.

Her grin widens, like a creepy-cute doll. 'No, I just didn't think he was as adorable as you. But he is . . .'

'I'm not a little kid. How old are you anyway?' I ask.

'Twelve.' She leans down to Lucas again and he steps back slightly behind me.

'Leave him alone.' One more move to touch him and she's getting dropped. I don't care.

She blinks, completely dismissing my warning and jerks her chin towards the cafe behind us. 'Did you guys just get some dessert?'

I quirk an eyebrow. 'Yeah we did, but where's Jada? Why aren't you with her?'

'I gave her the slip.' Layla shrugs.

'You can't just run away though,' I say.

She tilts her head like she's confused. 'Why not? I got bored. Don't worry, I'll find her again in a bit.'

*'She is supposed to keep an eye on you for a reason. You can't build trust if you sneak off,'* Nox remarks, and her

eyes shift to him.

'You guys pretty much trust me though, don't you? After all, I told you about your little traitor and you've met my friends in the cave, so that means we're good friends now. Even though I still don't agree with you taming umbra.'

Not once does her creepy grin waver. I take a hold of Lucas's hand and tug him away, but I hear her footsteps annoyingly click after us.

Lucas trips over a rock and his hand slips out of mine. I catch him before he falls but a loud cackle bellows behind us.

Lucas looks back at Layla in disbelief. I shoot her a glare and she claps a hand over her mouth, barely making an effort to cover her laughter.

'What? It was funny. His little face when he tripped. It was HILARIOUS.'

'Come on, guys, let's go,' I say to Lucas, Lux and Nox, and we pick up the pace.

'Wait! Can't we hang out for a bit?' Layla calls after us and I stop in my tracks. She plonks herself on the pavement and I look as people pass around her, puzzled by the sight of her just chilling on the cold, hard ground. Whether Layla notices or not is beyond me, but if she does, she doesn't seem to care.

'You're just going to sit there?' I ask.

'Why not? Come on. Sit with me. Let's get to know each other.' She pats the space next to her. Sighing, I sit on the ground. Lux and Nox's eyes are firmly watching us and Lucas sits beside me. *Well, this feels weird, but whatever floats her boat.*

I clear my throat, trying to think of what to talk about.

'So, you really don't have any idea where your parents are?' I ask.

'Yep, I really don't know,' she says and my heart tugs a bit. I can't imagine what that'd feel like. 'I remember we used to travel a lot, but we got separated. Then I lived with the umbra in a cave for a while. They basically raised me.' She sways a little, smiling dreamily at the memories. Her eyes look far away, but she truly looks happy. 'They were the best, but then Magnus and Maria took me in and they taught me stuff too.'

'But how did you end up going with the Elite?' I ask.

'I was out on the plains with one of the umbra when I saw them. I told the umbra to run away and then Maria asked if I wanted to come with her and I said yes,' she replies.

'So, you went with them freely?' I don't know

whether to be impressed or unnerved by this girl. The way she does things is just so different from anyone I've ever met, but maybe she isn't all that bad.

'Well, if I said no, they might have taken me by force. Either way, I knew I'd be able to get away, but it seemed like it could be fun in Astaroth,' she shrugs.

*Fun?*

'And you never thought about escaping back to the cave umbra? They're worried about you.'

Her eyes light up. She clasps her hands together and leans eagerly towards me. 'I'm really glad you met them. I knew they'd be all right! I didn't tell the Elite anything about them, so they should stay safe.' The joyous grin on her face brightens her eyes even more and suddenly the walls I put up between us slowly crumble away.

She grins at me again. 'Anything else you wanna know? I'll answer anything. Within reason, obviously.'

The cold of the pavement starts to bite through my clothes and I shift uncomfortably. 'Is there anything else you can tell me about the Elite?'

She sways side to side, tapping her lips. 'The Elite always had a backup plan in case their original one failed. So, be careful of who you trust in this city, Mia.

That's all I know.'

'What's the backup plan?'

'No idea, but as soon as things mess up, I'm outta here,' Layla says.

A shiver runs down my spine at that little nugget.

'Yo! Didn't I tell you to stay put?' a voice yells.

A sudden gust of wind and there's Jada leaping off Ruby. She lands between me and Layla. Her pretty afro hair whips furiously in the wind and her nose flares. Looks like Layla slipped away before Jada could get her hair rebraided. It's a cool look for her.

'I swear I don't get paid enough to babysit. Why'd you run off? I really don't want to have you locked up again, but I'm losing patience,' Jada fumes.

Layla hops up to her feet and sniggers. 'Well, looks like I got caught. Sorry.'

'Just quit running,' Jada says, and her eyes flicker to me. 'How you guys doing?'

'We're good. Just heading home before we go to help Mum in the lab,' I say. She nods and bumps fists with me.

'How you holding up?' I ask.

'I'm gettin' there. I visit Mum every day in the hold, but you know ... It's not the same,' Jada says.

'You should come and play with us sometimes,'

Lucas says and a smile spreads across Jada's face.

'I will. I promise.'

*'We should get going,'* Ruby says and she bumps her head softly against mine and I stroke her black feathers.

Jada slaps her hand down on Layla's shoulder, ensuring she can't scoot off again. 'Catch you guys later!' Layla says.

'See ya,' I say, waving back, and we head home.

It isn't long before Mum and Spike come to fetch me and Lucas. Nerves and excitement flutter in my stomach as we reach the lab.

I follow Mum through the sliding doors. Our shoes squeak against the clean shiny white floors. The powerful waft of cleaning solution burns my nose first, but the sounds of all the scientists working buzzes in my ears. Some examine shadow matter with crystal scopes, while others work on travel pods and moonlight inhibitors.

Lucas jumps up and down, holding Mum's hand. He loves going to the lab. This place is pretty cool, aside from the umbra research, which used to freak me out when I was younger. The constellation and energy research conducted here has a special place in my heart though. The fact that we can learn so much of our history through stars is something out of this world. One day I want to be an expert at reading the stars too, just like Miles and Layla can.

We pass Samuel Walker's room and my chest tightens when I catch a glimpse of him.

'I still think we'll bring him back,' Mum whispers and I smile up at her. We carry on walking and thankfully the umbra holograms aren't active today, making the lab feel more spacious and brighter.

We stop at the opposite side of the lab where the umbra health scanner is. A moon-glass wall separates the scanner room from the lab so you can see right inside, but the umbra or person inside can't see out.

'Mia, do you want to go first?' Mum asks, but I catch the edge of nerves in her voice.

'Yeah. I don't mind,' I say confidently. *What's the worst that can happen, right?*

'I scanned a few of the scientists earlier, and Mikasa and Lincoln too. So we have a good range of comparisons,' she says.

She opens the door for me and I step inside the huge echoey room. I stand in the middle, staring up at the tall white walls. *Well, here we go.* I face forward and imagine Mum, Lucas, and our umbra staring back at me. *I'll be fine.*

'I'm going to start the scan now, honey.' Mum's voice booms from the white speaker box above the door. 'Keep still.'

I give her a thumbs-up and suddenly the room vibrates. The floor rumbles against my feet and I flinch expecting pain, but instead my body gently lifts off the ground. *Woah!*

My body floats up and slowly spins against my will. A bright red light shines and scans me from all angles. After a few seconds it shuts off, and my feet return to the floor. I give my legs a shake and the door opens.

'Good job, honey. That's it,' Mum says.

Lucas bounces over to me.

'I saw the big red light go up and down, up and down. I waved at you, Mimi, but Mummy said you couldn't see me,' he says, hugging my legs.

'Yep, it wasn't scary at all. Wanna give it a go, Lu-Lu?' I ask and he lets go of me with a giant grin.

'Yes! I'm ready, Mimi! It's my turn now!'

Without any need of encouragement, he runs into the room and Mum shuts the door.

'I'm ready, Mummy!' he calls out.

He playfully hops on one foot to the middle of the room and waves his arms up and down, pretending to fly.

'OK, it's going to scan now, sweetie,' Mum says through the mic. 'Keep still.'

She winks at me and presses down on a yellow button. The room hums like it did when I was in there and the scan commences.

'Have you looked at my results yet?' I ask, watching the red light scan Lucas up and down.

Mum shakes her head, keeping her eyes on Lucas. 'We'll check both of your results together. It was very tempting to take a peek though.'

The scanner stops and when Lucas floats back to the floor, I open the door to let him out.

'That was fun, Mimi!' He beams, holding my hand. He swings back and forth and I twirl him around, making him giggle.

Behind us Mum gasps and we both turn to see her staring at the screen. She ushers over the other scientists and they all stare too. I tug Lucas across to take a look.

'What is it?' I ask, trying to look past all the adults and see the screen. Mum turns to me and moves out the way so I can see, and on the screen are the outlines of four small figures, one shorter than the rest, which I guess represent Lincoln, Mikasa, me and Lucas. Apart from the size, the scans all look pretty much the same to me. I don't know what they're all so psyched about.

'Fascinating …' one of the scientists mutters, rubbing his chin.

'We had always thought that the difference in your genetic make-up compared to the average person would be larger, but it isn't,' Mum explains.

'What does that mean?' I ask, still not getting it.

'It means that our understanding of lightcaster powers doesn't need to be so complex. It appears to be more emotionally linked than genetic, which means learning to control your powers may be easier than you think.'

She ushers me closer and points to one of the images and a chart beside it. 'This is your reading. There was a spike right here for a second. Were you nervous when you were in the room?'

'Yeah. I wondered if the scan was gonna hurt,' I say.

'And it shows here. Lincoln was the most nervous when I scanned him earlier, but it doesn't show in his results, or Mikasa. Lucas was excited throughout and his results are all spiked too.' The joy in Mum's voice makes me feel relieved.

'See, told ya we'd find something. You did raise a very intelligent daughter after all,' I say, lifting my chin in pride.

Mum laughs. 'It appears I have, but you get your cockiness from your father,' she retorts.

I grin and pop an imaginary collar. 'I'd call it confidence rather than cockiness.'

Mum and the other scientists read through everything, filled with fascination, but the data all looks like gobbily gloop to me.

'It's so interesting. There is truly only one difference between you and the other children. One particle in the brain within the limbic system,' Mum says. Most of this goes over my head, though I'm pretty sure the limbic system has something to do with emotions. But that explains a lot about the times when my powers flared up.

The lab doors slide open and Dad walks in with Bolt. My stomach drops at the sight of their stern faces. Seeing his face too, Mum immediately meets Dad and Bolt halfway across the room, away from the other scientists.

'How did it go?' she asks.

Dad leans down and kisses my head then Lucas's.

He gives Mum a quick peck and I swear they're the only two people in the world that don't give me the ick when they kiss.

Dad sighs. 'Not good, honey. I think I'm going to have to interrogate Maria and Magnus again,' he says. 'We're no closer to figuring out who the traitor is.'

'Do you want me to do it? Maybe I can get Magnus to talk to me,' Mum suggests, but Dad shakes his head. He hates putting Mum in any potentially dangerous situation even though she's a tamer too. I guess it's a dad thing.

'It's OK, honey. I got it,' he says.

'Dad, I want to come with you,' I say.

His attention shifts to me and I stare back at him, curious what he'll say. Waiting to see what happens next doesn't feel like an option any more. With each passing moment it seems that the Reaper King and that woman are finding new ways to get stronger, and I'm ready to see the Elite face to face again. I want answers. And I want to help figure out who the traitor is.

'Honey, I don't think that's a good idea,' Mum interjects, but the way Dad rubs the back of his neck, he's definitely considering it and I fight back a smile.

'All right. You can come. I'm trusting you on your first official tamer mission, OK?' he says. 'It isn't going to be easy and it could be scary, but I'll be with you.'

'I know, Dad.' *You've always got my back. I've got yours too.*

'Daniel,' Mum warns.

They share a look. Mum's eyes fall to me, examining my motives, but I can't fight back the grin any more. Finally, she nods.

'OK, fine, but the moment you feel uncomfortable—'

'I leave. I always have control,' I finish.

Mum smiles and hugs me. 'That's my girl.'

Lucas reaches up for Dad and he's immediately scooped up. He giggles and hugs Dad tight.

In the distance, the other scientists continue to examine the scans, and me, Mum, Dad and Lucas all stand together with our umbra. We hold out the star pendants we always wear as a family and I close my eyes. *Everything's fine.* I breathe in the lab air.

'What are the family promises?' I start.

'Always remember the good times,' Mum says.

'Always do good listening,' Lucas adds, puffing out his little chest proudly like he always does in Dad's arms.

'Always stick together,' Dad adds, leaving the last line for me and I smile.

'And it's never goodbye, only see you laters,' I finish.

We bump our fists together and the pendants flash with the promise, sealing the deal.

'Be safe,' Mum reminds us and Dad puts Lucas down. He winks and fist bumps me. He's finally trusting me with something important and I won't let him down. We'll find out the Elite's plan together.

'See you later,' Dad says.

'Bye Daddy, bye Mimi! Bye umbra!' calls Lucas, who has somehow managed to climb on top of Spike.

'See ya!' I say and together Dad and I leave with Bolt, Lux and Nox to where the Elite are being held . . . The hold.

# CHAPTER FIFTEEN

The hold is a dark underground prison located near the centre of the city, away from any major shops and houses. A place with bleak black walls and only umbra mice for company if you're lucky. A place riddled with negative vibes. Even time feels like it's at a standstill there.

I've never been inside before, but I've heard stories of what it's like. It's the last place you ever want to be, even worse than the Nightmare Plains.

We come to a stop outside the entrance and a lump builds in the back of my throat.

'Lux, Nox, Bolt, you three should stay above ground. Just in case the Elite try to control you,' Dad says.

Lux growls but fights the urge to argue back. *I think it's a good idea too guys.*

*'If something goes wrong, you tell us, Mouse,'* Lux says.

*'And remember your training – block out the voices of any other umbra who tries to talk to you,'* Nox adds.

*Good point. Thanks.*

'I'll see you guys soon.' I reach up and hug them close. 'See you soon too, Bolt!'

*'Be safe,'* he says, and I pet his head before joining Dad at the doors.

The armoured guards step aside for Dad and I catch a glimpse of the rope guns and crossbows in their grasp. I try to ignore the rapid beating of my heart. *It's OK. You got this.*

At the inner door he stops and glances over his shoulder at me. 'Are you sure about this, Baby-girl? It could be scary.'

'Yeah, but the Reaper King was scarier. I'll be OK,' I say, patting my thigh strap.

A smile of pride spreads across his bearded face and he keeps me close as we walk down to the hold. Our shoes clang against the metal stairs. With each step the cold stone walls either side of us feel like they're closing in and my grip on Dad's arm hardens.

A long corridor stretches ahead with holding cells on either side. There's a nasty smell of damp and disinfectant. Thick metal walls separate each of the cells and a crystallised glass wall stands in front of the bars, protecting us from the prisoners inside. Just like in the lab, it stops them from communicating with each other and means that we can see in but they can't see out.

Beside each cell a touch panel glows. I wonder if that's how the guards remove the glass. It looks as though they've just given the prisoners their meals because there's muffled activity and noise behind the glass. Some are yelling and one woman throws herself against the bars, as if she can sense we're there.

Dad keeps a protective arm around me. 'She can't see us,' he reminds me, and we keep walking. In each cell is a small single bed nailed to the floor, a toilet and a pile of books.

'Do they stay in the cells all day?' I ask, trying not to stare too much.

'Twice a day they're allowed out in the recreation room. It's the only room down here that has natural moonlight through a skylight.'

He hesitates by one of the cells and stops. 'They're sent out in small groups and the prisoners can walk around under strict supervision. They may have done bad things but we still need to treat them with a level of humanity.'

'Even if they've hurt people?' I ask.

He nods. 'We have to be better than them. The very least we can do is allow them to have a tiny bit of moonlight inside and some human interaction.'

I look into the cell beside us and do a double take. A woman with worn-out frizzy braids and light brown skin sits silently on her bed. Her fingers shakily clutch a photo and her eyes are slightly sunken from obvious lack of sleep. I realise suddenly that it must be Ms Halliwell – Jada's mum. It's like looking at Jada if she was thirty years older. Ms Halliwell glances up for a second and I quickly follow Dad as he carries on walking.

Towards the back of the hold, the Elite umbra are held behind the barrier Mum and the scientists made of crystallised steel. It's almost completely unbreakable but it doesn't stop the telepathic link between umbra and their tamers. They can still talk to each other through their thoughts, which is why the hold is so heavily guarded.

We walk to the very end of the corridor where a woman with dishevelled brown hair sits cross-legged on her bed, leaning against the wall. Her green eyes peek through her hair as we approach.

Dad presses his finger on the panel and a green light scans his face. After a beep, it stops and the glass is raised. My palms start to feel sweaty as the extra protection between us and the woman disappears, revealing us to her.

'Hello, Maria,' Dad greets.

His arms stay firmly at his sides, but he gently taps me with the back of his hand. A silent warning to stay behind him, and I do.

Maria slowly looks up, then stands to her feet. 'How is my son?'

*Miles.*

Dad's back stiffens. 'He's fine. Under watch but not in a holding cell like you and Magnus.'

Her glare is fixed on Dad, but when I lean closer, her eyes flick to me. They're full of rage, dangerous and terrifying. My jaw clenches but I stand my ground.

Her eyes stay pinned on me. 'Hello, Mia.'

A shiver prickles across the back of my neck. I always thought Miles's dad was the scary one, but his mum is ten times worse.

'If you think you're gonna use me like you used Miles, you can think again,' I say with a calmness that I'm proud of, despite the rapid beating of my heart.

Maria doesn't speak but steps forward. The words clearly ruffled her feathers and I almost smirk. *That's right. I'm not afraid any more.*

She presses her forehead against the bars. 'We never used Miles. We were protecting him,' she bites back.

'From what?' Dad asks, taking over the conversation and ensuring we're both out of grabbing reach. Her wild eyes snap to him.

'You don't understand, Daniel. You say the queen doesn't do her job in protecting the kingdom, yet here you and the tamers are protecting *her*. Welcoming her to your city. The tamers were created because of her incompetence.'

'I'm protecting my family.'

She yanks at the bars. 'And so am I. If you knew what the queen was doing you would be on our side too. You would want the king to reign over the kingdom. Complete darkness is the only way.'

Dad rubs his jaw. 'You're wrong. I'd choose neither to rule. But seeing as you refuse to tell me all that you know, you'll stay locked up until we decide what to do next.'

'That's a big mistake.'

'Why do you want to bring back the Reaper King?'

I ask. I want to – no, *need* to – hear it from her mouth. Her sharp eyes shift to me again.

'And why should I answer you?' she taunts.

I brush past Dad and step closer to her. I take in her dangerous eyes without fear.

'Well, it's kinda the least you can do after all you've done to the city,' I say.

'I owe you nothing, child. You shouldn't even be here. The Reaper King should have eaten your soul and then *he* would be here to reign—'

'Watch your mouth with my daughter,' Dad growls, but the fire is ignited inside me. She tried to kill me. She used – *abused* – Miles. If they had just left Miles in Nubis he would be OK. He wouldn't have turned bad and constantly have that tortured look behind his eyes. They're selfish and deserve to be punished!

*'Young one, what is going on?'* Nox's voice echoes in my head.

*They need to pay for what they've done.*

*'Mouse!'*

Something grabs my arm and I snap out of my thoughts to see Dad staring down at me, concerned.

'How fascinating. You still don't have control of your powers,' Maria says, eyes wide with glee. I look down to see the last little glow of purple dimming in my hands.

'Why did you and the Elite hurt my grandparents?' I ask, through gritted teeth. 'Why involve them?'

For the first time I see doubt flit across her face. 'What are you talking about?'

'Answer the question!' I yell, kicking the bars. Dad pulls me back, but I fight free of his grip.

'I don't know what you're talking about.'

Dad firmly tugs me behind him once more. 'Look, Maria, this is your last chance for any sort of redemption. Tell us why you want to bring back the Reaper King.'

Why isn't he asking her more about Nan and Grandad? She has to be the woman Nan was talking about. Who else would attack them?

Maria stretches her arms and yawns. 'I'm not going to waste my breath. It's too late for you anyway.' She waves a dismissive hand at us.

Dad steps back. 'Then so be it.' He pushes the button and the crystal glass wall slides down between us again. Even though she can't see us any more, she continues to stare with a sickening smirk.

'Come on, Baby-girl,' Dad murmurs.

He doesn't say another word the whole way back through the hold, not even bothering to interrogate Miles's dad, Magnus. I quietly follow him until we're outside and when the door closes behind us, he turns to face me. The look on his face scares me.

'I'm sorry my powers almost—' I begin.

'The traitor's been leaking information to the prisoners.'

'Wait, what?'

*Where did that come from?* The look of worry in his eyes makes me tug nervously at my sleeves. *What did I miss?*

'Mia, I need you to head home,' he says. He must have silently communicated with Bolt too because they immediately start walking in another direction.

*'Young one, what happened?'* Nox asks.

'I don't know. I didn't think Maria said anything that weird. Come on, we're going after them.'

I try to keep up as Dad speed-walks through town, messaging someone on his holophone.

'Mia, I told you to go home,' he sighs.

'How do you know someone's leaking information?' I ask. 'You didn't even mention the traitor.'

He stops and places a hand on my shoulder. 'If I had

asked about the traitor then she would know we're on to them. They'd warn whoever it is and we'd be no nearer to finding out who the traitor is. Maria was just making empty threats. There's nothing the Elite can do while they're in the hold.' He starts to walk again and I trot alongside him. 'I didn't tell her that Miles was back though, nor about the queen visiting Nubis. So someone else told her. Someone with access. Which narrows it down considerably.'

I stop abruptly. *That's right!* She didn't ask WHERE Miles was, she asked HOW he was.

I pick up the pace again to catch up with Dad, but for every two steps I take he's ahead by one.

'Do you think one of the guards let it slip?' I ask.

Dad shakes his head. 'We can't rule it out but I'm pretty confident it wasn't a guard. It's not like them to make that kind of mistake with such high-profile prisoners. One of my main suspects is Miles himself, but listen to me carefully, Mia.'

He stops again to stare straight into my eyes. 'Do not trust any tamer until I figure out who the traitor is. Not even Jada.'

*What? No way. Not Dad saying this too.*

We carry on walking, but I know Miles wouldn't be

that clownish, knowing he's under strict supervision, and it just couldn't have been Jada. It had to be . . . *Wait.*

I slow to a stop and Dad quickly stops too.

'Dad, the umbra! What if Shade communicated with the Elite umbra, or even Maria herself?'

The colour drains from Dad's face. 'You could be right, Baby-girl, but no one person and an umbra can go against the tamers as a whole. Whatever they're planning can't be in motion already.'

He pulls out his holophone and speaks so fast that it's only when I hear Mum's urgent voice on the other end that I realise who Dad's talking to. 'OK, I'll go get them.'

Something about the way Dad says those words sets my teeth on edge. He hangs up and turns to me, but I beat him to speaking.

'I'm coming too,' I jump in before he can tell me to go home again. 'To talk to Miles.'

'All right then, come on. I suppose you've proved yourself a fine tamer so far, but let me do the talking first. OK?'

'OK!'

'And watch Riley. Remember what I said. Right now we can't trust any tamer.'

We zigzag through the bustling market and Maria's words ring in my mind. *It's too late for you anyway.*

I slow down, seeing Miles ahead with Riley, talking with Shade and Myla. From the bored expression on Miles's face, Riley is scolding him about something.

'Miles, do you mind if we talk?' Dad asks. Miles raises a brow. He looks at me for a second, but silently nods. Dad waves for me to come but a hand on my shoulder stops me.

'Hey, Mia, what's going on?' Riley asks. He looks from me to Dad. I strain my ears to listen to Dad and Miles talk, but as hard as I try, they're just outta earshot. 'Does Daniel suspect Miles of something?'

'Not sure,' I lie, carefully watching his face. 'But we just came from the hold.'

Riley's eyebrows furrow. He chews the inside of his cheek but doesn't look away from Dad and Miles.

'And he thinks Miles did something? Or someone else?' Riley asks.

'Dunno,' I shrug, looking at Dad and Miles too.

He scratches the back of his head and I give him the side eye again.

'Well, if Miles is up to something, I'll find out,' Riley adds.

I force a nod but continue to secretly watch him. Funny how he suddenly wants to talk to me after accusing me of lying about Nox. He hasn't even spoken to me since then either, so what's with all the questions now?

I head over as Dad tuts and crosses his arms.

'Miles, everything will be easier if you're just honest.'

I look at Miles and mouth, 'It's OK.'

Dad's eyes connect with mine but I nod to Riley and shrug discreetly. He wants to know if Riley did anything suspect while he was speaking to Miles. I'm not a hundred per cent sure Riley's the traitor, but he's definitely suspicious. Dad acknowledges my response and switches his attention back to Miles.

Miles stuffs his hands in his pockets and stares at the ground. Dad can be rough around the edges sometimes, but he and Miles used to be really close. He looks at me with a huff and looks at Dad. 'Yeah, it was me.'

Dad lets out a sigh. 'Why?'

'Because I had to let Mum and Dad know I'm safe. That's it. I figured you wouldn't let me see them, so getting Shade to tell them was the only way. They already knew I was back though.'

Dad doesn't speak, but his eyes soften.

'What's done is done, but Miles, if I catch you trying to speak to your parents secretly again there will be consequences.'

Miles's jaw tightens. 'Yes, sir.'

'I really am sorry it has to be this way, Miles.' Dad pats him on the shoulder and then heads over to Riley.

Miles looks downcast, defeated. I tilt my head to meet his gaze.

'Hey, wanna hang out for a bit?'

'Sure, but the guard dog will probably have to follow,' he says, nodding to Riley. I turn around and catch Dad giving me the nod of approval.

'I think it'll be fine. Come on,' I say, tugging his arm. 'Let's go to the park.'

He scrunches up his nose and shakes his head. 'I'd rather go to the secret garden,' he says.

'Sounds good. Remember where it is?' I tease, and he smirks.

'Of course. How can I forget? We were literally there the other night. I always remembered roughly where it was,' he says.

I wave goodbye to Dad and Riley like nothing happened and we leave with our umbra.

Our steps fall into sync and we walk side by side. Just

like old times. He playfully bumps me several times and my stomach flutters every time our eyes meet. I'm so happy he's still here and I feel certain he won't leave again.

A huddle of bushes creates a purple leafy path that leads to our hideout. I squeeze through first, breaking out into the beautiful garden again. Miles walks over to the silver hollow tree and climbs up with ease. I follow behind and sit beside him on the thick branch. Below us, Lux, Nox and Shade rest on the grass.

'I missed this place a lot,' Miles says. 'I thought it would've been covered by weeds and stuff by now.'

I lean against the trunk of the tree, softly smiling to myself. 'I still came here a lot, even after you left. Whenever I wanted to just get away from everything.' It was the only place I still felt connected to him, as cheesy as that sounds, but I keep my mouth shut on that.

Silence falls between us and my smile falters. Until I saw that drawing in Astaroth I thought he had forgotten all about me.

The flowers bounce in the breeze and little bunny-rat umbra hop alongside normal rabbits. Our secret garden is the only place they're found. A question burns in the back of my mind and I gulp, hoping in my gut that I don't regret asking. Apparently being in the garden encourages me to ask about the tough stuff.

'How did Shade become your umbra? I mean I know *how*, but of all the umbra in the world, why tame her?'

I take a peek at his face and see that sadness in his eyes again.

'I never told you, but when we first saw Shade . . .' He hesitates, then carries on. 'Well, I never really got over it. I snuck out into the plains again.'

'Wait, what?'

'It was a few years later, a couple of months before we left the city. Remember I was training so hard?'

'Yeah, to be a tamer. I was too,' I say, but he shakes his head.

'It wasn't just because of that. It was so that one day I could go back out to the plains and hunt down the umbra that almost killed you.'

'She tried to kill both of us. Lucas too,' I add, hardly believing my ears. Why would he risk his life like that just to get revenge?

I close my eyes and I'm thrown right back to that moment. Shade's blood-red eyes, the violent hunger in them. It doesn't scare me as much as it did then, but it still hurts to think about what could have happened if it wasn't for Bolt rescuing us.

'Obviously I found her again,' Miles says. 'And this time her eyes were gold.' I look down at said umbra and she nods, confirming it. Miles carries on. 'We just stared at each other and then she left, saying we would meet again at another time. So, as I got better at my training, Mum and Dad said I should try their way of taming umbra with their shadow powers, and sure enough . . .'

'You found her again,' I say, clearing my throat, 'and forced her to eat a human soul.'

The wind whistles and the clouds stir in the sky.

*'Yes, he did,'* Shade says. *'But he did not force me to eat a human soul – I did that with complete free will.'*

The cockiness in her dark red eyes nearly makes my stomach hurl. Lux and Nox growl. Their shadowy fur bristles as they glare at Shade.

'She was helping the Reaper King and one of our members,' Miles says.

'So, she was possessed,' I say.

'Possessed isn't the right word,' he says. He rubs his chin, trying to think of another word, but I throw my hands up.

He blinks. 'What?'

'I point-blank saw one of your "members" use their powers to control a wild umbra against their will. That isn't right.'

Little rain droplets start to fall and my nose wrinkles as the air turns damp. The tree branches above us take the brunt of the shower, and neither of us makes a move to leave.

'How is it different from a spirit calling?' he asks.

'They have a *choice*. That's how it's different. They don't have to turn up in the Spirit Plain, or they can even eat your soul.' *It isn't rocket-science, mate.*

*'We don't always get a choice when it comes to being called by your spirit calling,'* Shade chips in. *'Sometimes umbra feel compelled to go towards the connection.'*

*'Maybe, but the tamers here do not force random umbra in the Nightmare Plains to do their bidding. We have free will. Compared to you. You just happen to enjoy eating human souls,'* Lux barks.

*'I am not forced to do anything,'* Shade growls.

*'Say that to your red eyes and the croco-umbra we met on the plains,'* Lux counters.

*'And me. I felt what it feels like to be controlled,'* Nox adds.

I drop down from the tree and, with a thud, Miles
lands beside me. We sit together on the lilac grass
instead. I sink my fingers into the dirt.

'Everything the Reaper King does is bad. He won't
even leave me alone in my sleep,' I mutter, watching
yellow birds fly above.

'So, you *do* dream about him too . . .' Miles's words
almost blend with the light sizzle of the rain, but I hear
his next set of words as clear as anything.

'The Reaper King's been in my dreams for as long as
I can remember.'

Goosebumps shiver up my arms. *All his life?*

'Do you . . . hear a random woman sometimes in your
nightmares too?' I say, finding my voice.

'No. But lately all my nightmares have been
about you.'

His eyes capture mine but they stare straight
through me.

'Funny . . .' I say, barely managing a pitiful laugh. 'I've
seen you in my nightmares too.'

My words linger like a bad cloud between us. He
picks up a stick and digs at the dirt.

'That's what he does. At first it was him in all my
nightmares, then they turned into you . . . but not you.

You always have sharp teeth and red eyes, but I know it's really him, tricking me.' He kisses his teeth and throws the stick out into the rain.

'That's what happens to me, except I see you!' I tell him. 'I've been practising how I can push him out of my thoughts. This woman seems to help me sometimes but I have no idea why, or who she is, and it's been freaking me out. And I've found things in my nightmare journal that I don't remember writing.'

'Do you think it has something to do with your powers?' he asks.

'I have no idea. I've just been pushing forward, pushing forward, but I'm really scared,' I mutter. 'And I don't know what to do.'

Something warm lands on my head and I peek up to see Miles's jacket on my head.

'Don't want your hair to get wet,' he murmurs. 'And don't be scared. I'll help you no matter what.'

The rain is now pouring down around us, but the warmth in my chest makes me feel almost on fire, and I smile. *Thanks, Miles.* 'Are you still having those weird nightmares about the Reaper King?'

'Sometimes. Not as often, but . . . I know he's there. Always at the back of my mind. It's like he's waiting or 'something,' he says. He shakes his hand, and what look like swirling shadows suddenly disappear.

'Is your hand OK?' I ask.

'Yeah, my shadow powers just flare up sometimes. No big deal,' he says dismissively. Just like me. I glance down and clench my hand into a fist. Guess I'm not the only one having trouble with their powers. It's kinda comforting.

'So, what do you think he's waiting for?' I ask.

'I don't know . . .' He smirks but I see right through it. He's scared. 'Why're you looking at me like that? You worried?'

I scrunch up my face. 'Aren't you?'

'Nope. So don't worry.'

*Yeah, but you're the one I'm worried about, mate.*

I let it go for now and sigh. Beyond the clouds, the constellations are already changing.

'Who do you think the woman is then?' Miles asks.

'I think she might be good. She helped me when Nox was being attacked and she helped me through some nightmares. I just don't get why. I hear her when I'm awake sometimes, and that's even creepier.'

'When was the last time she spoke to you?'

'A couple of days ago. She just said, 'Astaroth'. I wish I knew—'

I interrupt myself and sit up suddenly. 'This is going to sound crazy, but will you come with me to Astaroth?'

He bursts into laughter and I look at him, confused.

'You're something else, Supernova. You really want to go back there?' he asks.

'Yes. I want to check out that castle. Layla said you can only get in if you have shadow powers – and you do!'

'So you wanna get me in trouble?'

'No, but . . .'

He smirks. 'Of course I'll go. I wanna know why my parents did what they did and I think those answers are in the castle too. Despite what you and everybody else thinks, there is a good reason for their actions.'

I pull a face. 'Like what?'

He shrugs. 'All they would tell me is that it was to protect me and everyone in the kingdom. But they couldn't risk the queen getting wind of it. Kinda sucks when your own parents don't trust you.'

'And you believe them?' I ask, raising an eyebrow.

He gives me a side look. 'Anyway, there's this book that I want to look at too. I think it gives you powers or something.'

'What?!'

He shushes me and I clap my hand over my mouth. The rain lets up and I look around and notice Lux and Nox have disappeared. I can faintly hear their voices in my head, talking to Shade. Well, more like arguing. From the sounds of it, it's about taming again. I focus back on my own conversation.

'I saw my mum with it in a strange room,' Miles continues quietly. 'When she opened it, this dome of light engulfed her. There's probably a bunch of other stuff in there. I can sneak out at any point, but how are you gonna convince your parents?' he says.

'I'll figure something out, but we're going. As soon as possible.'

Something tells me this isn't something Mum and Dad will agree to. I've already broken their trust once by going to Astaroth, and my stomach churns thinking about doing it again. But this is all to keep us safe and find answers.

'Then we meet just before sky connect inside the main gate. Is that still one of the times when the tamers go on a perimeter run?' he asks.

'Pretty much, yeah,' I confirm.

'Then that's when we'll escape. Just like old times,' Miles whispers with a toothy smile.

'You mean when Shade almost killed us?'

His head tilts to the side. 'Fair point. Not the best memory to think of,' he says, but his smile doesn't falter. He stands up and I give him his jacket back.

'Thanks.' I smile. 'By the way, don't you wear anything else other than black?'

'What? You don't think this looks cool on me?'

I shrug. 'You look good, I guess. Just wear something bright every once in a while. Spice it up a bit.'

'Nah, I like black,' he smirks. 'Anyway, catch you later, Supernova! Don't be late!'

'See ya, Prince of Darkness!' I yell back.

He laughs, jumps on Shade's back and rides into the night leaving me to my thoughts.


I decide against telling Mum and Dad. Is it the smartest decision? Definitely not, but there's no way they'd let me go. Anyway, right now all of their focus is on finding out who the traitor is, so it's best I handle this. For them and for me.

I hurry and pack my backpack with water, my digital reader and scream spray, just in case. I stuff the backpack under my bed and dive on to it as my door clicks open.

'Mimi?'

I sigh in relief, seeing Lucas. 'I thought you were with Mum making dumplings for dinner. Are you OK?'

He stands by the door, clutching a toy, which I recognise as *my* favourite old red panda bear with wings and three little horns poking from his head. Willis. I gave him to Lucas ages ago when he had trouble sleeping and he grew attached to him like I did. Not gonna lie, I've been missing Willis lately.

He hands the toy to me. 'Willis will protect you from the nightmares, Mimi.'

I open my arms and give him a big hug. 'Thanks Lu-Lu.'

'You can sleep in my room too. I'll pre-tect you from the monsters.'

'Thanks. I should be OK tonight.' I give him another squeeze and he gives me a big smile.

'I'm gonna go play now, Mimi. The dumplings are almost ready.'

'OK, Lu-Lu. See you at dinner.' *That pipsqueak can be so sweet sometimes.*

Something taps against my window and I instantly recognise the sound of a holobot trying to get in. I quickly open the window and let it in.

'You have a call from Tyler-James Johnson. Do you wish to accept it?' the robot voice crackles.

'Yes,' I say.

It opens its beak and there's TJ sitting on my floor.

'What's up?' he chirps, immediately putting a smile on my face.

'I'm good, but there's been a lot going on,' I say, sitting down on the floor with him, and at the same time scooting the backpack further under my bed.

'The Reaper King and the Elite again?'

'Yep.'

TJ huffs and rests his hands on his head. 'You know what? That guy is like that final boss at the end of a game that has like a thousand HP. Geez.'

His serious face makes me burst into laughter.

'That's literally the best example,' I snigger. Perfect actually. Only TJ could make a scary situation that funny.

'And what about Elite boy? He still hanging around? If he messes with you, I know you can handle yourself, but I'll smack him up,' he adds, eyeing me with suspicion.

'You're actually too much,' I laugh, waving my hand at him.

'Well, not gonna lie, your judgement kinda goes down whenever Elite boy is around.'

My jaw drops. 'No, it doesn't.'

'Yeah, it definitely does.'

My smile falters and I draw my knees to my chest, hesitating to say the next thing. It'd be good to have an extra person know where I'm going in case something goes wrong. TJ raises an eyebrow at my sudden silence.

'So . . . Miles says there's a magical book in Astaroth. We're gonna go check it out.'

TJ throws his hands up. 'Really Mia? No. Don't go running off with the reason our parents were parent-napped in the first place. The VERY reason we had to travel across the Nightmare Plains with scary red-cloaked gutterslugs after us for like three days. You're asking for trouble!'

'But what if there IS something there. Like *why* the Reaper King keeps trying to come back, or possibly a way to—' I cut myself off. I can't tell him about the traitor. Not yet.

*'We think it's a good idea too,'* Nox intervenes. *'This could be vital information.'*

'And when we get back with it, they'll see how it's helped them,' I say. Kinda.

'I don't know, guys,' TJ says. 'What if you get ambushed?'

'Then we run. I'm not silly. I know when to run and when to fight.'

He doesn't look convinced and I don't know whether to feel hurt, annoyed, or both.

'Fine, but I'm leaving the holobot with you. Send it as soon as you get back home to let me know you're safe,' he says. 'I'm kinda ... borrowing it, so I'll definitely need it back, and if I haven't heard anything by this time tomorrow, I'm snitching.'

'Fine, deal. I'm leaving a note for Mum and Dad anyway.'

'Good. Well, I guess you should get some sleep then. But remember to send that bot back, OK?'

'I will. I promise. Night, TJ.'

'Night, Mia. Night, Lux and Nox.'

*'Goodnight.'*

The hologram switches off and I hide the small holobot next to my backpack. I head downstairs with Lux and Nox for dinner and afterwards climb into bed and close my eyes.

My alarm vibrates and I wave my hand, silencing it. I whip off the covers, fully dressed, wide-eyed and ready to go. I sit up and notice Lux and Nox staring at me. Hard.

'What is it?' I ask.

'*Young one. An hour ago you got up while still sleeping and wrote something in your journal,*' Nox says, pointing his horn to my drawer.

'I did what?'

I grab my nightmare journal and flick through the pages to the latest entry. My fingers tremble, and my heart skips a beat. A single sentence is written in the middle of the page:

Please find me.

# CHAPTER SIXTEEN

'Here goes nothing.'

My back presses against the cold brick wall and my feet hang a little off the ledge. Lux and Nox stay quiet below so I can concentrate and resist the urge to look down. The freezing wind pierces through my clothes and pushes me, coaxing me to go back inside. *You've done this before, you can do it again. You got this, girl . . .* I keep my chin up, ignoring the niggle of fear and guilt creeping in. I slide one wobbly leg after the other across the ledge, away from my bedroom window. *One, two, three. One, two, three.*

Maybe I should have risked going through the front door. The further I go, the more the cold of the wall burns my palms, and the fresh smell of crisp clean air turns heavy and damp. Rain's coming. Shoot. I hold my breath sliding past Mum and Dad's bedroom. I peek in and they're both in bed, with Bolt curled up on the floor by the door. Spike must be sleeping downstairs. *Good thing we did go out the window then.* I reach the drain pipe and sigh. *Made it.*

'Well done, Mouse!'

I smile at Lux and slide down to safety, high-fiving their horns. We race down the road until we're far enough from the house and a bright flash engulfs my umbra. They walk towards me in their adult form, I jump on Lux's back and we disappear into the night.

We slow down reaching the gate. Of course, it's guarded. Rosé and Peter lean against the wall, talking. I scrunch my nose when they start kissing. *Ya nasties...*

'Psst.' I turn my head to see Miles across the way, hidden in a bush. He grins and the red eyes of Shade are just about visible within the purple leaves. We sneak over and crouch in the bush beside them.

'So, how shall we do this?' Miles asks.

I look ahead at the two tamers again. They're so engrossed in each other that anyone could enter or attack the city and they wouldn't even know. *The muppets.* If Jada was on patrol this would be ten times harder. Could Rosé or Peter be the traitor?

'We go when they open the gates for the perimeter run,' I say.

The only thing Peter and Rosé are vigilant about right now is each other. We should be able to slip right past when they go out.

I crouch down as the gate opens up. Oblivious to our presence, Rosé and Peter head out on their umbra and we make our move. We dash through the gate before it closes, making it with plenty of time to spare.

'Nice,' Miles says. He gives me a toothy grin and I can't help but smile back, bumping fists with him.

Miles leads the way riding on Shade's back across the plains while I ride on Lux. Despite the guilt, I can't control the strange happiness in the pit of my stomach. Just seeing Miles's grin, and the look he gave me just now, reminds me of old times. But underneath, there's a feeling of dread. What are we gonna find in that castle? What is that woman trying to tell me? The niggle of fear in the back of my mind warns me to stay alert. We're about to go into the den of nightmares.

A few hours later we arrive at the dark, abandoned city and it's just as intimidating the second time. I walk through the gates with Lux and Nox by my side, fully alert. Every twig drop, crack of the wind and bang of a door makes me almost jump outta my skin. My fingers fidget by my thigh strap where my bo staff sits.

Miles hops off Shade. His hands sits casually in his pocket and he strolls ahead like we aren't in one of the most dangerous places in the kingdom.

'If you get scared you can stay close to me,' Miles says.

My eyebrow twitches at his overly smug face. He offers his hand but I slap it away.

I hear a light chuckle in my mind and Shade passes by with a side glance. I know she can't hear my thoughts like Lux and Nox, but still ... It's weird hearing her voice sometimes. I hadn't even realised she was behind me.

We head under a small bridge and Miles takes us down a random alley. Almost making a point of not going down the one that has his drawing of me on the wall. We keep a healthy distance between us but I remain vigilant at all times. Those eight-legged monsters could be lurking around any corner.

'I guess you really can see in the dark,' I murmur, tripping over a crack in the pavement.

'Perks of the king's powers,' Miles calls back.

'Don't sound too happy about it,' I mutter. He looks back and arches an eyebrow, but I shrug in response.

Our footsteps echo along the cobbled path and we pass the fountain where I first met Layla.

'So, did you have other friends when you lived here?' I ask.

'Nah, only Layla. There wasn't any other kids,' he says.

'You're telling me that none of the Elite had kids,' I ask, tilting my head.

'Nope.'

*Geez.* It must have been so lonely here.

A long stony path stretches out before us and we slow to a stop. Weeds pop out of the cracks and red-eyed bats screech and flap away overhead. A warning to leave. The tiny hairs on my arms shoot up at the sight of the giant castle at the very end. The tall glass windows reflect the moonlight, making the castle look like it has lots of creepy eyes.

Miles ushers me up the steps.

'Whose castle is this anyway?' I ask.

He looks back with a solemn look in his eyes, then he says three words that make my heart stop beating. 'The Reaper King's.'

I halt in my tracks.

'You OK?' Miles asks. He walks back to me, offering his hand again.

'I'm OK,' I say, marching past him. 'I was just a little shocked.'

*What the flip have I got myself into?*

I reach the doors and Miles stands beside me. He shakes his arms and stretches out his hands, curling his fingers like he's gripping a ball of air. Darkness swirls around him and shadows appear out of nowhere, crawling along his arms and hands. His lips part, revealing sharp teeth. His eyes blacken, and my fingers clench around my staff in horror. Miles yells, thrusting the shadows forward against the doors. Slowly but surely they creak open.

Miles lowers his hands and looks like himself again. 'Welcome to the king's old home,' he says, breathing heavily as the shadows vanish.

'Are you OK?' I ask.

'Yep. Come on.'

He walks inside without a care in the world, and Shade swiftly follows. I share a suspicious glance with Lux and Nox, but we enter too.

The clicking of our shoes echoes against the stone floor, loudly announcing our presence. *So much for being discreet.*

Along the walls, lots of moving portraits hang. Each

depicts the same creepy, bony creature: the Reaper King. I glare at all of them and throw a rock at the last one of him on a throne. Eat mud, jerk.

Miles walks over to a wall. Hundreds of keys, all different sizes, hang from it. He presses his palm against a big silver one and it sinks back into the wall. I suppress a gasp as the whole wall slides away, revealing an entrance. I take a few steps forward to get a better look. A secret staircase reveals itself, leading down to somewhere that can't be good.

'I saw my mum do it,' Miles says over his shoulder.

'What's down there?' I ask, suspiciously.

'You'll see. Come on.' He makes his way to the bottom with Shade but my feet stay planted.

'If there's someone down there, Miles . . .' I warn.

'There's not.'

His chuckle echoes from down the stairs. *There better not be, you clown, or you're the first I'm taking out.*

I give Lux and Nox one last look and we follow Miles and Shade down the stone stairs. I stick close to the walls with one hand on my staff. Well prepared to fight anybody who tries to jump me and my umbra.

What we find at the bottom surprises us all. Unlike upstairs, the room greets us with a warm glow. The floor is plush with a thick red carpet and the walls are painted a dark blue.

Something glints in the corner of my eye. A closer look reveals this to be a small shrine. My fingers brush the blue-cloth table. Above it, the still image of a beautiful woman with long braids tied up in two bunches smiles back at me. Her smile shines bright as the sun and even in the portrait her brown skin glows, but my eyebrows furrow. Despite the smile, something is oddly unnerving about the portrait. My heart jerks like it's familiar somehow. Maybe this is what Mum means by deja vu. The feeling of already having experienced something you're supposedly seeing for the first time.

'We don't know who she is,' Miles says, suddenly beside me. I almost punch him, but stop myself in time.

'Geez, don't surprise me like that,' I mutter, and he jigs his eyebrows at me.

'Sorry, didn't think you were so jumpy,' he muses, then jerks his chin up at the picture. 'She's pretty though, right?'

I roll my eyes and my attention shifts to the little lanterns on the table. Small crystals glitter around them and a blue star hairclip sits in the centre.

'She must have meant something to the Reaper King if he made the mourning shrine,' Nox says.

'Maybe it's not a "mourning" shrine,' Shade suggests. 'Maybe it's a tribute to her, or a yearning? She could simply be missing.'

I guess she could be right, but if we can find out who this woman is, then maybe we can figure out more about that gutterslug king.

'Hey, Mia, I found something!' Miles calls from the other side of the room. He crouches in front of a huge chest and lifts the lid. A giant waft of dust explodes from inside. He coughs and waves it away.

'Here.' He pulls out a small book and hands it to me. 'I think this is what Mum was hiding.'

'*That's* the book?' I ask, puzzled.

He shakes his head and points at it. 'Remember, it only looks like a book. It does this weird hologram thing. Open it. You'll see.'

He sits on the carpet next to me and my hand stays firmly on the book. I watch his face for any sign of a trick. He rolls his eyes and offers out his hand. 'I can open it if you want.'

*Here goes nothing.* I take a deep breath and open the book. A bright light bursts from inside, encasing us in a white glowing dome. I jump to my feet as walls and chains stretch around us. The whole world changes, transporting us somewhere new. The ceilings are high and completely black. The plush red carpet that was once beneath us is now hard steel, like we're in a strange sort of tank. *Why does this feel familiar?*

I hear a groan behind us. I spin around, shielding my eyes as another bright light engulfs our faces. I peek just below my arm and see a woman glowing before us. Her eyes flash gold like the sun over Stella, but long chains of light trap her wrists to the wall, as if they were made of metal itself. The hairs rise on the back of my neck as I instantly recognise her. It's the woman from the shrine.

*'Katiya … I'm tired'* Her voice shakes.

*Katiya? As in the queen? Why is she talking to the queen?*

I look at Miles, who is just as shocked.

*'It's been decades, let me rest. He won't stop until I'm freed,'* the chained woman says. *'I'm tired, so tired …'*

'Do you think she can hear us?' Miles whispers.

'Don't know,' I whisper back. *But there's one way to find out.*

'Hello?'

My voice bounces off the walls and her head jerks up.

'Who's there?'

Miles yanks me behind him and I almost trip. Her gold eyes bore straight into mine and I step out from behind Miles. *That voice . . .*

'What happened to you?' I ask. *I know that voice.*

'I'm trapped. I want to get out but if I do, the cities will fall . . . I'm running out of strength. I'm so tired.'

'Young one . . .' Nox's words float in my mind but he sounds far away and I realise he's nowhere in sight.

The woman's eyes pin me to the spot and my whole body feels heavy, as if my energy is being sapped away. *What's this feeling? Is she doing this to me?*

I look down and my body glows all over, just like her. The world around me fades to black. Miles disappears and I'm left with this woman. Alone.

'What did you just do? Who are you?' I ask.

'Ria . . .' the woman mutters, but it's like every word she speaks drains her more. 'But you know me. At least you know my voice.'

It feels like time itself slows down as her words echo

in my mind. My knees buckle but somehow I manage to stay on my feet. All this time, it's been *her*.

*Ria* . . . Her once lovely face looks sunken, like all the life is being sucked out of her. Her golden eyes reflect mine, but I don't know where to look.

'But why?' I ask, finding my voice again. 'And how? *Who exactly* are you?'

She looks at me and her lips part, trembling. My heart thumps louder and louder, beating in my ears.

*'I'm a lightcaster and a founder of Lunis.'*

# Chapter Seventeen

Thousands of thoughts race through my head.

'I don't understand. Are you real? Or is this just a weird dream? Why did you mention Queen Katiya? Did she do this to you?' I ask, trying to make sense of it all. Maybe this is all just another dream.

She jerks forward but the chains of light yank her back.

'You're like me. It's why I've been able to reach out to you. All lightcasters are connected. He is one too. He was once human, like you … And he won't stop until I'm free, but don't let any of them take you.'

'Don't let who take me? The queen?' I ask.

'Katiya, my brother, everyone. Keep your powers to yourself. Don't let anyone exploit them. Tell that boy too, your friend. I sense my brother in him. The legend is coming true and it cannot be stopped.'

Does she mean Miles?

'Wait, slow down. Who is your brother?' My brain feels ready to explode and I rub the sides of my head.

*You have a book that talks about the legends of the lightcasters, am I correct?* she asks.

'Yeah, at home.'

*Show me.*

I blink at her. 'It's ... It's at home.' I repeat.

She jerks against the chains of light that shackle her again. *We are communicating in your mind right now. You control more than you think. Imagine the book in your hands and will it to you.*

'Can I imagine you without the shackles?' I ask, but she shakes her head.

*Sadly not. I can only appear to you in my current state. That's why I only ever used my voice to speak to you. Your mind cannot affect me. It can only push me out, should you wish.*

'And it was you, wasn't it? The one who wrote all those nightmare journal entries,' I ask. That's why this place feels so familiar. I remember something like this described in one of the entries.

Ria grimaces, but nods. *I needed you to find me. I'm sorry I scared you,* she says. *Now focus on the book ...*

345

Every breath she takes sounds painful, but I do as she says and close my eyes. I imagine the book from Dad's office, the weight of it pressed against my palms and the way it looks with the notes inside. The brown cover and tiny note that had the title written on the front is as clear as stars.

'*There,*' Ria says.

My eyes flutter open and a book rests in my hands.

'How is this possible?' I mutter.

'*Open it.*'

I turn the pages and stop somewhere randomly in the middle. Her tired eyes scan it.

'*This is Arien's hand.*'

'Arien? As in one of the other founders of Lunis?' I ask, and the way her eyes shift to mine sends a nervous chill down my spine. So, *he's* the last one.

'*Yes. Your ancestor.*'

My body suddenly jerks back and the air rattles. The world around us morphs from black to white.

'Wait, what's happening?' I yell.

The book vanishes from my hands and my arms flail in the empty space around me.

'*It's OK. It's just the holoport breaking. It is only stable for a short amount of time.*'

'But I have more questions!'

*Just beware of my brother and Katiya. They believe they're doing the right thing, but they're wrong. Don't let them use you. Use your powers on that book! Learn the truth about who you are!*

'But who's your brother?' I shout.

Her face turns solemn. *He's the one you call the Reaper King.*

I reach out to her but the world around us collapses and she fades to black. 'Wait!'

I'm sucked into the darkness like a vacuum and spat out into nothingness. My body floats, just like the way it felt in the Spirit Plain. Empty.

A white light rushes towards me and I'm thrown back against a plush red carpet. The walls of the castle return and the gentle hue of the fading light shines on Miles's frowning face.

'You good? What happened? Everything went dark for me, then I was suddenly back here, but you were still frozen,' he says.

I scratch the back of my head, disorientated. Worry is written on the faces of Nox and Lux, and Nox brushes his snout against my cheek.

347

'We couldn't reach you,' he says.

'I was speaking to a woman. The same one you saw, Miles. Her name's Ria.' I try to catch my breath. 'She's trapped somewhere, but that's not all.' I juggle my thoughts, making sure what I'm about to say is accurate.

'What is it, Mouse?'

'She's the one who's been talking to me all this time, and she's one of the founders of Lunis.'

'So, she is a lightcaster. We were worried, young one. Our connection was blocked,' Nox says.

'I was about to destroy that thing, but Nox stopped me,' Lux gruffs.

I smile at him, but he harrumphs, looking the other way. 'Don't get a big head, tiny mouse. I was only a little concerned.'

'Geez, what is this thing?' Miles says.

He shakes the book upside-down before closing it. 'I thought it was some magical book that gave you powers, but it was like we had actually been teleported somewhere. She actually spoke to us.'

'She did. It wasn't a holographic illusion.' My eyes fall back to the book. 'She called it a holoport.'

My throat runs dry at the thought of her. Trapped

like a prisoner somewhere. Then it hits me like a lightning bolt.

'We have to go. NOW.' I scramble to my feet. *It's her!* All of this has always been about *her.*

Miles stands up and raises his eyebrow. 'What's the sudden rush?'

'Just before she disappeared, she said that the Reaper King was her brother. He wants to free her. That's what all this is about and somehow the queen is involved. We have to tell Mum and Dad right now.'

'Wait!' Miles brushes past me and blocks my path. Shade bares her teeth and Lux and Nox growl. Their shadowy bodies bristle, ready to fight.

'Wait a second. You can't just tell them everything,' he says.

'Er . . . yes I can.' I go to move left but he blocks me again. 'What are you doing? Move.'

'If you tell your parents *everything* then they'll know we were here and I'll be locked up. We need a story.'

I look him up and down. You've gotta be kidding me. 'Move.'

'No.'

He stands his ground, towering over me. His dark

349

eyes bore coldly into mine and black shadows waft from his body.

'If you think I'm gonna keep all this from them, you can think again.' I step towards him so close his breath lightly brushes against my face. 'I'm telling them about this book and about Ria. End of.'

I try to sidestep him again, but he gets in my way once more, and I barely hold back a growl. He clocks my fingers resting on my staff and a crooked smile spreads across his face. He steps back, letting me pass.

*Let's go, guys.*

# CHAPTER EIGHTEEN

The journey back to Nubis feels flat in comparison to the way out. Miles and I barely speak to each other but at least we're gonna do the right thing. The closer we get home, the more the nerves pile up in my stomach. I still don't know what to believe about this situation with Ria, but one thing's for certain – she's the voice that's been helping me so far and I want to return the favour.

We slow down at the front door of my house and I slide off Nox's back. Miles jumps off Shade and joins me.

'You ready?' I ask him.

'It's now or never, I guess.'

I walk inside, slip off my shoes and quietly close the door behind us. I head into the living room, where Mum, Dad and Lucas are laughing together. They're sitting on the floor looking at a book together. Lux and Nox follow close behind but I gesture to Miles to stay hidden.

'Morning,' I greet.

'Morning,' Mum says.

I glance over to see what they're all looking at and it's another photo album – one filled with pictures of me and Lucas. I shake my head at the one where baby Lucas is tugging at my hair, and smile at another where we're both sleeping but I'm on the floor holding his small hand through the bars of his crib.

'I'm so tiny . . .' Lucas whispers. *You still are, mate . . .*

'You two were the cutest babies,' Dad says, patting the space beside him. My stomach does flips and I sit down uncomfortably. Across from me, golden eyes burn holes into me. Spike and Bolt are staring so hard it makes me almost gulp. *Shoot! They know! Did they hear the front door?*

*'They probably sensed the mutt in the hallway, but if they guessed our plans it appears they didn't snitch,'* Lux says.

*'Probably giving us a chance to come clean first,'* Nox adds.

My hands start to turn clammy but the thought that

Miles is in the hallway with Shade stays centre in my mind. I have to tell them now.

I clear my throat. 'Mum, Dad. I have to tell you something.' The cue I agreed with Miles.

'What is it, honey?' Mum asks, then she and Dad stand up as Miles enters with Shade.

'What's going on?' Dad says. I wince at his tone.

'We went to Astaroth.' My voice is barely above a whisper.

Mum and Dad freeze and look at each other, and even Lucas recognises the serious turn things have taken.

'And?' asks Mum. The calmness in her voice sets my teeth on edge.

I close my eyes and take a deep breath. 'I know I should have told you first but I did leave a note, and it was all my idea—'

'No, it was my idea,' Miles interrupts. 'But we've found out why the Reaper King wants to come back.'

Mum presses her fingers against her head. The silence and the look she gives consumes me with guilt.

'Mia, you made a promise to us. Now, you break your word, *and* with someone whose actions are still under question?' The tone in Dad's voice makes me want to sink through the floor.

'I knew you wouldn't let me go, and you and Mum have enough on your plate already,' I say, stumbling over my words. 'I wanted to save time. And now we have answers.'

'Carry on,' Dad mutters, but the warning is clear in his voice. If what we say next isn't good enough, I have no idea what the consequences will be.

'We went to the castle and Miles showed me this secret basement where his mum used to go,' I begin.

'Every month, my mum would go to the basement and open this book that would engulf her in a weird sort of light, so I wanted to see what it was,' Miles adds.

'We found this strange shrine to a woman, and the book. But it wasn't actually a book. It was a thing called a holoport and it transported us somewhere,' I say.

Both Mum and Dad stay quiet, so I continue. 'It was like a holding room, or a tank, but I recognised it from a description in my nightmare journal. The woman from the shrine was there. She was chained to the wall by this light, somehow, and was asking for help. Her name is Ria and she's the one who's been talking to me.' I clear my throat and stare directly at Mum and Dad. 'She's a lightcaster and one of the founders of Lunis, and ... she's also the Reaper King's sister.'

'What!' Mum screeches and I almost leap outta my skin.

'She told me that all lightcasters are connected and that the Reaper King won't stop until she is free, and ...' I trail off, finally out of energy.

*'It looks like Queen Katiya has her captured somewhere. She warned Mia not to let the queen or anyone take her,'* Nox finishes for me, reading my thoughts. I smile in gratitude.

'I'm sorry we went behind your back, but if what Ria says is true, we can stop the Reaper King if we find her,' Miles says, stepping forward. 'I really don't know what my parents' plan is, but I think they might have found another way and are going after his sister too. That's what the king wants, to free Ria, but maybe if we do it first, he'll stop.'

'Where's the holoport now?' Mum asks.

'Here,' Miles says, handing her the device.

'Ria also said something about the lightcaster book. She said that it was written and passed down by our ancestor, Arien. He was one of the founders of Lunis too, and all of the information is in that book. My powers should help us understand it,' I say.

'Daniel, can you get the book from the office?' Mum says.

Dad rushes past us but stops in the doorway.

'Look, Mia, I understand why you did this. You've proved time and time again that you are intelligent and strong, but if something had gone wrong, things would be even worse now,' he says. His eyes flick to Miles. 'And you should have been honest with us too. If you had told us your plan we could have gone with you, or sent Bolt or Spike as extra backup. How can we trust you if you don't trust us?'

Miles nods. 'Sorry, sir.'

'I'm really sorry too,' I say.

'Just remember, you're not just responsible for yourself, but also for Lux and Nox,' Mum says.

She's right. They're not invincible . . .

*Do not worry about us, Mouse. We are stronger together. The three of us will always have each other's backs,'* Lux says only to me.

*Thanks guys . . .*

'Do you want a hug, Mimi?' Lucas asks. I nod and he

squeezes me tight. Dad fetches the lightcaster book and when he returns he kisses my head. Mum hugs Miles and whispers something to him that I can't hear, but it makes him hug her harder.

Then she rests the holoport book on the carpet. While the rest of us stand back, Mum flicks it open. Just like before, a giant transparent dome surrounds her and Dad and they freeze in a trancelike state, their minds transported to Ria.

'What are they doing, Mimi?' Lucas whispers.

'They're contacting a woman called Ria,' Miles answers. Lucas tilts his head back and his brown eyes intensely inspect the boy beside me. I rub his back, letting him know that it's OK.

The dome suddenly disappears and Mum and Dad gasp back to life.

'She didn't speak to us but we saw her,' Mum says. Dad glances at the time and stands up.

'Mia, can you take Lucas to school? Miles, go back to Riley's house, pack your things and bring them here. He's supposed to be on town patrol before teaching, but no need to tell him where you've been if you bump into him – leave that to me,' Dad says. 'I need to hold a meeting with some of the tamers about

357

the queen. But for now, you two to keep this quiet. Pretend everything's normal. We don't need the city panicking. Mia, come straight home after your class, OK? Remember what I said.'

Everyone nods and I make sure to send the holobot back to TJ before we all head out.

I drop Lucas off and then go to tamer class in the gymnasium. Everyone is surprisingly quiet.

'Glad you made it on time, Mia,' Rosé says. The saltiness in her tone makes me narrow my eyes. I force my fingers to connect and bow to her in greeting, wondering why she's taking class instead of Riley.

'Hey, Mia, do you know what's going on?' Margaux asks.

'I was hoping you'd know,' I reply.

'The tamers have been acting weird since yesterday,' Elijah says, joining us. 'I saw Jada arguing with some of the guards outside the hold, and Riley's a no-show.'

Why would Jada be arguing with the guard? My heart skips, thinking the worse. *No. She can't be the traitor.*

'OK, guys, gather up,' Rosé calls, bringing our conversation to a halt.

We line up in front of her and our umbra stand behind us. Margaux stands next to me and winks. She playfully budges me and my eyes connect with Elijah, who smiles. *Wow, maybe we are becoming friends.*

'Riley is busy on a mission so I'll be covering your class today,' Rosé informs us.

*A mission?* Dad never mentioned a mission earlier.

'We're going to practise your third transformation forms. The only form in which you and your umbra become one. You all know it's the most difficult and the most powerful form, so let's see how long you can last,' she finishes. 'Let's begin.'

'But I've only done it once before!' I protest.

'Then you obviously need the practice,' she says, almost tauntingly. I give her the dirtiest look I can muster.

Lux snaps his teeth at her and his shadowy fox tail bristles dangerously. I open my mouth, but stop myself. She's not even worth it.

*'That's right, young one. Let it go,'* Nox says.

*'Watch your tone,'* Lux growls and I realise he means Rosé. Her zebra-like umbra picks up on this and flares her bushy tail in response.

Rosé rolls her eyes, but keeps her mouth shut and gestures everyone to begin.

Bursts of bright lights explode in the room as everyone prepares to transform with their umbra. Margaux and Elijah go first. Cocky smiles spread across their faces as their umbra turn into shadows that zap to their bodies. The shadows pulse and blend with the tamers in training. They successfully merge with their umbra and chills run down my spine.

Margaux stands with two baton-like bladed shadow weapons in her hands, and upon closer inspection I realise they're bladed tonfas. Dragon wings sprout from her back too and four horns pop from her head between fluffy ears. Elijah stands taller in shadowy armour, horns also poking from his head, with spiked brass knuckles around his hands.

They make it look flippin' easy.

Lux and Nox gently nudge me. 'Ready to try?' I ask.

I close my eyes and feel a gentle push of energy against my cheeks, where their snouts touch. Like a quiet flame the energy spreads, running along my face, arms and legs. *We got this.*

Warm shadows engulf me as their presence suddenly intensifies and a bright light flashes. Their shadows swarm my body, twirling around my arms and legs until they reach the centre of my heart. A burst of energy pulses through me and my eyes burst open. Their shadows mesh and become a part of me. A shadowy sword forms in one hand, and a shield in the other. Power surges inside of me and I sense and see everything. The tiny cracks of paint on the walls across the room, the faint smell of pine that wafts through the windows. Everyone around me highlighted in gold. I feel it all, fully connected to my umbra.

*'Because we are meant to fight as one,'* Nox says.

*'And because we're the greatest,'* Lux muses.

I spin around and my tail swishes in the wind. I tap the two horns of my head with the back of my hand and jump for joy, wondering why I was ever afraid of doing this. Adrenaline pulses in my veins like electricity, and I backflip. *It feels like I could run for hours, or climb a mountain!*

Elijah raises his fists, inspecting his brass knuckle weapons, and Clara dances around with a spear. My golden eyes flicker to Abigail next, and the gutterslug wields nunchucks. Lastly, Aaron attacks the air with daggers.

'Pretty good, well done. Now we'll—' Rosé is interrupted as her holophone buzzes. She picks it up and her eyebrows furrow. When she hangs up she still looks worried. 'Guys, sorry, but we gotta cut this lesson short. There's an emergency tamer meeting.'

We all transform back to our separate selves and watch Rosé rush out the door with her umbra.

'OK, something is definitely going on,' Margaux says, and as much as I wanna say something, I keep my lips sealed.

I walk out of class with Lux and Nox. We head towards the Missing Tree, and the paper crescent moons dangling from house and shop windows remind me about the Lunar Lantern Festival tomorrow. Things have been so hectic that I've lost all track of time.

By the Missing Tree, I meet Miles carrying two bags.

'Hey, is that all of your stuff?' I ask.

'Yeah. Riley wasn't even there. Left a note saying he had to go on a mission with Bently.' He plonks the bags on the ground. 'Your mum and dad are at the tamer meeting. Your dad told me to tell you "he'll figure out Nox's attacker today".'

My breath hitches in my throat. Does that mean he's going to confront all the tamers?

I really want to know what happens. A large shadow

flies over our heads and I narrow my eyes at the sky. Isn't that Jada and Ruby? Aren't they supposed to be at the tamer meeting?

*'They're probably heading there now,'* Nox says. But ... I recognise the direction that they came from and my heart sinks. The direction of the hold.

'Hey, guys!' A voice yells and we turn to see Layla running towards us. 'Jada said I could have a free day exploring as she had to rush out. Apparently your dad gave permission or something. Wanna play a game or something? Long time no see, Miles.'

She stops a few metres away and winks at him.

'Can't. I'm literally grounded. I have to get home or Spike will come after me,' I say, jerking my thumb towards the direction of my house.

'Come on!' she whines, then stops and changes tack. 'By the way, did you ever find the traitor?'

'Traitor ...?' Miles quirks an eyebrow at me.

'Well? *Did* you?' Layla presses.

'Not yet, but we're close. Thanks for the tip,' I say and she high-fives me.

'Anytime you wanna spar, hit me up. I'll happily give you more information if you win,' she muses, giving Miles a strange look.

'Well . . . I guess we could have a quick match outside my house,' I say, changing my mind.

'I don't think this is a good idea,' Miles says as we stand outside my house. I ignore him.

'What kind of sparring do you want to do? No cheating this time,' I say, and Layla's eyes light up.

'The game is this. If I grab you with both hands, I win. You win if you can get me to fall on my butt.'

'Sure.' Sounds easy enough. 'What's the prize?'

Layla taps her lip, pacing back and forth, and I stare at her with a raised eyebrow as she stops.

'How about if I win, you gotta take me to see my friends in the cave?' she suggests.

'I can't promise, but sure. I'll try,' I say.

A grin crawls along her face. 'OK, cool. And if you win, I'll tell you something about good ol' Miles over there.'

'Wait, wha—' Miles starts to protest.

'Three-two-one, GO!' Layla yells, cutting him off.

She springs off her feet and I gasp, backflipping away, batting my staff at her as her hands go to grab me. Before I can think, she's on the move again. I block her left, right and centre, thrusting my hand forward, pushing her back.

'Woah! That's a new one.'

I jerk my hand out again and feel my powers stirring. I feel invigorated. This time I know I'm fully in control of it. My light flashes and smacks against her, but she grinds her feet into the ground, unmoving. A devilish smile spreads across her face as she takes one step after the other, pushing against it.

I try harder and the energy bursts out of my palms.

The door behind me swings open and Spike's voice roars, *'Mia, break it up. Time to come inside!'*

I jump at the sound of his voice and my powers vanish. Layla stumbles forward, crashing to the ground.

'Sorry,' I say to both him and Layla.

'Geez, well technically I'm on my stomach, not my butt, so I guess it's a draw,' she muses, standing up. She turns to Spike and bows her head. 'Please forgive us. I begged her to spar because I was lonely. It's my fault.'

I don't blame Spike for looking confused. I'm just as baffled, and she grins at us. Miles just sighs, obviously used to Layla's strange behaviour.

Thankfully, Spike doesn't snitch on us, but after dinner, Dad pulls me aside to chat while Mum asks Miles and Lucas to help her in the kitchen.

I sit beside Dad on the sofa and his eyebrows knit together. 'I'm going to take Riley and Jada in for interrogation during the festival tomorrow.'

'What? Dad—!'

He cuts me off, raising his hand.

'Jada's been caught sneaking off to the hold several times during midnight star hours, and these last few days, Riley has been going missing when he's supposed to be on duty. They're now my top suspects.'

*No, no, no!* 'It can't be Jada. I wouldn't even be alive if it wasn't for her,' I say.

'Then let me ask you something,' Dad says. 'How many times have you actually spoken to Jada in the last month?' My mouth opens and closes. 'Her students have reported that she leaves in a rush after class all the time, and when I confronted her, she made excuses, saying it's about finding out more about the Elite.'

'Maybe she's been trying to get her mum to talk,' I say.

'Then why not report that to the other tamers?' Dad reasons, but I can't agree with his logic. I may have only seen Jada a few times, but that doesn't mean she's guilty! I mean, why would she run those special classes for me, Mikasa, Thomas and Lincoln if she was a traitor? I mean, I can't even think it's Riley – he's such a stickler for the rules. But outta the two of them . . .

'Look Baby-girl, I don't want to believe it either, but I have to look at the facts and some things just aren't adding up,' Dad sighs.

'Do all the tamers know about Ria now?'

'No, I told them about what Layla said about the umbra seeing the attacker though.'

*'Jada and Riley had the most questions, which was interesting,'* Bolt chips in.

But why interrogate them during the Lunar Lantern Festival, I wonder? As if reading my mind, Bolt answers.

*'If the traitor is planning to make a move, what better time than when everyone is busy celebrating, including the tamers,'* he explains.

'And because we don't know who it is, this is the safest thing to do,' Dad says. 'It's complicated, Baby-girl. Technically, I shouldn't imprison either of them without solid evidence, but I can't risk them succeeding in whatever plan they have going on.'

*'A festival would be a good time to do something bad,'* Nox agrees.

'I'd rather find physical proof or catch them in the act, but time is running out,' Dad says. 'If there's anything you think would narrow it down, that'd help.'

I try to think.

'I saw Jada flying from the direction of the hold when you had the tamer meeting,' I say, my heart sinking a little.

*'Yes, she and Ruby were late. They said they were lesson planning,'* Bolt says.

I rack my brains about Riley. 'The weirdest thing I can think of is all the questions Riley kept asking me when you were speaking to Miles after we had been to the hold.' I hum, trying to think back. 'He did seem . . . worried, but that's it really. I also saw him on a sleep patrol with Bently.'

'A sleep patrol? When was that?' he asks.

'Umm – the night I snuck out with Miles,' I tell him.

'OK. That's great information.' A new look of determination strikes his face. He reaches over and hugs me tight. 'Mia, no matter what happens. Just know that I'm proud of you.'

I freeze at his words and a soft smile is on his face, but a new expression that I can't read is in his eyes. Worry?

'I'm proud of you too, Dad,' I say back. His eyes widen for a second before he smiles again and holds me tight.

We talk for a bit longer and then I head upstairs to sleep, with Lux and Nox following. I lie down in bed when someone knocks at the door and it clicks open. Mum walks in and the strong whiff of chocolate catches my nose before I see the mug in her hand.

'Hey darling. I got you a hot chocolate. Did your dad fill you in on everything?'

'Yeah … Thank you.' I sit up, accepting the hot chocolate with a smile. It's just how I like it with the little marshmallows and honeycomb cream.

I take a sip, but my smile falls. 'Mum, do you really think Jada could be the traitor?'

She sighs and leans against the wall. 'Honestly, I don't know, darling. My heart doesn't want to believe it, but she has been going to the hold a lot. Maybe she's been visiting her mum, though I don't know why she wouldn't have told us.'

'OK,' I murmur, staring down at the hot chocolate, enjoying the warmth of the mug in my hands.

'Stay on guard tomorrow, just in case.' She kisses my head and I nod.

'Night, Mum.'

'Goodnight, darling.'

When the door clicks shut again, I turn to Lux and Nox.

'Are you guys OK?' I ask.

*'Of course. We were just reflecting on events thus far. How are you, young one?'* Nox says.

'I'm OK – just wanted to check in with you guys. A lot seems to be happening all at once.'

*'We get it,'* Lux says.

*'But you have us, so you don't have to handle it alone,'* Nox adds.

I stare down at the hot chocolate and my chest tightens. 'It just feels like something's gonna happen any time now, doesn't it?'

I chew my lip and feel a horn conk me on my head.

'Hey!' I hiss, rubbing the spot. Lux chuckles.

*'Whatever happens, we'll get through it together,'* he says.

'Yeah, you guys are right. Thanks.'


I'm flicking through my reader in my pyjamas when TJ's robot bird holobot comes through. I jump up, quickly accepting the call and TJ sits on the floor in my room. A big grin is plastered on his face and I can't help but feel happy to see him.

'So, what happened in Astaroth?' he asks.

'Are you alone?' I ask.

He raises an eyebrow, but nods. 'Yeah, I am.'

I tap my ear and nod to the side and TJ laughs. 'No one can hear, Mia. It's just me. What's going on?'

I rise to my feet and pace the room. How do I word this? 'Have you seen anything weird at the castle since you've been staying there? Like a huge tank or . . .'

'No, why?' He stands too, and his eyebrows furrow. 'What's going on?'

My hands shake and I rest them on my head. 'When Miles and I went to the Reaper King's castle in Astaroth we found this book thing that transported us to a strange tank. There was this woman and, long story short, she says she's the Reaper King's sister, and I believe her. She's a lightcaster, but she's trapped somewhere and I think she might be in Stella. She warned me that . . . the queen can't be trusted.'

'Woah, what?' He stares me dead in my eyes. 'Are you serious?'

'Shhh, not so loud!' I shush, but I can tell from his eyes that he doesn't want to believe it.

'Do you even know what you're saying? What do you mean the queen can't be trusted? How do you know that woman was telling you the truth? How can the Reaper King have a sister? He isn't even human.'

'TJ, I saw her chained up and trapped in a room. She mentioned Queen Katiya's name before even seeing me. She told me I can translate the lightcaster book with my powers. Ria said lightcasters are all connected so—'

'So, the Reaper King could be one too,' TJ interrupts.

'Exactly. There's a telepathic link, just like with the umbra. Lucas too.'

TJ falls silent and slumps to the floor. He throws his head in his hands, staring at the floor. I don't say a word, and let everything sink in. After a moment, he finally looks up and our eyes connect. A sea of emotions rushes through his and I crouch down in front of him.

'Mia. This is big.'

'I know,' I say, narrowing my eyes. 'The queen has a lightcaster imprisoned.'

TJ closes his eyes and rubs his temples. 'Have you told your parents?'

'Yeah. It's just a lot, and we're trying to piece

everything together.'

'Geez ... OK, OK. Just be safe. All right? I'll ... I'll try and see what I can find out on my end.'

'TJ, you don't have to—'

'I do.' I almost make a joke when our eyes meet again, but his seriousness throws me off.

'If you need me, just call. Keep the holobot for now. I'll do what I can to find out about Ria and the queen on my end.'

'OK.'

'I mean it, Mia. Be careful.'

'I will.' I say. We wave goodbye and the hologram cuts off. I fall back on my butt, sighing at the ceiling. *What the flip is going to happen tomorrow?*

There are two knocks at the door and I call at the person to come in. It slowly pushes open, revealing a sleepy Lucas. His favourite dragon umbra plush is tucked under his arm with its twin tails dragging along the floor.

'What is it, Lu-Lu?' I whisper, wondering why he's out of bed at this hour. He should've been sleeping ages ago. 'Did you have a nightmare about the scary man?'

He shakes his head and yawns. 'I'm here to pretect you from the night monsters, Mimi.'

I raise an eyebrow, but before I can say anything he climbs on to my bed and snuggles in. 'Don't worry. You won't get nightmares. Me, Willis and Timmy will shoo them away,' he says, pulling my old bear Willis into a hug along with his dragon. He yawns again. 'And Lux and Nox are here too. We'll pretect each other.'

A bemused look appears on Lux's face as he rests his head on Nox's back, the two of them curled up on the floor. I climb into bed too and run my fingers through Lucas's curly locks. My heart tugs. No matter what happens tomorrow, I'll protect him.

'We'll be OK,' I whisper, but there's no response. Instead, light snores sound beside me.

I lie back and close my eyes, hugging Lucas and the teddies tight.

# CHAPTER NINETEEN

Today I'm supposed to act like everything's normal for the festival this afternoon. But I can't sit and do nothing. I won't. Not while the Elite could make an escape attempt at any moment.

Maybe translating the lightcaster book will help. It will at least help me feel like I'm doing *something*. I gotta get to Mum's lab too, and see if my powers will work on Samuel as well.

But first, I have to convince Mum and Dad that everything is fine. I tie a hoodie around my waist and leave the house with Mum, Dad, and Lucas. Outside, music booms and people cheer. The Lunar Lantern Festival is a celebration that combines the lantern festival previously held in Lunavale and the light festival we used to hold in Nubis. Everyone decided to join the two when Lunavale fell to the Darkness.

The air is rich with the smell of sweets and lavender. Mixed with the usual stalls in the marketplace are games and activities, and neon lanterns and paper boats hang from shop stalls. Children run around with their parents, everyone happy, celebrating. The whole city bursts with even more colour, from the moon decorations that dangle on walls and houses to the glitter confetti lining the pavement.

Lucas playfully swings between Mum and Dad's hands. Dad wraps his free arm around me, and I chuckle seeing Mikasa and her parents playing at the ball-bucket stall, trying to win a wolf-fox umbra plushie.

'Mia!' I spin around. Behind the food stall, Thomas and Lincoln wave and gesture to special bread art their parents are selling.

'Mum, Dad, can I go say hi to Thomas and Lincoln?'

'Of course, sweetie. We'll be right here,' Mum says, scanning through all the shiny trinkets and jewellery.

'Come on, Lu-Lu.' I offer out my hand and he grabs it.

At the stall, I ogle the bread on the table. All different colours and shapes. 'These look so cool! Did you actually make them?'

'Well, I made most of them with Mum and Dad.

Thomas helped a little bit,' Lincoln says, puffing out his chest.

Thomas slaps him upside the head. 'Hey, I made plenty!' he argues. Lincoln winces and mouths, 'He didn't,' behind Thomas's back.

'Mimi, can I have one?' Lucas asks. I put some tokens on the table and point at the bread.

'I'll take five mini crescent-moon breads,' I say and the boys look at each other with a grin.

'Of course, thanks!' they say in unison.

I pass Lucas a moon bread and he cheers, nibbling on it. He hums with enjoyment and takes my hand again. I'm glad I can make him happy with something so simple when so much of his childhood has been tainted by the Reaper King. I wave goodbye to the twins and look around. I've gotta think of a way to get to the lab.

No one seems to know a thing about what's going on with the tamers. We head back to Mum and I spot Layla, Miles and Jada by the giant lanterns. My heart leaps, seeing Jada. *Dad must be taking Riley in for questioning first!* They wave me over and Mum takes Lucas's hand. She gives me the nod and I'm off like a bullet.

'Remember what I said,' she calls after me and I do

a front handspring, bouncing off the ground with a thumbs-up.

I catch a glimpse of Dad leaving the festival with Bolt. He's about to find Riley and take him in for interrogation. I chew the inside of my cheek and try to ignore the nerves that well in my gut.

'Hey, Mia! How are you Lux, Nox?' Layla greets. Her arms open to hug me, but she quickly drops her arms and connects her hands together and bows. I smile and bow back.

*'We are well,'* Nox answers, and Lux just wiggles his snout. My eyes slyly shift to Jada.

'How are you doing, Layla? Sorry I haven't been able to hang out much,' I apologise, but she waves a hand. 'No worries, I get it. After all, you've been *busy* with other things.' She winks and randomly dances on the spot. 'And Jada has been fun to hang around with. It's like we're best friends.'

'All right, enough of that,' Jada muses. When my eyes meet hers, she says, 'The tamers agreed that Layla deserved to have a bit more freedom.'

'So, you guys have been hanging out a lot?' I ask, trying to wrap my fingers in my sleeves.

'Yeah, she's actually been teaching *me* about how to

read the stars, and about umbra behaviour too,' Jada says. 'Hey, wanna talk?' It throws me off guard, but her face doesn't give anything away.

'Uh, sure.' I gesture for her to lead the way and we leave Miles and Layla. The clicks of our shoes fill the silence between us. A few times Jada glances at me, but I never meet her gaze. We stop at the bridge and I sit by the river. Ruby circles over us and Lux and Nox keep their distance.

Jada sits beside me, resting her arm on her knee. The river fills my vision but a hollowness in my chest grows.

'So, what's been—'

'Jada, are you the traitor?' I look at her. I wasn't planning on asking her about it – and my stomach drops, thinking about how I ruined Dad's plan – but we've been through so much together. I have to know, to see her face as she answers.

A hush falls. Neither of us speak. A knife could slice through the tension, but Jada's eyes bore into mine as I wait.

Jada inhales a breath and a calmness I've never seen before washes over her face. She takes my hand in hers.

'Mia, I am not the traitor.'

The soft grip of her hands as they warm mine and the sincerity in her eyes reinforce the feelings I had all along. I believe her.

She's innocent.

'But why have you been going to the hold so much?' I ask.

'To see my mum.' Her hands slowly let go of mine. 'She's not doing well in there. I've been trying to see her more, to try and reconnect, I guess.'

I get that. Jada was raised by her grandparents for so many years, but when they passed away she had no one left in her family, until now. It makes sense. 'I'm sorry for being a little suspicious of you.'

'Don't worry about it, sis. When Daniel told us what Layla said, I knew I might be a suspect. I should've just come clean about visiting my mum so often,' she says. 'It's weird though, because I saw Riley coming out of the lab before he went off with Daniel somewhere. For some reason Myla wasn't with him.'

Footsteps near us and we turn around to see Miles.

'Hey, Mia, I really need to tell you something,' he says.

'Erm, sure,' I say.

He grabs my wrist and pulls me up.

'Woah, wait!' I say, trying to pull away, but he drags me along. 'I'll see you soon, Jada! Thanks for the talk!'

*'If he doesn't let go of your wrist, I'm going to bite his hand off,'* Lux growls, but Miles lets go when we're further down the river. He crouches down to stare at the running water and then after a quiet moment, he speaks.

'I'm sorry.'

I blink, realising he's talking to me. I crouch beside him and watch the silver leaves floating down into the water.

'What for?' I ask. His messy hair almost covers his eyes as they meet mine in a soft gaze that makes my heart skip a beat.

'About everything. About capturing your parents, the Elite taking over your city, all of it.' He glances back at the river. A pool of emotions swimming through his dark eyes.

I shrug awkwardly. 'It's OK.'

*What am I supposed to say?*

*'Tell him to kick rocks.'*

*Get outta my head, Lux!*

I rub the back of my neck. 'What's done is done. Besides, you didn't force the Elite to invade Nubis.

They did it on their own,' I say. 'But thanks. Your apology means a lot.'

His hands slide into his pockets and he mulls over my words. 'I need to ask you a big favour.'

I wait for him to continue.

'I know this is gonna sound weird, but if I ever do something that puts you in danger, don't hesitate to take me out,' he says quietly.

The look in his eyes almost scares me. I want to ask why he's saying this, but my mind goes blank and no words come out.

'Promise me, OK?' he insists.

I reach out to him but he gets up to dodge me. 'I won't let anyone hurt you, or Lucas, but if *I* do, don't hesitate to attack me.'

I see it, only for a moment. The pain. The same pain I've noticed for a while now. I first saw it when we met during the Elite's attack and again when he left after we beat the Reaper King. Even when he came back to Nubis, I kept seeing a glint in his eye. Something's going on with him. I wait, wide-eyed, heart pounding, but he doesn't say anything else. He clenches and unclenches his fist and shadows waft in his hands.

'OK,' is all I manage to say, and he nods.

'Sorry . . . I just haven't been feeling myself lately,' he admits, this time avoiding my eyes.

'Is it the nightmares? The Reaper King?' I ask.

He sighs. 'Sometimes it doesn't feel like *I'm* the one thinking in my head. Like someone's voice is whispering in my mind or something,' he says, but then his crooked half-smile returns. 'I don't know. Don't worry about it. I'll be fine.'

*The last thing you sound is fine, you muppet.* We stare up at all the colourful lanterns floating up in the sky, carrying the hopes and dreams of everyone in the city.

'Look Mia, I don't want you to end up like—' He cuts himself off and looks to the ground.

'Like what? Who?' I urge, shaking his shoulder.

'Ria.' He shrugs my hand off and scoots away, widening the gap between us.

I sigh and look at the people walking up and down the street.

'You never stopped being my best friend, Mia. I don't want to lose you. I can't.' *What?*

I struggle to form words in my brain. The seriousness in his eyes rattles my core and it's my turn to look away. I clutch my hands together and stare ahead.

'I don't know what you're on about, but I'm not a princess who needs saving,' I tell him, keeping my eyes anywhere but him. 'I'm brave and strong and I flippin' travelled across the whole Nightmare Plains to save everyone. I'm all right. I don't want you risking anything for me. You're great just as you are.'

I reach over and flick his cheek. He hisses and cups his cheek, grumbling under his breath. I laugh, gently nudging him with my shoulder.

'All I need is a friend, not a saviour,' I say.

I raise my pinkie finger up and he blinks.

'What are you doing?' he asks, staring at my finger.

'I read it in an old book once,' I say. 'Raise yours too.'

He looks down at his pinkie before copying me. I smile and hook my pinkie with his.

'We'll promise that no matter what happens, we'll be there for each other,' I say. He quietly smiles, tapping his forehead against mine, and nods.

'Promise.'


'All right, you lot. It's time to hang out with me too!' Layla says, suddenly muscling in between us.

'It's so pretty, isn't it?' she says with her full attention on the stars above. 'Do you ever just find yourself lost staring at the sky? It's so big. Bigger than we can ever imagine. I wonder what's up there.'

She looks at me with a gentle smile. 'I'd like to travel to the stars one day.'

'Maybe you will,' I say. 'Anything's possible.'

'You got that right,' Miles adds.

'Would you guys come with me? To the stars?' She points up, then spreads her fingers out like she's trying to catch one.

'Maybe,' I say. 'If you buy me some honey cakes.'

Miles laughs and Layla grins. 'I miss them, ya know . . . The umbra in the cave.'

I sit up properly but she doesn't look at me. 'Sometimes I wonder if I have a little brother or sister, like you, Mia,' she says.

For the first time, it feels like I glimpse into who she is beneath the constant smiles and cheers. Would it be OK for me to take her to the cave umbra again?

'Do you want to see those umbra again?' I ask.

Her eyes connect with mine again. 'More than anything.'

'OK, then me, Lux, and Nox will take you one day. I promise.'

I ignore Lux's caution in my head.

'Why are you being nice to me all of a sudden?' she asks. She leans so close to my face that our noses almost touch.

'I've been separated from my family once too, and it's the worst feeling in the world.'

'Does this mean we're finally best friends? I knew it, I knew you liked me.' She pulls me and Miles into a hug, choking my neck.

'Let's not go too far. We're just friends, for now.' I wiggle out of her death grip and she laughs.

'But I gotta get going,' I say, standing up. It's probably too late to go to the lab now. Not without an after-hours code. But we need to tell Mum and Dad about my conversation with Jada.

At home, Mum and Lucas are in the living room and I run inside with Miles after leaving Layla with Jada.

'Is Dad not back?' I ask, puffing for breath.

Mum shakes her head, frowning.

'Not yet. He's still questioning Riley. Why?' she asks.

'I know I wasn't supposed to interfere with the investigation but . . . I spoke to Jada. It's not her. Dad can even ask her. I really don't think she did it. Dad can even ask her mum to confirm it, or one of the guards.'

'Are you a hundred per cent sure she wasn't lying?' Mum asks.

'Trust me, Mum. I know it's not much proof, but I felt it. And if it's not her then—'

'There's a huge probability that it's Riley,' she mutters, finishing my sentence.

'Jada said she saw him coming out of the lab before Dad found him, but for some reason Myla wasn't with him.'

'I need you to stay here with Lucas. Your Dad's phone will be off because he's in the hold, so I have to go there and tell him,' she says. 'I'll check the lab as well.'

'Got it. Leave Lucas with me.'

I turn back to Miles and he stares at the floor, frowning.

'You OK?' I touch his arm and he jumps.

'Yeah, sorry. Just . . . tired,' he says.

'It is late. Get some rest,' Mum says, grabbing her coat. 'I'm going to talk to Jada too and gather the tamers. If Riley took something from the lab, I'll know about it.'

She walks over and kisses my head and then Lucas's. She opens her arms to Miles next, and he hesitates before hugging her tightly.

'*We'll be back soon, children,*' Spike says, and the front door clicks shut.

'Mimi, I'm tired,' Lucas whispers, and I wave him over as a yawn slips from my own lips.

'Come on, I'll take you to bed,' I say, walking him to the stairs. I stop by the living-room door. 'You coming, Miles?'

He blinks. 'Yeah.'

We head upstairs and Lux, Nox and Shade follow. I tuck Lucas in and Miles waits for me in the hallway with Shade.

'You sure you're OK?' I ask him, and he nods.

'I hate falling asleep, that's all,' he grumbles, stuffing his hands in his pockets.

'Me too,' I say. 'But I learned something that helps. Before you go to sleep, imagine a wall blocking the Reaper King out of your mind.'

He tilts his head to the side. 'You sure that works?'

'It has for me,' I shrug. 'Doesn't hurt to try though.'

He nods again and his eyes shift towards the guest room where he used to sleep. 'Hey, remember what I said at the festival?' he says.

'Don't hesitate to take you down if you try to hurt me,' I repeat. He smiles but the faraway look in his eyes makes my stomach lurch. Even Shade is more quiet than usual.

'Yeah. But don't worry, everything's gonna be OK. No matter what happens ... you're my best friend and I'll always try and protect you. Goodnight, Supernova.'

'Night,' I say and then he's gone, the guest-room door shut.

*What's that all about?*

*'He was definitely acting strange,'* Nox says.

*'Even the mutt was acting shifty,'* Lux adds.

*Think we'd better keep an eye on them tomorrow.*

*'Agreed,'* they say in unison. We walk into my room and I get changed into some PJs and throw myself on my bed.

*'You're not going to sleep until you hear your parents come back, are you?'* Lux asks.

'That's right mate,' I say, and he gives me a bemused look. I lie back in bed and switch on the star light, watching them dance across my ceiling, fading in and out, and my eyes slowly close.

I'm surrounded by a grey mist. If I wasn't sitting on something hard, I'd be sure I was floating in an endless void. There's not a single person in sight and I stand up, looking around.

'Mimi...'

'Lucas?' I spin around.

I squint and see, within the mist, my little brother standing alone, half dazed. He reaches out for me before turning around and walking off without a word.

'Wait!' I move towards him but every movement is slowed and stretched, gravity pulling at me. He continues to walk, getting further and further away. 'Lucas!'

Ahead of him, something disturbs the mist and bony fingers stretch out toward him.

'LUCAS, WAIT!' I scream at the top of my lungs. My legs scream for mercy, but I push through the pain. I have to reach him. I HAVE TO REACH HIM!

He keeps walking, trapped in a trancelike state. Within the shadows, a mouth filled with shark teeth smiles. 'LUCAS!'

*He's mine ...*

Skeleton hands burst into my peripheral vision from behind, snatching my arms and legs. They crack and twitch as I yank my way forward. Little voices whisper and sob in my ears in a language I don't understand. My body cries and aches to give in. Through my wet blurry eyes, I see that Lucas is just in sight. I reach for him.

'Take my hand, Lucas!'

He stops right between the bony arms and I snatch him back. Slowly, he turns around with his eyes closed and I crouch down to his level. 'Are you OK?' I ask.

His eyes burst open to reveal black endless pits and I scream, falling back and scrambling away from him. He grins with shark teeth.

*'You're next . . .'*

I jerk myself awake. Looking around, I'm back in my room. Safe. Sweaty PJs sticking to me. I'm struggling to catch my breath, but I stumble out of my bed and run to Lucas's room. I burst through the door and the whole room's quiet. I squint my eyes in the darkness and his cuddled-up form sleeps peacefully. The covers hide his face and his toys lie all around him like a king's guard of his own. I sigh in relief. *He's safe.*

'*Mia, what happened?*' Lux asks, joining me in Lucas's room with Nox.

'He had him. The Reaper King had Lucas,' I say through my dry throat. I slump down beside his bed, leaning my head against the soft mattress. *Thank Lunis he's safe.* I look up and for some reason Lux and Nox stay by the door.

'What's wrong?' I whisper.

A weight of worry nestles inside me, but it's not my emotion. It's theirs. Nox takes one slow step towards me, and nerves tingle down the back of my neck.

*'Young one . . . We do not smell the little one's scent.'*

'What do you mean? He's right—' I pull the covers back and cut myself off. My heart stops. Pillows fill the space where he should've been sleeping. My hands tremble, dropping the covers.

*'Young one, we should—'*

'Lucas? LUCAS!' I yell, scrambling to my feet. My knees buckle as I crash into his wardrobe, yanking open the doors. I rummage through it, throwing out clothes and toys, but he's not there. Under his bed, nothing. Behind the curtains, nothing. I grip my hair, spinning around the room. He's not *anywhere.*

'Lucas!' I run into the hallway. *Where is he? Why isn't he in bed?*

*'I don't think Lila and Daniel are back either,'* Lux says, nodding his horn at their door. My heart pounds against my chest. *Miles!* I run across the landing and burst into his room.

'Miles, Lucas is—' I freeze in the doorway. His room is empty. Not a single sign of him or Shade. His curtains flap in the wind as his window sits wide open and my blood runs cold.

Miles has taken Lucas.

# CHAPTER TWENTY

No. no. NO! Why did he take Lucas? Why did he take my brother? Was he working with the traitor this whole time?

I throw on my hoodie, slip on my trainers and run outside with Lux and Nox on my heels. A bright light flashes and then they're galloping in their adult forms. *We have to sound the alarm!* I vault on to Lux's back, and his shadow hooves tear through the street in a frenzy. I grip his fur, my head spinning.

'Nox, can you go to the hold and tell Mum and Dad about Miles taking Lucas.'

*'On it,'* he says, and I nod.

'Lux and I are going to activate the alarm.' The closest emergency announcement beacon is by city hall, and I telepathically direct Lux there.

The sick feeling in my stomach refuses to go away.

I wipe my hot tears with my sleeve but they won't stop falling.

I leap off Lux's back when we reach the alarm, and I swing open the door to the small red dome. Inside there's a lever protected by a glass with a huge blue button beside it. My skin crawls at the thought of what could be happening to Lucas. *Please be OK!*

I push the button and a bright light scans me up and down. I repeatedly tap my thigh, waiting.

'State your name and emergency.'

'M-Mia McKenna. Lucas McKenna is missing!' I yell. The light switches off and instantly the glass in front of the lever slides open.

'Please pull the lever to activate the emergency announcement.'

I yank the lever before the robotic voice can finish and the whole city engulfs in red, just like it did when the tamers announced the queen arriving. Sirens blast from speakers across the city and the emergency announcement sounds.

'Attention. Attention. This is an emergency announcement. Lucas McKenna is missing. Lucas McKenna is missing. This is an emergency announcement.'

I run outside and all around us the lights inside everyone's houses turn on. I vault on to Lux's back, feeling my pulse racing a thousand times a minute.

*'Young one, meet me in the fields by the bridge. I'm with Lila and Daniel!'* Nox says in my mind and we set off.

We weave in and out of people on the street. Everyone around us yells for Lucas, joining the search.

I take it back. I'm so glad these announcements are so loud. Everyone looks in the alleyways, under market stalls, buildings, everywhere, yelling Lucas's name. The entire city searches for him.

Lux slows to a stop by the bridge and Mum and Dad are in a panic by the purple fields.

'Mia!' Mum cries out. I throw myself off Lux and run straight into her arms. She pulls me into a hug and I choke on my tears, burying my face in her chest. Dad leans down and tenderly strokes the back of my head.

'Mia, do you have any idea where Miles would take him?' he asks.

I shake my head. 'He didn't tell me anything. Before we went to sleep he was acting weird though. During the festival too. He said he didn't feel like himself but told me if he ever did anything to hurt me or Lucas, not to hesitate to attack him. I had no idea *this* was what he meant.' And I'll get him for this. No hesitation.

'We'll find him. They can't have got that far,' Dad says.

'The other tamers are already looking across the city. Let's get—'

A loud squawk sounds over our heads and Ruby lands next to us. Jada jumps off with Layla coming down right after her.

'You believed me,' I say to Dad.

'Of course. She told me everything,' Dad says. 'Riley is still in the hold for now though.'

'What's going on? Is Lucas really missing?' Jada asks.

'Yeah, Miles took him,' I tell her.

'Mia! We're here. We'll help!' I turn around and Mikasa, Thomas and Lincoln run up to me, all in their PJs and with their parents. My eyes burn with tears and I nod.

'Thanks guys.'

My eyes connect with Layla's as she walks over and I suddenly see red. I march over and push her so hard she stumbles back and hisses but doesn't fight back when I grab her by the shirt. 'Do you know anything about this? Where is my brother?!' I scream. My hands shake and pulse with light.

'Mia, don't!' Mikasa yells, grabbing my arm. I shove her away and stare into Layla's eyes.

'What are you talking about? I don't know where he is.' Her voice is so calm, my light flares, angrier.

'Liar!'

'Mia!' Dad pulls me off her and I struggle in his grip.

'I'm telling you the truth. I don't know where he is,' Layla says. 'I mean it.'

*No, it's all lies!* I can't think straight.

*'Mia.'* I hear Nox behind me.

*No. She has to know something!* My body boils all over and heat rushes to my hands.

*'I don't believe she's lying, Mouse. Stop before you hurt your father!'*

My eyes well up and my vision blurs. I scream.

*WHERE IS HE?*

'We'll find him, I promise, but you have to calm down, Baby-girl.' I almost don't recognise Dad's voice, but I stop fighting and the light around my hands fades. He lets go and I heave, clutching at my hair.

'Mia?' Margaux calls out. Behind me, she, Elijah, Clara, Aaron and Abigail stand with their umbra.

'We'll help,' Elijah says, but all I can do is nod through my puffy eyes.

'Let's all split up,' Dad orders. 'They may even be out of the city.'

'Lila, Samuel is gone. He's not in the lab!' One of the scientists shouts, racing over to us.

'What?' Mum says, her eyes wide.

'I went to check the lab just like you said, and … Samuel is gone too,' he explains.

Suddenly, without warning, a loud explosion booms, cutting off the scientist, and the sheer force pushes us back. Mum grabs my arm before I'm blown away and the ground shakes. The air rattles and a girl screams. Panic strikes my core and we all turn around.

'That sounded like Rosé,' Dad shouts. Mum checks me over as my ears ring.

'What was that bang?' I shout.

'It came from the direction of the hold,' Elijah says, gravely. He stares behind us and black smoke bursts into the air.

'What the—'

I see Mum and Dad look at each other, making a decision. And in an instant, we're racing towards the hold.

*

Shadow smoke wafts from doors that have burst off their hinges. Shattered glass litters the floor from the busted skylight that leads down to the day room in the hold.

'They're free! The Elite are free! They're coming!' Rosé yells, running up to us from the doors. Her clothes and hair are charred and there are scratches on her arms and legs. 'It's Riley! He broke out of the interrogation room and freed them!'

The ground rumbles and the hold guards dive out the way, barely dodging the red-eyed umbra that flood through the doors with the Elite riding on their backs, Maria and Magnus leading them. Riley and Myla are with them, with Samuel Walker slung across Myla's back in front of Riley. They head towards the main gate.

'After them!' Dad orders. 'Don't let them leave the city!'

Light flashes around us as the other umbra turn into their adult forms and give chase, tamers beside them or on their backs. I follow swiftly behind Mum and Dad with Lux and Nox.

'If they get out of the city, they're probably heading to Astaroth. That must be where Miles is taking Lucas. We need to make it there first and find him!' Mum orders from atop Spike. Lux speeds up until we are beside her. My heart skips with an idea.

'Mum. Me, Lux and Nox can make it to Astaroth faster if I can use my powers like I did before,' I say. 'When I hold the staff Queen Katiya gave me, it gives us extra speed. If we do it again we can get there before those gutterslugs.'

Mum frowns. 'Mia, you'd be playing right into their hands. Even with Lux and Nox.'

'We can do it. We'll even make it before the Elite if I try it now,' I say urgently. I pull the staff from my thigh and it glows at my touch.

Mum looks into my eyes and I stare right back, determined. *I have to try.*

She sighs. 'All right, fine. I trust you but if you get there and the Elite have already arrived, wait for us. Your Dad and Bolt should make it there to you first.'

'OK. I'll find Lucas,' I promise. No matter what. I'm saving my baby brother.

'Be safe,' she says, looking to Lux and Nox next. 'All of you.'

We break apart and I tighten my grip on the staff. My eyes close and I focus on the purple light inside me, calming my mind. It sparks, travelling through my arms straight to my hands, and the staff draws it in, absorbing the energy.

*Lucas, I'm coming.*

I open my eyes and the staff explodes with light, engulfing me, Lux and Nox. Power surges through us as we burst through the city like a rocket slicing through wind, closing the gap between us and the Elite ahead. They all raise their hands and shadows shoot at the main gate, blasting it open.

Soon enough we're on them. Nox thrashes his horn, knocking one of them to the ground, and I kick out my foot, pushing another off their umbra.

'MIA!' Maria roars as I pass her.

I whip my head back, face glowing with a giant smirk. *Gutterslugs! Eat my dust!*

We steadily continue to draw ahead of them and once we have a good lead, I take a deep breath and my light dims. Just like with dance, I slow my breath and feel every inch of my body and calm my light as we make it to the top of the mountain that overlooks Astaroth and the Nightmare Plains. The plains are silent and still, the crooked trees barely flinching in the wind. The snapping carno plants don't even move, like nature itself is on edge.

It's time to save Lucas.

'Mia, Mia, Mia, Mia. Mia, Mia, Mia, Mia, Mia, Mia, Mia, Mia, Mia, Mia, Mia, Mia, Mia, Mia, Mia, Mia, Mia, Mia, Mia, Mia. I'm waiting ...'

# CHAPTER TWENTY-ONE

We burst through the gates of Astaroth. I look around the abandoned streets. Not a human soul in sight.

'Lucas! Lucas!' I scream.

I swing my staff, blasting the gigantic spiders and creatures out of our path. We look through windows of busted shops and houses, but there's no sign of anyone. *They have to be here.* The buildings and the houses give nothing away and we stop, seeing wafts of black shadow smoke ahead. I know exactly where they're coming from.

'Let's go!' I yell.

We gallop towards the Reaper King's old home, dodging huge spiderwebs and leaping over fallen logs until we stop in front of the creepy, dust-ridden castle.

'When we're done, I'm burning this place down,' I mutter.

'The tiny one is in there. I can smell his scent,' Lux confirms.

'We must approach with caution, young one. I smell Miles's scent too,' Nox warns.

I slide off Lux and we walk up the cracked stone steps. The giant doors are already wide open. Once inside I gasp, almost dropping my staff. At the top of the basement steps is Lucas, his little fists clenched. A long red hooded cloak drapes over his shoulders, and I don't recognise the blood-red eyes that stare out at me from his sweet face.

'Lucas ...?' I take a slow step forward, putting my staff away. My heart pounds in my ears. 'We're here to take you home now, OK? Mum and Dad are on their way too.'

I open my arms for him, but he doesn't move. Not a twinkle of recognition in his eyes. He makes no movement to run and hug me. Just dead red eyes staring back at me. Like I'm a stranger.

His hand shifts and I catch my breath. Something inside his cloak glints in the moonlight. His boomerang.

'Mimi,' he finally says. His voice is as emotionless as his face. 'Come with me.'

He turns to walk down the steps, but I yell out,

'No, Lucas, come on. Let's get out of here before the Elite come!'

He pauses mid-step, casting his eyes over his shoulder at me. 'The kingdom needs to be fixed and we have to find *her*. You can help too. He needs your help.'

'Lucas—'

'Mia.'

A chill shivers down my spine. *Did he just call me . . .?* Someone runs up the stairs from the basement and my anger flares seeing Miles and Shade.

'What. Did. You. Do?' My tone is almost feral as I stare at him, but he raises his hands.

'Mia, the Reaper King made me do it, but I have a plan that will—'

The staff is back in my grasp and aimed at Miles before I can even think. My hands burn with power and rage.

*'He accepted the Darkness. It's your time too,'* Lucas says, but it's *not* his voice. This voice is deep, dripping with danger. It's the voice that's haunted my nightmares. The Reaper King.

'Leave my brother alone,' I warn. Lux and Nox's shadow fur bristles and they bare their teeth.

*'This boy will be the key that brings me back into*

*this world once the dead one arrives. I will drain the last bit of his life and walk amongst my people in Lunis again. Little Lucas has a tiny bit of control now, but that will soon change. He is mine.'*

His chaotic laugh bounces off the castle walls, and my blood runs cold. *It can't be too late.*

'Lucas, if you can hear me, put the boomerang down. You can fight him. You're strong!' I yell.

'No!' he snaps, dashing past me before I can grab him. He dodges Lux and Nox, spins on his foot and punches his fist forward. A blue light bursts towards them, throwing them back against the walls.

'Guys!' I scream.

*'We are fine, get the boy!'* Lux yells, shaking his body. *'We'll hold off the Elite brat and the mutt.'*

Without a second thought I burst through the doors outside after Lucas, leaving Miles and Shade to my umbra. 'I'm taking you home, Lu-Lu!'

'I'M NOT A BABY! I don't want to!' He flashes forward and his boomerang clashes with my staff.

'Lucas, stop!' I yell, gritting my teeth. Has he always been this strong?

'No!' he shouts.

The city is quiet except for the clashing of our

weapons, and I hope Dad isn't far behind. The intensity of his words ripples through the air.

'You're being controlled! Fight it!' I yell, batting away his boomerang again.

'NO!' he screams.

His boomerang flashes in front of my eyes and I jump back, knocking it away. He leaps and catches it smoothly.

'Stop it, Lucas!'

He raises his boomerang again. I chew my lip. *This isn't working, but I have to try something!* Suddenly an idea comes to me. *If this doesn't work ... I might be finished, but ...* I dig my feet into the ground, take a deep breath. Lucas yells and I let my staff slip through my fingers. It clatters to the ground as his boomerang strikes me.

Pain shoots through my stomach and I scream, smacking into the wall. I thud to the ground. I roll on to my stomach, hunched. Sharp pain radiates through me.

Lucas freezes and his hands shake, dropping the boomerang that had already returned to him. His eyes flash to brown and if it weren't for the shooting pain, I would've sighed in relief.

'Mimi . . .? MIMI!'

'You finally snapped out of it, pipsqueak. It's about time.' I heave. Blood splatters from where I bit my tongue and spews from my mouth as I cough.

He finds his feet and runs over. 'I'll help you, Mimi! I'm sorry! I'm really sorry!'

My body cries out, begging me to stay down on the ground, but I force myself up.

'We need to find Mum and Dad,' I manage to say. My ribs ache with every breath but his eyes are still normal and that's all that matters. But there's no way it was that easy to stop the gutterslug king.

'Let's find Mummy and Daddy,' Lucas says, holding my hand.

*Lux, Nox, are you guys OK?*

*'Yes, we're coming, young one. We're making sure Miles and Shade stay away from you,'* Nox's voice sounds pained and I turn around to face the doors of the castle. Suddenly Lucas jerks back, crying out.

*Where do you think you're going?*

He clutches his head and stumbles backwards. Shadows flock around his small body, twisting and wrapping around him like tentacles. I go to him and some of the shadows turn to me. I grit my teeth and ready my staff.

'Mouse!'

'Stay back!' I shout at Lux and Nox by the castle doors.

I close my eyes, flexing my arms like a dance warm-up. The light swirls in my core as my mind relaxes and I hold on to the feeling of calm. Fluttering my arms like ripples in a river, I push the energy out, and a bright purple light bursts from my staff, colliding against the shadows. They flare in a fiery rage, swallowing my light like it's nothing. *What?*

*You will witness my revival. One that you cannot stop. I will be set free!'* Lucas says in the Reaper King's voice. Shadows burst from his arms and his screams of pain cut my heart.

'Lucas!' I yell, pushing through the shadows. 'Stop it! If you have to use someone then use me! Not him!'

'Mia, don't! I have a plan!' Miles yells, running down the steps of the castle. He grabs my arm, but I break out of his grip and push him back.

'USE ME!' I scream at the Reaper King, slapping Miles's hands away. 'USE ME INSTEAD!'

*It's a deal.*

'Young one!'

'Mouse!'

I drop my staff and throw my arms out. *I have to protect him.* The shadows around Lucas morph red and zap from his body to mine. I gasp, feeling my body go numb. The shadows race along my arms like a burning fire and my energy drains out of me. A thousand invisible flames burn up my neck, arms and legs. I scream, then suddenly it stops and my whole body feels heavy.

*'Just as there's light in your soul, there is darkness. Embrace it.'*

The shadows slither through me and my thoughts blur, no longer my own.

'There they are! Riley, place Samuel down and give her the crystal!' I hear Maria yell faintly as my vision goes blurry. The Elite are here now. Are the tamers? I can't think. I can't feel.

The warm purple light of my powers inside me turns cold and black. I turn around and catch a crystal without telling my body to do so. A tear runs down my cheek. I'm a passenger in my own body. This is how the umbra feel when they're being controlled. This is how Lucas felt.

*'Just what I was waiting for,'* I say, but it's not *my* voice. It's HIS.

Then his voice echoes in my head, saying evil taunts just for me. *Recognise this? It's from your mother's lab. This crystal fragment is the link to the Spirit Plain along with that boy. It's a fragment piece of the crystal I found long ago.*

My throat burns, wanting to speak, but none of the words I want to say come out. Only his. My hand, holding the crystal, hovers over Samuel and shadows rush from my body to his. When they reach him, Samuel's eyes burst open. He screams at the top of his lungs, conscious for the first time in years. He twists and turns on the ground. I scream inside my head, but no one can hear.

The crystal leaves my hand and hovers above Samuel, lifting him into the air. A huge black portal spins open in front of him. I walk over to the portal against my will.

*'Now for the final piece: Blood of a lightcaster. Now you won't be able to stop it with that same silly rock from Katya.'*

My hand moves to my mouth and I bite down. Pain shoots through my hand as blood drips from it into the portal.

Shadows burst from the opening in response and

ghostly hands begin to claw their way out. A true entrance – or exit – to the Spirit Plain.

'*Rehan, STOP!*' Ria's voice suddenly screams in my head and a burst of energy flashes inside me as a sword slashes the crystal, and the connection between me and the shadows snaps. My eyes close and I fall back, but someone catches me just before I hit the floor.

I open my eyes to see Dad hovering over me, transformed with Bolt. Their third form. He smiles, but something's wrong. I look down and he grips his side with his free hand. '*Mia, I managed to push his shadows from your mind but only temporarily. He could force his way back in.*' Ria's voice whispers in my head.

'*You're too late.*' The Reaper King cackles, but this time the voice comes from the portal.

Dad stands up, carrying me and my staff, backing away from the portal. I squint to see something slowly begin to step out.

'He's coming!'

'We have to stop him now!'

'But how?'

My mind spins and suddenly Mum is holding me and Lucas close. The Reaper King's possession has left me foggy, and I struggle to hold on to my thoughts. *What's going on?*

'Don't worry, Mia, we got you!' *Margaux?*

'Take the kids and run.' Dad enters my blurry vision again, having transformed back to normal with Bolt by his side. 'He needs a vessel, a lightcaster. You have to get them away.'

'No, you're hurt. We're fighting this together. You can't do this alone,' Mum begs.

I blink, trying to see clearly. Swarms of shadows rush out of the portal, and a creature straightens to full height, his skin made of shadows itself. A crown of bones sits on his head and a black cloak flaps in the wind. But he's not truly *here*, not yet. Trails of shadows pull back towards the portal and I can see through him.

Dad places a hand on Mum's cheek and something wet drips on my face. Is Mum crying? I blink twice, trying to focus. *No . . . it's Dad.*

'Lila, you've trusted me for twenty-one years. Trust me now. I have to close the portal.'

'Mum, Dad.' I can barely make out my own words, but things start to appear clearer. My body feels like a thousand bricks are weighing me down.

I slowly reach for Dad and he looks at me with a smile, but something is off again. Very, very off. In my dizzy mind, I hear Lucas's cries ring in my ears and feel the gentle press of Dad's lips against my forehead.

'I love you, Baby-girl.' *No wait . . .*

The Reaper King's shadows creep closer. Bony feet scrape across the ground, coming towards us. Dad goes to Lucas next, and kisses his head, telling him he loves him, before giving Mum the longest kiss of all. They part and the bright light causes me to squeeze my eyes shut. He merges again with Bolt and his eyes burn gold and pointy panther ears poke from the top of his head. He takes Mum's hand and holds it tight.

'The portal needed a sacrifice to be opened, and it's fuelled by lightcaster blood. So, non-lightcaster blood could corrupt the energy and close it.'

'We don't know that, Daniel,' Mum argues, still holding me. 'Even if it works, the portal would be so unstable, anything could happen.'

Dad smiles. 'Either way, we have to close it. Trust me, Lila. Let me do this.'

His hands fall from Mum's and he kisses her lips.

'Dad . . . Wait . . .' My lungs burn, wanting to shout,

and I push myself up from Mum but Dad dashes towards the Reaper King. He slices through the king's shadows with his sword as I stumble after him.

'Mia, wait!' I yank my wrist from Mum's hand and drag my feet across the ground as fast as I can – as Dad heads straight for the portal.

*'Where do you think you're going?'* the Reaper King growls.

Like vipers, the king's shadows snap at Dad's body, but he pushes through, and stops, reaching his goal. For a second, Dad looks back at me and our eyes connect. The shadow armour that protects his arm vanishes. He mouths something, but I can't make it out from so far away. He smiles, then he lifts his sword and slashes his arm. Blood splatters into the portal and instantly it bursts into black flames.

'Dad!' I yell.

He screams as the flames engulf him, and my eyes widen as suddenly Bolt separates from Dad, thrown aside as if on purpose, as Dad changes back to normal. Then the portal shuts, leaving my dad motionless on the ground.

*'His filthy, dirty blood! Reapers! Bring me a vessel! NOW!'* the Reaper King yells.

But I don't see what's happening. I can't rip my eyes away from Dad.

Moments after the portal disappears, Samuel gasps for air a few feet away. He looks down at Dad beside him and drops to the ground too.

'Daniel!' Mum screams. She runs past me and falls to her knees, cradling Dad in her arms, trying to prop him up.

'He's OK, right? He'll wake up. Right, Mum? MUM!' I yell.

'I love you ... so much.' Dad breathes and I gasp, almost tripping over my feet, running towards him.

He coughs violently and Mum props him up more. His glassy eyes meet mine and a hand slowly reaches up to touch my face. 'I'm so proud to have been your dad. Look after Lucas and your mum.'

His breath rattles in his chest and Mum cradles him closer. Tears run down her cheeks.

'Stay awake,' she begs.

'You have to stay awake, Dad. Remember the number-one family rule?' I whisper, clutching his hand on my cheek. His eyes glaze, but he manages a weak smile as he looks from Lucas, who's behind us, to me.

'We'll always be together, Baby-girl.'

His hand falls from my face and suddenly his body goes limp in our arms as Bolt cries out. Tears flood my cheeks and I scream at the top of my lungs.

'DAD!' The back of my throat burns and I shake his body over and over. *NO! NO NO NO NO!* 'Open your eyes!'

'Mimi . . . Why isn't Daddy waking up?' Lucas asks, walking over with Spike, and I hug Dad tight.

'He's gone!' I cry out. He looks from me to Dad and his eyes start to well up.

'Gone? But he's right here.' He kneels on the floor and nudges Dad. 'Daddy, wake up.'

'Quick! Get one of the lightcasters!' an Elite woman yells, and I look up. My insides burn and light explodes from my body. *They took him away! They need to pay!*

I'm on my feet before I know what I'm going to do. Nox races by my side and I vault up on his back as Lux joins us. Fire and rage fill their cores, one thought screaming in our minds. Revenge.

My powers bubble and another scream is unleashed from my throat, shattering and quaking the earth and the air around us.

My purple light zaps like a lightning bolt, following

my every command. It shoots through every Elite in sight, filling the air with their screams.

My vision is red as they all fall to their knees, feeling the pain that Dad must have felt. Pain I want them to feel. A woman screams as Nox knocks her back and I thrust my hand forward, engulfing her in my fiery light.

The anger burns me up, but a sickly grin spreads across my face as more Elite arrive with their umbra. I jump off Nox, ready to fight the gutterslugs myself.

'Mia, that's enough!' Mum yells, but I push her back with my powers, readying my next attack. *They'll all pay!*

'Mia! If you do this, then you're no better than them!' I hear Layla's voice. My attention snaps in her direction.

'I thought you wanted revenge on them, Layla. This is revenge!'

'No. There's better ways to get revenge that don't include hurting people!' she yells. 'I know that more than anyone!'

'Mimi, stop it!' Lucas cries. I push him back with my light too. *They don't understand. I'm doing it for them. I won't let the Elite take anyone else. NO. MORE!*

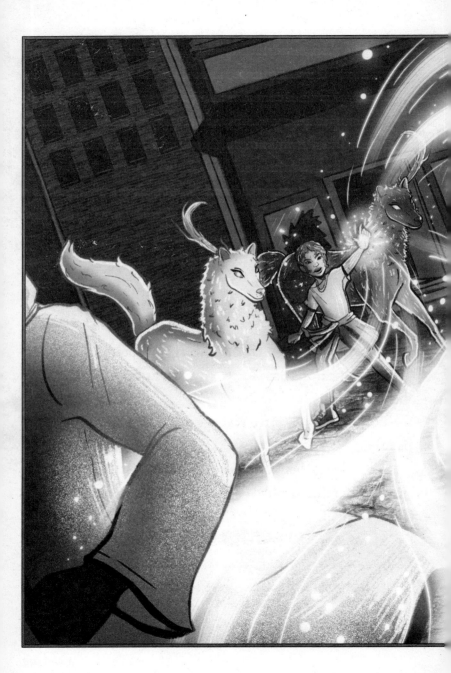

'Mia! Stop!' Someone tackles me and we crash to the ground. Like a cord snapping, the light vanishes from my hands. I hiss as pain shoots through my side. My head pounds as I try to get up from the dirt.

'OK, you're really heavy. I'm gonna need you to fully get off.'

I blink, looking down to see who pulled me to the ground, and my eyes widen.

'TJ? How?' I roll off him on to my feet. *When did he even get here?* He stands up, dressed in the Queen's Guard uniform with his signature trainers. Lucas runs and hugs my legs. 'Mimi! No more!'

Lux and Nox get to their feet, their faces solemn as they look onwards. I follow their gazes and freeze. Countless men and women are spread out on the ground, crying out in pain and gripping their bodies. Pain I have inflicted on them.

'Are you OK?' I jump as TJ touches my shoulder. His voice is tender, but I just stare at him with the same shock. He opens his arms and I fall into him without a second thought, gripping him tight. *What have I done?*

'Mia, honey . . .' Mum's gentle voice calls and I look over TJ's shoulder at her. I quickly let go and race to hug her.

'I'm sorry ...' I whisper as my eyes sting with tears that won't stop falling. I almost want to throw up. 'I hurt them all.'

'But you stopped,' Layla says.

Mum squeezes me close as the world turns quiet, but she whispers the two words I needed to hear the most in this very moment. 'It's OK ...'

A loud noise booms, and the sky fills with a dark red smoke.

'This still isn't over though. The Reaper King needs a vessel and won't stop until he has one now. We have to go help the other tamers.' Worry seeps through her voice, but I clench my fist. I will not let Dad's death go in vain.

# CHAPTER TWENTY-TWO

'We're going together,' Mum says, but even with the little energy I have left, I push her back with my powers. The blood on her clothes and the shadows dripping from Spike and Bolt tell me they're in no shape to fight. Bolt slumps to the floor, completely emotionless. He stares blankly at the ground, unmoving.

I look at Samuel next and he shivers, sitting on the ground with Mum's lab coat around him.

'I'll stop him,' I promise. 'TJ, Layla, stay here and protect everyone.' I turn to walk off when Lucas runs and grabs my leg again.

'Mimi!' I turn around and crouch down. He hugs me tight and I kiss his head, brushing away the tears from his little cheeks. 'Go get him, Mimi. I'll help TJ and Layla pretect Mummy, Spike and Bolt.'

He throws off the red cloak from his body and stamps on it. He clutches his necklace and I clutch mine with a smile.

I hop on to Nox's back. I nod at my family and instantly gallop off with Lux in the direction of the Reaper King.

We bound over the rubble and fallen buildings. As we get closer to the source of the red smoke, I see Margaux and my classmates with the tamers, clutching at wounds and tending to each other. My heart pounds harder. Each second that passes feels like we're racing closer to our deaths and yet ... I feel strong. Determined.

Lux's shadows twist around me and the connection between the three of us strengthens. My eyes squeeze shut, channelling their thoughts and feelings. I hold on to them until they blend and become my own. And we become one.

My eyes burst open and the world explodes with detail. Every speck of dust, every bug and spiderweb all become visible. I see it all. The Elite are in sight, and ahead vicious red shadows swirl, ready to strike us, growing as the Reaper King regains his powers.

Nox disappears from under me, his shadows wrapping

around my body and I drop to my feet, running at superspeed. The cold wind is nothing compared to the adrenaline that pumps in my veins. Nox's shadows mesh with Lux's, forming black and white armour along my body. A sword and shield form in my hands and shadow horns grow from my head. A long bushy tail swishes back and forth behind me and we run at the speed of light, connected in our third form.

We break out of a dark alleyway, and ahead, in the middle of the street, Miles stands in a triangle with his parents. Their hands press down on his shoulders, keeping him from running. He bows his head in defeat, but I understand now what he meant at the festival. The Reaper King used him. Just like he used me and Lucas, but I'll stop him. For all of us. I won't rest until he's gone.

In the centre of the triangle, the Reaper King's powers flock together, slowly forming a body. I skid to a stop and his red eyes light up with a disgustingly joyous look that makes me sick.

*'Mia ... You came ...'*

I shake my head, getting his gutterslug voice outta my mind.

'Mia, I—' Miles begins.

'It's OK. Leave,' I warn him once and only once. He and his parents aren't my focus right now.

'*That's right. We're only here to fight him,*' Lux says in my mind.

'*Your father may have stopped the portal, but I can take your soul and regain the rest of my strength . . .*'

The Reaper King smirks, flexing his shadows.

'That's a lot of talk coming from a lump of shadows,' I spit out.

Miles and his parents break apart, leaving me free to point my sword at the monster. It glows a mix of white shadows and my purple light.

'*You're mine!*'

He strikes and I block his shadows with the shield as we race past Miles.

'Hey, you jerk! You want me? Come get me!' I scream. The shadows chase after us and my heart pounds a thousand times a minute. But I'm alive. I'm doing this. I'll defeat him!

The air thickens, clogging my throat, but I jump and flip out of the way of his shadow attacks. He roars and the force of it blows me back, forcing me to plant my feet.

*'Mia MaKenna! Your soul is mine!'*

The king rushes towards me again, and I brace myself.

*If this is the last for me, I want you guys to leave me and keep everyone safe.*

'No. *You will get out of this alive, we will make sure of it, Mouse,'* Lux says.

'*We got you,'* says Nox.

I smile as a tear slips down my cheek. *I love you guys.*

We dash forward as one and I push off the ground, catapulting high into the air, boosted by my light. The Reaper King launches into the air too but I have the high ground.

'I'll destroy you!' I scream.

*'I will devour you!'* he yells.

I fall towards him, screaming at the top of my burning lungs. Dad's gentle smile, Mum's soft laugh and Lucas's sweet giggle echo and fill my mind. They're counting on me.

Mum, Dad, Lucas, Spike, Bolt, Lux and Nox. Miles. Everyone. *I got this!*

Light bursts from my sword. Purple collides with red as our powers meet. His shadows tear at my light, but I grit my teeth, fighting back, pouring out every ounce of energy in me.

My pulse races as the power of my light keeps my body suspended in the air.

*Just hold out ... a little longer. Don't give up, girl! Don't give up!*

Lux and Nox sonic scream through me and it blasts from my mouth at the king.

He roars, shaking his head and covering his ears. I feel his powers waver. *That's right, you gutterslug! Have that!*

*Now!* I drop to the ground as his shadows dwindle and my feet move before I can think, slashing through the miasma of his shadows, fighting against them with my light and sword. I cartwheel and front flip towards the shadow king, rage burning through my arms and chest, lighting up my body. *Time to end this!*

His skeleton hands thrust forward and shadows explode in front of me, throwing us back. My head bangs against the concrete and Lux and Nox cry out. They separate from me and I hear their bodies smack against the ground behind me.

'Mia!' someone yells out. My mind spins and I slowly sit up, feeling dizzy. I press my fingers against my head, but it's sticky. Red drips from my shaking hands.

I can barely focus on what's in front of me as the shadowy mass of the Reaper King dashes forward. My gasp traps in the back of my throat as I scramble backwards to Lux and Nox.

*Your light is mine!*

His shadows race towards me. Suddenly black shadows burst from behind me, pushing back at the Reaper King's. I look behind me and with gritted teeth Miles forces the Reaper King back.

'You can't have her!' he roars. His eyes snap to me and my heart skips a bit.

'Mia, finish him!' Miles cries out. I clench my fist, but the light inside me doesn't spark. Miles struggles to keep the shadows away. His dark eyes gloss over completely black as he fights back and I struggle to stand.

'MILES!'

*'If I can't have you and come back in my full form, then I'll take him as my vessel instead. I will live through my descendant.'*

Miles freezes as the king's red shadows overpower Miles's black ones. They latch on to Miles's arms, yanking him from just within my grasp. Shade bites and claws at the shadows, but they engulf her and she howls out in pain.

*Come on! Come on!* I jerk my hands forward, panicking, trying to force my light out, but it barely sputters out of my hands. My legs give in and I fall back down, completely drained. *I have to keep trying.* I shakily raise my hands, but the dizziness makes it hard to concentrate. I push harder, screaming, throwing out every bit of energy I can, but the shadows don't stop.

'Wait! You aren't supposed to hurt him! We had a deal!' Maria yells.

'You can't use him as your vessel!' Magnus yells, joining in with his umbra, but they're thrown back in seconds.

*'He is my descendant and I will do what is necessary.'*

Hands grab me from behind and I scramble to break free until I look behind me and see Mum and Lucas. 'Mia! We have to go. It's starting. He's taking over Miles.'

'No, I can help him! Let go!' My arms burn as I push more light towards Miles. 'Lucas, try too!'

'I can't Mimi.'

'JUST TRY!'

He jumps, trembling.

'Mia, go!' Miles screams.

'No! Not without you! I can't lose anyone else! Fight it!'

He gasps for air and the shadows twist around him like chains. His eyes change from brown to red. 'Miles!'

'Mia, we need to go!' Mum yells. 'Lux, get her!'

I scream as Lux grabs the back of my top with his mouth and my feet lift from the floor. The wind whips around me as Lux throws me up and catches me on his back, sprinting off at full speed.

'NO! Stop! We can't leave him!'

*It's too late, Mia. The king's shadows already have him. We have to get out of here,'* Nox says.

*No, we can still save him. It can't be too late. We're all he has left!*

'We have to try!'

*I'm sorry, young one.'*

I look over my shoulder as we get further and further from Miles, and through stinging eyes I see him engulfed by the shadows, but a single hand reaches out from them. My grip on Lux's shadow fur softens as I reach out too. *Miles . . .* Lux increases his speed just as I'm about to jump off, forcing me to hold on instead. *I'm sorry . . . I'll find a way. I'll keep my promise.*

We pass through Astaroth's gates and I burst into tears.

*'Be strong,'* Lux says.

*'Life will always reveal itself to you in how you need,'* Nox adds.

'But what does that mean?' I ask, feeling my cheeks cold from the tears.

Leaning over, Nox presses his shadowy soft nose against my cheek and a ray of warmth fills my heart for a single second.

*'It means everything always works out in the end. You may not see it now, but it will, Mia.'*

I hope they're right. But one thing's for certain. This war is just beginning and I'm going to finish it.

# EPILOGUE

It's been a few days since the events in Astaroth. I watch as Mum and the tamers prep the ceremony field. A field in the eastern part of the city used for weddings . . . and funerals.

My frizzy hair is tangled and unkempt, and I clutch the second necklace that hangs from my neck. Dad's necklace. The cold air on my face feels weird. It's the first time I've been out in days, but I have no choice with the funeral coming up. It's tradition that all immediate family members help in the preparation. Mum said I didn't have to, but I could at least be present. For him. Especially since Nan and Grandad on Dad's side aren't around any more.

Margaux and Elijah look back at me with a sympathetic smile as they scatter star dust on the grass, meant to help send spirits on their way. Thankfully, all the tamers returned safe from Astaroth and only a few had to get a check-up at the medicentre. I don't return their smile but Margaux and Elijah continue to help out. I've pretty much been avoiding everyone since we've been back.

The tamers all agreed to regroup and come up with a plan after the funeral. With the Elite and the Reaper King now free, we need time to fully reassess the situation before striking back. We have to make sure our city defences are strong when we leave and go on the attack.

Mum and Lucas plant lily seeds in a huge circle with the other tamers. By tomorrow, they'll grow into beautiful soul lilies to symbolise the life of the one gone.

I stand at a distance with Lux and Nox. Right now, Miles is out there somewhere, possessed by the Reaper King. We only got away because of him. Again. But I couldn't even save him. Now he's trapped and being used by that monster and there's nothing I can do. My jaw clenches thinking about it.

*'There's always a way, young one,'* Nox mutters.

Footsteps slowly walk up behind us, but I don't bother looking.

'Hey . . . Long time no see,' TJ says.

'Hey,' I murmur, keeping my eyes ahead on Mum and Lucas. In the corner of my eye I see TJ rub the back of his head.

'I know you've been out of it lately, but I've got something I really need to tell you,' he says. I respond with a hum.

'You were right about the queen,' TJ says suddenly. I break my stare to look at him, and he continues. 'She's been tracking you all this time.'

'How?'

His eyes trail down and I suddenly become very aware of the weapon that presses against my leg.

'It has a tracker in it. That's how I found you in Astaroth. I found you with this.' He pulls out a small tablet screen from his backpack. 'The staff has been showing the queen your every movement. I stole it and followed you here with Mum.'

No wonder she told me to always keep it close! The hollowness in my heart dominates my feelings, but anger inside me sparks and I throw the staff to the ground. *That gutterslug!*

'That's not all,' TJ says, hesitating. 'I think I've found proof that Queen Katiya was behind your grandparents' attack too.'

His words hang between us and time feels like it's stopped, but the anger bubbles in my veins.

All this time. It's been *her*. Ria was right. I remember now. Back when we first met the queen, I heard a scream. I thought I was just imagining it, but maybe that was actually the first time Ria tried reaching out to me. She's been calling for help for so long. Tortured for years and Queen Katiya and the royal family have been behind it for generations.

They're the ones who imprisoned Ria, and the reason for the Reaper King's rampage. Worst of all, Queen Katiya is the one responsible for the attack on Nan and Grandad and we never knew it. My emotions turn cold and my fist clenches so hard my nails dig into my skin, and I grit my teeth. Both the queen and the Reaper King are gonna pay for everything they've done. I won't stop until I get my revenge.

# ACKNOWLEDGEMENTS

I still find it hard to believe sometimes that this trilogy series created from my love of gaming is really out there in the world for people to read – and now we're on the second book!

First, as always, I want to thank my amazing mum for being the best support system ever. Through the ups and the downs, she's always there and helps me stay motivated.

Second, I want to thank YOU, the reader. Thank you so much for taking the time to delve back into the world of Mia and the kingdom of Lunis. I appreciate every single one of you and I hope you enjoyed this book.

Next is Rachel, my superstar agent, who continues to champion me every step of the way in this amazing career I have as an author. I wouldn't have made it this far without her and she's my rock in this literary world.

Then there's my amazing Faber Children's team, who continue to work so hard to help bring this series together. My editors Leah and Stella are the absolute best. I have so much love for all of my Faber team too, including my publicity, marketing, rights team and project manager. I can't thank everyone enough.

Ana Latese, the superstar behind the illustrations has done it once again. She's brought this story to life with her amazing illustrations and it's an honour to share this book with her.

Finally, I want to acknowledge how much music has helped me when writing this book and the series as a whole. Music is a part of my writing process and I want to thank the legendary Hiroyuki Sawano, a composer who has created music for some of my favourite anime. Many of the epic scenes written in this series were created whilst listening to his music, as well as Hans Zimmer's. Samuel Kim is another amazing composer, who has put together amazing playlists that include music from some of my favourite anime and movies. A lot of the emotional moments in my books were written to his music.

Once again, thank you so much for taking the time to read my books! This journey has been a wild ride in the best way, and I can't wait to share the final book in the trilogy with you.